WHAT TIME IS IT THERE?

What time is it there?

GLENICE WHITTING

POESY QUILL PUBLISHING

Poesy Quill Publishing

poesyquill.com

First published 2020

This book is based on fact and woven with fiction. I have created a cast of
fictional characters and used an amalgamation of real and imagined
letters. Some of the events described in these pages did happen, others are
pure invention, others still a blend of both.

Cover design
Luke Harris
www.workingtype.com.au

Interior layout and design
A Distant Mirror
adistantmirror.com.au

*There are no faster or firmer friendships than those
between people who love the same books.*

– Irving Stone

'Come with me. We can go together.' It sounds as if Hank is inviting her on a holiday, or one of the scientific excursions they so enjoyed. This isn't a trip. Maggie can see it, has read this ending in many books. The younger doting wife dying in her elderly husband's arms. The end. Close the book. This is not a story with a tidy ending. This is life. To die with him would put an end to her pain, but there is no reincarnation.

No happy Christian afterlife. Dead is dead. Finished. *Muerto.* One of them a murderer, one a suicide.

Goddammit, she's fifteen years his junior. Has he forgotten? Has he forgotten his granddaughter? What about Elizabeth? His death will be enough for her to try and understand without losing both of her grandparents. Maggie's mind whirls in every direction. Stay, go, no. Stay, stay. Stay and be free. Free to live her life how she wants to live. Finally do what she wants to do.

'You bastard,' she mutters and suddenly feels guilty. This is not just about him or her.

'What about Barb? Does she have to lose a mother as well?'

*

25.9.2018: Diane's Journal. Australia

The night belongs to the novelist. You straighten your back and stretch weary muscles. A bold, bright lamp highlights the desk. In the shadows, folders and documents festoon every inch of the floor. The filing cabinet a hanging garden of paper. The only time available in your busy life to write The Book is between three and six a.m. Snores, loud and sonorous. Sound sleep for him at last. A cough. He will soon stretch, yawn and reach for you.

You glance at the folder marked 'Maggie', containing how many years of letters? Can it really be thirty-five?

The last two years of her letters are in loopy script scrawled on bright yellow paper. Why yellow? Maybe the lone general store in Gateway, Arizona only stocked one colour? Why didn't she buy a white pad on her monthly shopping trip to the larger town of Geriton? Maybe yellow was easier on ninety-year-old eyes.

The first rays of sun gild the topmost leaves of tall melaleuca gums and spread a promise of hope beneath dark clouds. It will soon rise above them, lost to you for another day. But today you know why you do this. Why you write until your eyes won't focus and your head tips towards the computer screen hoping for some support. You lean back in your padded chair and smile. The black words beam back at you. Half an hour ago they were blood red, chaotically dripping and slipping down the screen. Now, they make sense and positively glow. The beginning of this work in progress finally feels right. Your fingertips caress the screen. How joyous when the writing flows.

*

Bacon sizzles in the pan. Two eggs over-easy. Toast slightly burnt, just as he likes it. Lashings of butter, cholesterol not an issue. Percolated coffee. It gives Maggie something to do, something to distract her from what is happening. His jeans hang loose, wrinkled like an old elephant's hide over his shrunken butt. Head bowed, she carefully buttons the anniversary shirt, adjusts the woven leather bolo tie, combs his hair and, on top, places his Stetson, all wrinkled and worn. Sweat stains add another pattern to the diamond back snakeskin band. Hank leans heavily against her, and they stagger to his old man's recliner. His fingers grip the arm, and she carefully eases him down, arranging his useless forearm on the armrest. He's like the statue of Lincoln, that distant look already seeing the future. Maggie places the loaded and

8

cocked Beretta in his lap. To be aimed at the base of the skull. He's never looked more handsome.

'Still time to change your mind,' he says.

'You too,' she replies, but knows the decision has been made and Hank is not a man to change his mind. Ever. She holds his head to her chest and strokes the shaggy mane. Life has never seemed more precious.

How can she leave him to do this alone? To die alone? It takes all her courage to look at him. They kiss. A long, tender, goodbye kiss. She knows she will have to walk to the door. But how to leave? How to walk away from fifty years of laughter, fears, tears and adventure? But there are also memories of other times, bad times. Maggie squeezes his hand, grabs her anorak and library backpack from their pegs, and closes the door behind her. She must walk the four kilometres to the Santa Fe library, be seen by people, have an alibi. She must ring her daughter, Barb.

And Diane in Australia? 'Goddammit,' she says. 'If only I could turn back the years.'

*

1975: Outback Australia

Maggies Journal

It should never have happened. And never like that.
There was sunshine, a hint of spring in the air. Darkness
should have hidden the enormity. Anna travelled every
day by train. Loved the click clack of wheels. Didn't mind
the graffiti, called it New York's urban art, but she only
glimpsed it. Saw what she wanted to see. Always had a
book two inches from the chunky glasses balanced on her
unforgiving nose. She swayed and jolted to wherever she
went, lost in another world, another time. Closed off from
strap-hanging folk on their way to windowless offices,
but she was coiled, ready to strike. Her lashing tongue,

*barbed words always found their mark. A thousand tiny
cuts. When she flew too close to the sun, my body bled.
After she tumbled to earth I tried to gather her in my
arms. Lift her out of blackness. She left me…. So like
Hank. Too much like…*

Maggie snaps shut her diary, words and heartbreak trapped
inside. She stares at her reflection in the window noticing
tanned skin, sad eyes, her downturned mouth and the grey
creeping through brown wavy hair. She glances at the solid
man wedged into the seat beside her. The large white
handkerchief covering his face rises and falls with each
measured snore. She wants to punch him. Hard. How dare he
sleep when her only relief is to scrawl her grief into a diary.
Below a dried up coopers creek staggers through shimmering
heat surrounded by ochre soil and sparse trees stretching for
miles. The vast open spaces and parched land reminds Maggie
of home. Only the ocotillo cactus and century trees are
missing. Maggie pushes a lock of hair behind her left ear and
glances out of the window. She spots a child waving near a
partially concealed pull-along camper and raises her hand in
a half- hearted greeting.

Beside her, Hank's large Texan frame fills the seat to
overflowing, his legs wedged under the seat in front. He's not
made for tiny planes. When she taps his arm, he removes the
handkerchief covering his face and glowers. 'What?'

'Buckle up.'

He caps his hand behind his ear. Maggie sighs, realising
he's turned off his hearing aids. Again. Or is this once again a
case of selective hearing? He never seemed to have any
trouble understanding her when they crouched beside a pond
at dusk trying to record the sound of mating frogs. She points
down. Hank glowers and fastens his seat belt. The plane
slowly circles and Maggie observes that the pull-along
camper is parked too close to a water hole. From her travels

in Africa, she knows that no critter in its right mind will drink there. Washing hung from a makeshift clothesline means soapsuds leaching into sand. A cloud obscures her view and she leans forward. Smoke. Burning wood. Mutilated trees? Crazy folk. She turns to Hank. 'Don't they know anything? Hank,' she shouts into his ear. 'Turn on your Goddamn hearing aids.'

Sitting on a log in pitiful shade beside the makeshift runway, Maggie reads her travel notes on Alan Moorhead's book Cooper's Creek. The tragedy of the story always saddens her. Explorers, Burke, Wills and King, on their return from the Gulf of Carpentaria, missed the expedition's back-up party by only hours and were too malnourished and weak to follow. They obeyed the blaze on a large coolibah tree —DIG 8ft NW April 21 1861— and found the supplies that lasted a month. Burke and Wills died of starvation. Only King survived. Such a harrowing tale.

Lionel, their tour leader, wanders over. 'We'll head off to see the Dig Tree in about ten minutes, Maggie.' He looks at his watch. 'We'll have lunch there.'

Maggie realises it will be at least another hour until she eats. Her stomach rumbles and she dreams of the cafe back home serving a two-inch-thick steak, smothered in crushed peppercorn sauce with a sprig of fresh parsley. She digs deep into her pack, riffling past passports, airline tickets and several books, hoping to find a spare cookie.

The story fills her mind as they stroll along the sandy track. Twigs snap and shatter under foot and a heavy blanket of heat saps her energy on the short walk to the Dig tree.

'On the way back we'll call into that camp we saw from the air,' Mike says. Hank nods, but Maggie curses under her breath. 'Goddamn tourists.'

*

A droning, buzzing sound tugs at Diane's thoughts. She swishes her hand in front of her face, but the gnat-like noise doesn't go away. Her barefoot daughter shouts and Diane hurries to the camper door. Kerry waves at a speck in the sky and laughs as it waggles its wings before disappearing beyond the tree line. Diane juggles two cans. Tinned sausages or baked beans? Big choice, but the nearest store is a day's travel away. But why worry? Kerry and her dad are a joy to feed. If Diane put a feather on a plate, they'd think it was chicken. She puts the tinned sausages back in the cupboard. What six-year-old doesn't like baked beans?

Theirs is the only camp for two hundred miles. The campervan shimmers in the energy-sapping heat. She feels like a gypsy. Everything they own—socks, shirts, pants, towels, sleeping bags— is securely pegged to hastily erected rope lines attached to two Coolibah trees. The luxury of an unlimited water supply means she no longer has to stand Kerry in a bucket, soap her down and rinse her with as little water as possible.

Kerry plays and splashes in the lagoon, her fair skin so tanned by lengthy days under the sun that, at a glance, blonde curls are the only difference between her and an aboriginal child. It has taken a long day of dirt, dust, cockatoos and kangaroos to travel from the outback town of Innamincka, population seven, to this oasis. Diane revels in the solitude. She doesn't have to answer to anyone. A hairdresser is always at someone's beck and call: you must fit me in. I must have my hair tinted, cut, permed, set, tipped, spiked. I'm going to a special date, dance, party, funeral, hospital.

The clients are always sharing their troubles with her. But Diane never shared hers with them. She ponders on her first marriage and messy divorce.

*

The squabbling of waking seagulls drags you out of your memories. You stretch aching shoulders before abandoning the computer, and the novel in progress. Under the shower you ponder whether to include your first marriage and messy divorce. Nineteen and ceremonially bound to a boy your own age. How young. How stupidly young. Your hasty wedding so reminiscent of long-gone war years. The borrowed gown, the romantic week in a family friend's cottage in the Dandenong ranges. His flight to Malaya to rejoin the 2nd Royal Australian Regiment commissioned to prevent Communist Terrorists crossing the Thai border. Two years protected by the army. The return to Australia to build a home and be told you couldn't have children. To be blessed three years later with a daughter, only for the dream to shatter. Eight years of marriage. Three years on your own. You pull your mind out of the past. No, better to leave all that out.

In 1974, at the local Baptist church, the sun shone, silk rustled and doves cooed when the Reverend Marks murmured a benediction. Both sets of elderly parents sighed with relief and toasted everything that moved at the reception at the Sundowner Hotel. Your little girl clung to Ron's knees as to a life raft in a storm. The adoption ceremony and three-month camping trip around Australia achieving the desired result, three different lives blending into a family. But there are parenting differences.

*

They are living their dream. Mum, Dad and daughter bonding in the isolation of the bush. Getting to know each other, testing strengths and weaknesses. Diane cannot resist Kerry's crumpled face and tear filled eyes and often, for the sake of peace, gives her the desired toy or chocolate. Ron believes the old adage, spare the rod and spoil the child still applies and that a swift hand across the buttocks does more good than harm. When crammed together in an old beat up campervan the differences in parenting techniques are accentuated.

'This sounds interesting.' Ron had pointed to an advertisement in *The Aussie Trader*. 'Much loved campervan. Needs repair. A thousand dollars.'

'Uh ha,' Diane murmured. Dishes clattered in the sink. To her, it sounded like a real estate advertisement for a 'renovator's dream.'

It took six months of sawing and hammering in the garage until after midnight before the camper, complete with new refrigerator and stove, was ready to transport them to what Diane referred to as, 'The trip of a lifetime'.

Kerry pesters Diane to distraction to play cards, or I Spy with My Little Eye, or help build a cubby. 'I'm bored,' she moans. Diane would kill for electricity, running water, and her twin tub washing machine features constantly in her dreams. But she would endure anything—dust, flies and even bindy burrs—to wake each morning to corellas squabbling in dead trees, a blue canopy of sky and no television. So much time is wasted on television and there is a constant haze of smog over the city. Out here, the stars at night are bigger, closer and almost touchable. She has everything she dreamed of, a husband and family she loved, a rewarding job, she is travelling the outback so why can't she shake a crazy feeling that there should be more to life than marriage, motherhood and work?

*

Mike leads Hank and Maggie down the sandy track. They are wearing battered khaki trousers and multi-pocketed vests. Binoculars and cameras swing from lanyards around their necks. Hank pulls off his floppy hat, runs calloused fingers through his thatch of greying hair, revealing dark eyes partially hidden beneath bushy eyebrows. He glares at the sun then drags the hat back on and, with outstretched hand, ambles over to Ron.

'Dr Livingston, I presume?'

Ron grins. 'Ron Simpson,' he says shaking hands.

'Where do you come from?'

'Melbourne.'

'You look like decent people,' Hank replies. Maggie smiles and shakes Diane's hand.

'What did you think of the Dig Tree?' Diane asks.

'Such a tragic tale.'

Diane nods and points to a canvas camp-chair tucked close to the camper. 'Take a load off your feet.' Maggie sinks into the chair, grateful for the sparse shade. Ron grabs a stick and lifts a battered kettle off the campfire. Michael tips his akubra back on his head and squats on his haunches. 'Glad to see you've kept the billy boiling.'

Hank, always ready for a cup of coffee, hitches trouser legs and, with a grunt, eases his bulky frame onto a log. 'Black, thanks.' He holds up two fingers. 'Two sugars.' He whisks away flies with the back of his hand. Holding an enamel mug, Hank noisily clangs the spoon. Maggie silently counts, four stirs clockwise and three anticlockwise, then waits for him to loudly sieve coffee through his bristly grey moustache. Once he settles down for a talk, there is no moving him. Maggie wants to see more than the blaze on the tree and hopes to wander off to a secluded spot to lie with her back on red earth and observe comical corellas bitch and squawk. Maybe catch a glimpse of the elusive blue kingfisher she'd read so much about. She resents the gruff male campfire talk. It sounds like a bar on a Saturday night. She licks dry lips.

She taps the chair beside her and Diane settles back with a thankful sigh. Maggie notes that Diane looks mid thirties, about the same age as Maggie's youngest daughter, Barb, but there the similarities end. Barb has olive skin, her thick black braid reaching to her waist. Diane is fair in a Nordic way, but her tight curly hair has dark roots. Maggie shivers. Hank's last fling had bottle blonde hair.

Kerry plonks herself at her mother's feet and Diane absent-mindedly strokes her daughter's curls. The gesture tugs at Maggie's heart. It is a long time since her children were small. How she wishes she could change places. To once again have two girls to love and cuddle. How different it is when they reach their thirties and you no longer have any hold on them. They come and go as they please and you count for nothing. She can't remember when she and her youngest, Barb, last expressed genuine affection.

'Coffee?' Diane picks up a mug, takes a heaped spoon from a jar of granules and adds water from the billy.

Maggie stares at the cup. What she needs at this moment is good strong coffee, brewed coffee made with real beans. She can cope, but life is too short for instant. She takes a couple of sips before placing the mug on the sand.

'Where are you from?' Diane passes Maggie a slab of fruitcake as big as a doorstop. In between bites Maggie sprouts like a glossy brochure as she promotes the glories of New Mexico. The blood red Sangre de Christo mountains, ice crystals turning trailing trees into frozen chandeliers, adobe houses high on a hill, Madonna-blue gates and the Palace of the Governors.

Diane listens intently. She waves her hand towards the little girl who has run off to play. 'I've always wanted to travel overseas, but with a six year old...' They watch Kerry happily add rocks to an already large cairn that is beginning to rival Machu Pitchu.

'An Afghan camel driver would be proud of Kerry's cairn.' Diane smiles as another rock is added. 'Got any kids?'

'Two daughters...' The cairn grows higher. 'And a

granddaughter.' Maggie nods towards Kerry. 'Older than your little gal'.

Diane offers more cake. Maggie shakes her head, grabs two imaginary waistline love handles before pointing to the camp oven. 'Smells delicious. What's cooking?'

'Damper.'

'What's that?'

'It's a type of bread and easy to make. Just mix together self-raising flour, water, a bit of oil and some salt.'

Maggie takes her journal out of her daypack and starts jotting notes.

'I'm the same.' Diane indicates the book. 'I always keep a record of our trips and I'm constantly making lists: shopping lists, things I need to do, things Ron needs to fix...Damper is great when I've run out of bread.'

Maggie tucks the journal back into her pack. 'Do you like to read?'

'When I get time.'

'Have you read Patrick White? *Voss* is a tour de force.'

Diane puts a log on the fire, pokes it with a stick and checks the camp oven. Maggie tries again. 'Marcus Clarke's *His Natural Life*?' There is no look of recognition. Diane asks who organised their tour.

'The Audubon Society.'

Diane shakes her head, so Maggie tells her that a rare first edition of John James Audubon's sumptuously illustrated *The Birds of America,* depicting more than four hundred life-size North American species in four monumental volumes, is her State Library's most valuable book.

Diane's face has a 'so what' look about it.

'It's worth over a million dollars.'

Diane raises her hands and shrugs her shoulders. 'A daughter, six days a week hairdressing, plus canteen duty at the school?'

They both smile. Maggie still remembers what it's like to

have young children.

Hank scuffs the red dust with his boot, picks up a fragment of bone, places it in his large palm, and prods it with a scarred brown thumb. 'Part of the mandible of a macropus giganteus.'

'Really?' Ron looks closely at the piece of kangaroo jawbone. Michael joins them in the shade. Diane can't keep her eyes off his bushy beard. She leans towards him. 'You look like Ned Kelly. Have you been to Glenrowan? Did you see the museum? Ned Kelly's armour was made out of ploughshares and they hanged him in the Old Melbourne Goal. He wrote a letter—'

'The famous Jerilderie letter.' Michael strokes his beard and laughs.

'Michael is also famous, Diane,' Maggie interrupts. 'He's the author of *Dingos, Wallabies* and *Painted Lizards*.'

'I've never met an author. It must take ages to write a book.' Diane smiles back at Mike as he whips a comb out of his pocket and removes crumbs trapped in his beard. 'Any dingos around here?'

'We hear them howling some nights,' Ron says. 'During the day, you can't get near them.'

'They get bad press,' Maggie says, her blood rising. 'Journalists write stories of howling Dingoes roaming the countryside and killing—

'It sells papers. You know that, Maggie,' Hank interrupts.
'But—'

'Drop it. Once you get started you don't know where to stop.'

Diane passes Mike the last piece of cake.

The men and Kerry wander off, their eyes scanning red soil while Diane and Maggie sit well back from the campfire and watch the billy boil. They chat about the weather, how quickly the washing dries and the outrageous price of a dozen eggs. The homey smell of cooking and the soft rustling of invisible creatures soothes Maggie's nerves, but Diane's needing- to- be-bleached hair tightens the stress knots in the back of her neck. It stirs a memory of her Anna when she tried to bleach her hair and ended up with an orange spiky crop that defied definition. Anna. Everything came back to Anna, reminded her of Anna...

'That must be cold.' Diane points to Maggie's mug. She shakes her head, but Diane throws the contents onto thirsty soil and makes another cup. 'Would you like powdered milk? More sugar?'

To cover the awkwardness Maggie prattles about books, poetry and writing limericks. Diane tries to keep up and nods occasionally while poking the already red-hot coals of the fire.

'You've lost me, Maggie,' she finally says. 'I'd love to be able to talk about books. Be well read and write poetry like you.' She sighs and glances at Kerry paddling along the edge of the waterhole. 'Maybe I can find time to borrow some books from the local library when I get home.'

'There are many famous authors, such as Virginia Woolf and Christina Stead, but I suggest you start off with *Jane Eyre* by Charlotte Brontè. It focuses on the emotions and experiences of a thinking, passionate woman. I'm sure you'll like it.'

'Jane?' Diane smiles wickedly. 'I know her well. She has a white minx rinse before her hairset every week.'

Maggie wriggles in her seat, appreciating the joke, because she's done it again. Let her passion for books override her sensitivity. 'That fruitcake was delicious. It's the best I've ever tasted.'

Diane smiles and eases back in her chair. 'I'll send you the recipe if you like. What's your address?' Maggie rummages around in her backpack until she finds one of Hank's cards.

> *HENRY. M. JACKSON*
> *11 Camino del Poniente*
> *Santa Fe, New Mexico 83565 USA*

Tearing a scrap of paper from the bottom of a *Woman's Weekly* magazine, Diane writes.

Diane Simpson. 57 Kingsley St Kubungi Beach
3192. Victoria Australia

Maggie tucks the address inside her journal, recalling many exchanges of addresses. Hank's cards handed out to networking acquaintances at conferences, in hotel lobbies, to wide-eyed students clinging to his coat tails desperate to tap into his body of knowledge. This time, Maggie wishes she had a card of her own.

*

Diane chews the end of her pen. What do you say to a well educated American woman? She glances at the clock on the kitchen wall. Any minute now, Kerry will bounce in, throw her books on the table and then it will be Mum this, Mum that, until tea time.

12/10/1975

> *Dear Mrs Jackson,*
> *I hope you are well we...*

She frowns, screws the page into a ball and tosses it amongst the other false starts littering the table.

Dear Mrs Jackson,

> *It was lovely meeting you at the dig tree and when you*
> *walked over that sand dune you seemed to come from*
> *nowhere and we must have looked so grotty with all that*
> *washing hanging everywhere and kerry was running wild.*

Diane bites her thumbnail as she stares at the brief words it has taken ages to write. At this rate she will never finish. She bends her head to the task.

*You will be pleased to hear that when we got home I
joined our local library and they got your tour guide's
book in for me. I thought danny was such a lovely dingo
its no wonder Michael wrote about him.*

Diane scratches her head seeking inspiration.

*Is it cold over their in Santa Fe. It is so hot hear and we
will soon be swimming in the bay. Kerry loves the beach.
Im expecting her in at any minute because it only takes
her a quarter of an hour to walk home from the local state
school. Ron is back working at vallor optics in the city and
Im still cutting and curling at christobell hairdressing
salon. I hope you like the photos and if you have the time it
would be great if you could write back to me.*

Diane leans back and sighs, remembering her mother
sitting at her green laminated kitchen table, head bent, pen in
hand, writing a letter, herself a child twirling and swirling to
a tune on the radio. *Pack up your troubles in your old kitbag and
smile, smile, smile.* The music stops. Her mother listens intently
to the news of the final destruction of Germany and shakes
her head. In the centre of the table are the makings of a food
parcel. An open tin containing fruitcake, biscuits, hand-
knitted socks and chocolate. Diane kneels on a chair and
reaches into the tin.

'Get your hands out of there, you little devil.' Her mother
laughingly pushes her away. 'This is for people far worse off
than us.' She sits Diane in the chair and takes the remains of
yesterday's large block-loaf of bread from out of the
cupboard. Holding the loaf against her chest, cut side up, she
spreads it with jam. When she hacks a thick slice towards
her large bosom, Diane holds her breath. Munching on her
jam piece she watches her mother carefully fold the letter,
then place it in an envelope and put it in the tin. She looks
around for the large roll of silver duct-tape, finds it, and

enthusiastically secures the lid. Diane helps her wrap the tin in a square of rough hessian material, then her mother, with a big bag needle and strong thread, sews it secure. In bold black marking pen she writes, Mr & Mrs Donovan, 54 Lee St Highams Park London. Tomorrow, she will post her bundle to Britain.

After the war, Diane's mum constantly checked the letterbox. When a blue-striped envelope arrived, she hurried inside. Holding the letter close to her chest, she made a cup of tea then settled into her favourite lounge chair with hand-crochet covers draped over the arms. A letter knife, kept especially for the occasion, slit the thin aerogram edge. The aerogram was so thin it looked as if it would crumble to dust if harshly handled. Diane knew whining, or temper tantrums would be ignored until every word was devoured.

'It's snowing in Higham Park,' her mum said, wiping sweat from her forehead.

'Margery sends her love,' she softly whispered to herself.

Diane glances at the letter in her hand and wonders if she is seeking the same friendship, the same connection to someone overseas as her mother? Maybe Diane wants a Margery of her own. And Maggie is a poet. Diane wishes she could distil her own feelings into words that paint indelible pictures. After adding a photo of herself and Maggie sitting together in the shade, Diane seals the envelope and then, in her best writing, prints: Mrs. M Jackson, 11 Camino del Poniente, Santa Fe. New Mexico, 83565 America. An offending thumb mark quickly erased ensures the letter is looking its best. Complete with colourful stamp she will post it on her way to work tomorrow. She crosses her fingers and hopes for a reply.

*

*You look in despair at the computer screen. Writing a
novel is like trying to drive a bulky four-wheel drive with
a flat tyre. It won't do what you want it to. You struggle
with what appears to be pages of useless drivel. At least
you won't be upset if you once again click some vague
computer key and lose two hours of work. Good riddance.
You can't think of more to write. Maybe a cup of
espresso, strong and black with just a touch of milk, will
help you concentrate.*

*A folder on the floor drags you back from the brink of
despair. There are some benefits to being a hoarder. At
least you have many of Maggie's letters. Some are in an
A4 folder, still others neatly filed in the cabinet under
Letter/Maggie/Dig Tree.*

*You didn't think to copy and file any of your letters.
There are some personal notes wedged between the cost
of petrol and details of where you camped each night in
your diary. Not letters as such, just rambling notes and
impressions with many missing years in between. Have
you recaptured the person you were back in the
seventies? Dug deep enough into your memory ten,
twenty, thirty years ago to that first trip to the banks of
Cooper's Creek.*

*

The wooden door slams behind Maggie, making the garland of
red chillies quiver. She can still hear Hank ranting and raving
that her research is incomplete, full of mistakes. Like always,
she followed his orders to the letter. As far as she's concerned,
he can type the damn essay himself.

Gravel crunches underfoot. It feels as if the snow will
arrive early this year, so Maggie is glad of her warm sweater.
She hates the cold, but it is still better than the humid
fecundity of the tropics. It's impossible for her to breathe

there. She needs the clear air of Santa Fe's high altitude to get air deep into her weak lungs.

The flag is up on the mailbox. Dragging a stack of envelopes from beyond the steel trapdoor, Maggie hurries inside and puts on the coffee percolator. It's the usual stack of bills. She systematically slits them open with the tapered letter opener that belonged to her mother. Everything is addressed to Hank, until, on the last envelope, she sees: Mrs. M Jackson. She has difficulty reading the longhand scrawl and the spelling mistakes grate, but the words transport her to another country where spring is the air.

The pleasure of the letter is astonishing. Diane considers her a poet. Maggie wonders if she can claim that title. She writes in her diary every day and lines of poetry constantly run through her mind. But If she is completely honest she only shares her verses with her writing group. To be published is Hank's domain. Diane's childish script has poor punctuation, the spelling is appalling, but it is wholesome and heart-warming. And Maggie feels that sort of effort deserves a reply.

11/13/1975

Dear Diane,
Usually at this time I am out doing my early morning
walk, but today I made up my mind to reply to your letter.

Maggie leans back in her chair. Why is she doing this? Why doesn't she simply ignore Diane's letter. Throw it in the bin. Maggie hates writing letters. It takes ages to check every word and it still doesn't convey what she wants to say. Poetry is so different. She leans forward and scrawls on a piece of paper.

How many hours have I spent. Thoughts beating in my mind, pinning down a sentiment when suddenly...

She peers out of the window, forehead furrowed, searching for exactly the words that convey how she feels.

She smiles and writes,

when suddenly I find that words, so nearly sentient
can die when too confined—

That's it. That's what she means, but she can't send that to Diane. She wouldn't understand.

Maggie knows she is not lazy. For every trip she has a typed and bound copy of her handwritten travel diaries. All are referenced, every detail meticulously recorded: time, place, temperature, people and addresses. But sometimes, she wishes she could be like her first-born. Anna filled book after book with thousands of imaginative words. But Maggie cannot write about wild, other worlds, of mythical flying beasts and fairylike creatures.

She reads Diane's letter again, the spelling mistakes like squeaking chalk on a blackboard. The Devil's fingernails scratching her intellect. She's spent too many years editing and proof reading Hank's papers. Goddamnit. That girl doesn't have a hope in hell of getting on in life if she doesn't learn to spell. Maggie's fingers automatically grasp the red pen and with a will of their own start circling, underlining and correcting.

I hope you don't mind me correcting your letter, Diane,
but we often don't see our own mistakes. Have you
thought of consulting a dictionary? I know a great many
people who have trouble with spelling, and I've always
wondered why they don't check...

Maggie glances at the photos on her desk. Diane and herself. Forever smiling, clutching that dreadful coffee in hot enamel mugs. Slouched in chairs in scarce shade, they are both at ease. What do they have in common? Nothing. Different interests, level of education, lifestyle, and an age gap of thirty years, not to mention a different culture and country. Enough to put off anyone.

She glances at the photo again. Sees the clothes line, dishes in a bowl of suds, the remnants of a once large fruitcake. Camp oven on the fire. Two women coping with the whims and needs of men. At least they have daughters.

The desert landscape reminds her that...

Hank and I are originally Westerners. We spent thirty-two years with the Department of Reptiles and Amphibians at the American Museum of Natural History in New York, but missed the West so much that he took early retirement. We moved back to Santa Fe to be close to our youngest daughter, Barb.

Maggie stares out of the window lost in her memories.

Mother beckons and Maggie runs. She hoists Maggie astride her ample knees and holds her hands. She starts to jig. Mother laughs and bounces Maggie. They chant; *I sprang to the stirrup, and Joris, and he, I galloped, Dirck galloped, we galloped all three.* Afterwards, they sit side by side at the dining room table cluttered with story books, colouring pads and pencils. Mother makes loopy letters. Later, she cleans Maggie's ears with the head of a bobby pin.

Father stands, arms crossed, staring at Maggie over horn-rimmed glasses. His friends call him Stony. A great nickname for a petroleum geologist. Hands on her hips, feet well spread and with clean ears, Maggie recites: 'The sedimentary aspects of the stratum,' she looks at Father to check if he is listening: 'Has internally consistent characteristics,' another check, 'That distinguishes it from contiguous layers.'

'Have you finished talking, Maggie, or are you going to enlighten us some more?' he sarcastically enquires. She runs and hides under the bed. His loud raucous laugh follows her. She saw the twinkle in his eye and discovered that a sure way to extract an approving guffaw was to recount passages of poems from the leather bound, gilt edged book with **RB** on the front. In a thick Scottish accent, accompanied by elaborate gestures she'd recite,

To a Mouse.

Wee sleekit, cow'rin', tim'rous beastie
O what a panic's in they breastie.
Thous need na start awa sae hasty
wi' bickering brattle.

Maggie's father liked to believe he was a direct descendant of Rob Roy. With a surname like Roydon, it could be truth. Her mother's maiden name was Finney. Scot and Irish. What a genetic mixture. When Maggie was born, her father took one glance, said she looked like a little Irish Mick, and named her, Maggie. Such an unforgiving name for a child.

*

Diane stands beside her brick letterbox and stares with amazement at the red white and blue edged envelope with the American stamp. She had hoped for but not expected a reply. Hot sun stings her skin and she hurries inside. Holding the letter close to her chest, she takes a mug of coffee to the kitchen table then carefully opens the envelope. A photo reveals Maggie standing in front of her snow-encrusted adobe home. Ropes of red chillies frame the door. Diane holds the photo to her nose, hoping for a whiff of the icy coolness of Santa Fe.

She reads the letter twice, savouring Maggie's childhood memories and family news. It is a generous response. But there is a sting attached. Neatly folded behind Maggie's words is the letter she sent. Every spelling mistake is underlined in red, the correct spelling in firm, minute script in the margin. Diane is shocked to see so many.

For years, she's been writing letters to friends and family. Loves the feel of the pen skimming across the paper, unable to keep up with thoughts tumbling onto the page. Little daily dramas, cute kiddie sayings, camping adventures with never a thought about spelling. If she had to spend time checking every word, she'd never write to anyone. Diane screws her edited letter into a ball and throws it into the pedal bin. Why bother? She doesn't have time for such nonsense. Leave correct spelling and well-crafted letters to ageing poets.

She pins the photo next to one of Kerry's drawings on a corkboard on the kitchen wall. While preparing the evening meal, and all through dinner she keeps glancing at the photo. Maggie's eyes challenge her.

*

Maggie pulls out the drawer in her writing desk and scratches around amongst paper clips, staples, and a two-hole punch. In amongst the clutter she finds her Father's leather wallet with the tooled Indian head on the front. Inside is a folded piece of paper.

*I hate to appear bumptious, or even so presumptuous, as
to talk about that taboo subject, money.*

Her father's doggerel. It always makes her laugh. So comical, so political

*It seems that some can't find it, and others never mind it,
and that, to me, is something less than funny.*

He travelled the world. In his letters to her, he would start a verse and she would write one back. It only stopped when he died. The date in the top right hand corner of this letter is 2/8/1965 when America was heavily involved in the space race and committed to the Vietnam War.

*It is time to be specific, either Space, or the Pacific, and
decide to give it everything, and soon. We are fed up:
can't absorb it. What use put a man in orbit: is anything
we need found on the moon?*

At the bottom of the page is her reply.

*I'm sending you this token of poetic spirit broken, Of high
ambitions buried in the ground. Since I've lost my rhyme
and reason And this ain't the time or season, I'm willing
to concede the latest round.*

Carefully folding the yellowing paper into its original
creases, she tucks it back into her Father's wallet. She misses
the old son of a bitch. She grabs pen and paper.

12/16/1975

*Dear Diane, Have you heard of doggerel poetry? If you
receive any Christmas letters in the form of bad poetry
then you certainly have experienced it. Why do people
insist on sending those inane Dear Blank Christmas
verses? You'll never get one from me.*

Strangely, she no longer feels so alone. Pouncing on a stray
thirty-one cent airmail stamp, she licks it and presses it on
the envelope addressing it to Kubunji Beach.

*

10/1/1976

*Dear Maggie, I looked up doggerel in one of two amazing
books I bought the other day from a second-hand
bookshop. They were only a dollar each. They have
brown leather covers with gold writing and a gold
pineapple in a circle for a badge. Together they make a
complete Funk and Wagnalls Dictionary. The first book
goes from A to P and the second one from Q to Z, but the
part I like best is the section with foreign words. First,
there is the English word, followed by French, German,
Italian, Spanish, Swedish and the last one is Yiddish.
Amazing. The books are so big I could use them for a
doorstop. According to page 375 of Part One, doggerel is
trivial, awkwardly written verse. I thought of trying to*

Diane rests her chin in her hand and rereads Maggie's letter. It is an invitation to share her life, but she's never had time to sit and think about the past. It's just that, the past. What can she tell Maggie? She chews the end of her pen. Her mind drifts to the clouds.

The train, nicknamed The Red Rattler, clicks and clacks its way from Taylor to Buntland. Half an hour's travel filled with schoolgirl giggles and daydreams. Diane stares out of the window from sleep-rimmed eyes at broken paling-fences, rusting swings, overgrown vegetable gardens and flapping washing. She makes up stories about the occupants based on their laundry. Nappies snuggle next to support hose. Flimsy night-dresses seductively flap. While on other lines, Yakka overalls overpower football socks, and grandpa long johns. All the stories have happy-ever-after endings. Diane looks for the spire of the Noblevale Girls Domestic Arts School. When the train pulls into Buntland station, old English beech trees block her view.

The school day is spent cooking cakes and buns, learning how to fold a nappy, sterilise bottles, sew floral pyjamas and crochet lace tablecloths. High on the agenda is how to organise a household budget for a family of four and to sing like an angel. After all, the girls are told, they will soon marry so why do they need to learn advanced arithmetic?

Diane soon discovers her mother is right. The way to a man's heart is through his stomach. Rock cakes, slightly out of shape, but with a daub of raspberry jam in the middle, are a boy magnet on the train going home. The rich smell of freshly baked cakes fills the carriage as giggling girls distribute culinary treasures to favourite ravenous boys. The girls don't keep any for themselves. Instead, they watch with parted lips and shining eyes as their gifts are consumed. With tilted berets, singing Fortis et Fidelis, they promise to be strong and faithful.

*

Diane's Journal: Australia

Leaving a domestic arts school at fourteen—after passing Home Management, Cooking, Sewing, mothercraft, first-aid, Music, Sport (how you hated those baggy Bombay bloomers), Geography and basic English, ensured you were well suited to a life of domesticity or for what your parents called 'a good trade'. Later, your world was quartering apples for the school tuck-shop, washing and ironing, Mum's Taxi Service and hairdressing. You had it all, a caring husband, a healthy child, a house, a car and a job you loved. So why did you yearn deep inside for something you couldn't name?

In 1955 this was just the way the world was for you. Most of the boys who ate the rock cakes on the Taylor train went to the local technical school to learn how to dig trenches, join pipes, saw timber and build houses so they could support a wife and children. Your mother often quoted Alfred Lord Tennyson's 'Ours is not to reason why, ours is but to do and die' as a fact of life. You now know different.

*

We love living at Kubunji Beach, Maggie. Lots of birds visit our yard. Ron made a fancy wooden birdfeeder complete with roof and tiny swings. He placed it on top of a tall pole so next door's cat can't scare the birds. Yesterday, two rosellas chased off at least five pigeons to get to the seed. I buy it by the bag from a seed merchant in Lockwood. If I get time, I love to walk along the local

31

beach picking up bits and pieces. On the mantelpiece is a
big glass bowl full of shells I've collected over the years.
But I don't get much time to go to the beach these days.
There is always so much to do.

The unfinished letter waits on the kitchen table. Diane sighs and dumps her shoulder bag and hairdressing kit onto the tiled bench. It had taken three days and twenty mesh sheets, each supporting a dozen two-inch tiles and a gallon of grout to finish the bench. The pleasing effect, spurred her on to renovate the entire kitchen. The antique olive and ochre colour scheme gleaned from television images of ancient stone Mediterranean villas and gossiping black-scarfed women. A terracotta fruit bowl completed the Italian kitchen theme. After successfully tiling the bench, the kitchen floor was next, followed by the floor of the thirty-foot-long family room. Not a perfect job, but better than worn-out vinyl and saved them a fortune in labour.

She glances at the huge kitchen clock above the refrigerator. In two hours, Ron will be home from Vallor Optics. Grinding spectacle lenses is a precise, painstaking job requiring a firm hand and unlimited patience. A lens pressed too hard against the emery wheel will explode and the whole process has to start all over again. Five years ago, he found the clock beside the workshop garbage bins in Old Hardware Lane.

'It still works perfectly,' he said, standing well back to admire the three foot round chrome creation.

'But it's big enough to hang at the Flinders Street Railway Station.'

'It'll grow on you.'

'The ticking will drive me insane.'

Years later, Diane has learned to live with it. He won't part with his clock no matter how much she complains.

She's got fifteen minutes until Kerry charges in waving her latest creative masterpiece. Where on earth will she put it?

The fridge door is already covered in crayoned butcher's paper and fridge magnets. Kerry's latest of Mum, Dad and self has huge belly buttons, podgy hands and fat sausage fingers. Diane looks for a spare spot. She decides to place it next to the four-wheel-drive chugging up a vertical mountain. Kerry's rays of a bright yellow sun, like fingers of God, bless the right-hand corner of every scene.

Diane glances at the clock. Ten minutes left of peace and quiet. Just enough time to finish Maggie's letter. The back door bangs.

'Hi Mum.'

Diane puts down her pen.

'I want a dog.' Kerry dumps her schoolbag on the floor. Her jumper next to it. She puts her arms around Diane's waist.

'Can I Mum? Everyone at school has a dog.'

'Who will look after it when we go camping?'

'Grandma loves dogs.' Kerry looks confidently at Diane. 'She'll take him.'

A chorus of barking welcomes them to the dog pound.

'I'd like a small, shorthaired bitch,' Diane says to the receptionist. Rows of cages stretch before them. Kerry heads for an Alsatian as big as a horse. Then she wants a Bull Mastiff that bares its teeth and growls. Diane snatches Kerry's hand back before she loses a finger.

'What about this one?' A whimpering brown and white wire haired terrier licks Diane's hand. Pink tongue slipping through gaps in the wire.

'What's her name?' Diane asks the attendant.

'Sally.'

They soon discover why Sally was left at the pound. She hovers three inches behind the heels of whoever is closest, and they are forever tripping over her. Throw a ball and she will fetch, but only in one direction. If, after throwing the ball left, Diane throws it to the right, Sally will still run left and keep going, forever chasing an imaginary ball.

They take her to the local beach, and she starts swimming to Tasmania. The local life saver has to paddle out on his board and bring her back. In Kerry's arms Sally's paws are still paddling. When Diane moves Kerry's bedroom furniture, they wonder if Sally has serious mental problems. Every morning, as soon as Kerry's door is opened, Sally jumps onto her bed. For the week after redecorating, Sally runs in, jumps and hits the wall where the bed used to be. Dumb dog. They jokingly agree that if by any chance she dies, they should have her stuffed and stand her, head leaning pathetically against the very expensive unused doggie door. That way they wouldn't miss her so much.

Whack. Crack. Yelp. Diane dashes to the back door.

'Sally,' she calls. The wire haired terrier, tail between her legs, runs to meet her. From the step, through the cyclone-wire back fence, Diane can see to the end of the golf course. Gum trees vie with wattles; mushrooms are plentiful and every year a cherry plum provides a dozen jars of jam. She laughingly calls the Greendale Golf Course her 'country estate'. It is Kerry's haven. A place where, every night after school, with friends in tow, she can run, hide and make cubbies. If only they could stop Sally digging under the fence and retrieving golf balls.

We have tried to continue the golf course theme into our own backyard. Two large flowering gums shade tree ferns and ivy-covered, rock-edged gardens surround a small patch of lawn. If we stuck a flag in the centre, it could be mistaken for a putting green. Life is so busy these days. We—

Time. There is never enough. The Valor Optics reject clock rules Diane's life.

Five a.m. Wave goodbye to Ron, who walks to the Kubunji Beach station to catch the five thirty-two a.m. train for the city. Six thirty a.m. Sing, *Wake up chickabiddie the morning is* bright. *The birds are all singing to welcome the light,* and drag Kerry out of bed. Six forty five a.m. Cook and cover the evening meal to save time later in the day. Seven thirty a.m. Pull back the collar of Kerry's shirt to check what's underneath. The memory of the last classroom Show and Tell still haunts Diane.

'Look everyone,' Kerry said, standing on the platform in front of the class and pulling up her woollen jumper. 'I still have my jamies on under my clothes.' Drop her at school and arrive at the Christobell Coiffure Hairdressing Salon at the Thrift Park at exactly 9:00 a.m. The first client in the chair impatiently taps her foot. No time to think. Elderly parents organised to pick up Kerry after school and keep her until Diane arrives home.

Maggie, I envy you your childhood surrounded by books.
The only book we had was the Bible and no one read that.
Any spare time was spent playing in our big backyard.
Did you ever play hopscotch or make jacks from lamb
knuckles? At night, we watched TV and split our sides
laughing at the series Dad and Dave. Most nights I'd pull
the blankets over my head, turn on the bedside radio and
shiver at the sound of a creaking door introducing The
Inner Sanctum Mysteries. During the day, there were
always chores to do. Reading was considered a waste of
time. Even now, I find it hard not to feel guilty if I sit and
read a book. I love hearing about your family. My
parents live ten minutes away...

She writes about her German ancestry. How Kerry never tires of the story of *Little Red Riding mit de Red Hoot.* Ex-military, Diane's dad is tall and stern, but keeps Columbine toffees in his pocket and spoils Kerry rotten. Australian-born Mum, short, tubby and as soft as butter. Knits dozens of jumpers for Kerry from discarded garments. The wool unravelled, washed and then knitted again in stripes to rival a bumblebee. Osteoarthritis means a walking stick. Jokingly, she brandishes her weapon at Kerry.

'Not the stick, Grandma.' Kerry laughs, dropping to her knees in prayer position. 'Anything but the stick.'

But that's enough about my family, Maggie.
I must tell you about Ron's parents.

She blurbs on the page that they live across the street and Pop is a real Cockney from the Old Country, who can barely write his name. He lost the top of his finger at the local saw mill and cut it down to the first knuckle with a breadknife. He got more worker's compensation that way. Ma insisting she is Australian. In 1917 both lied about their ages to do their bit for the war effort. Pop gassed in France. Ma nursed him in an army hospital and both of them seventeen. Most days finding Ma crocheting rugs and listening to classical music, Scamp, one of her two cats, curled on her knee. How she is the most tolerant person Diane knows. If Ron said, 'Ma, I think we'll go to the moon tomorrow,' she'd say, 'Have a nice time, Dear.' Every Sunday, the family gathers for lunch at Diane and Ron's Kubunji Beach home.

Diane glances at the clock, where has the time gone? She hastily scrawls, *Six o'clock. Must run.* Signs the bottom of the letter in a flourish and stuffs it into the stamped-addressed envelope, the glue stinging her tongue.

*

3/20/1976

Dear Diane, I am a very curious person and was
interested to hear about your life. There is something
indulgent about revisiting the past. I often wonder if my
memories are true. Did things really happen that way, or
is it a construct of my imagination? Some people yearn
for the good old days, but my memories from when I was
young are of my family constantly on the move. I went to

Maggie looks back at the last sentence. Miserable is the word. Her father was constantly assigned to different locations, and they were forever packing their bags and following. She hated high school in Glendale, California. All that false glamour and gossip parties. In laced up boots and old baggy jeans, she adopted a John Wayne swagger and thumbed her nose at prissy girls.

And Phil Schutz? Maggie dredges up memories of pumping worms out of the muddy bank of the local stream. Ignoring sticky goo oozing through their fingers when threading fishhooks down through worm heads. The death throes irresistible to rainbow trout. Two Huckleberry Finns strutting home. Catch slung over their shoulders.

She lost days reading books, captivated by the lives of people in the stories: the struggles of artists in dreary attics, the hungry years of couples in tiny apartments and anything she could lay her hands on about the natural world. She was a whiz at the natural sciences; only studied subjects that she liked and managed to avoid anything to do with math. Even now, Hank looked after the finances.

When she won a full scholarship to Mills College in Oakland. She thought it could be the answer to her prayers but it was more misery: no boys, except on weekends as dates. Horrors. No wonder she told the college they could keep their scholarship, went back south and enrolled at UCLA.

The auditorium was filled to overflowing. Students dropped pens, discussed plans for the weekend, and shuffled papers, but when the famous herpetologist, Charles Mathew Jackson strode into the room it was possible to have heard the flutter of a butterfly's wings. A single tap on the microphone, one look from glowering eyes, half hidden beneath bushy eyebrows, ensured complete silence. And Maggie, his university-appointed research assistant—the one who toiled though microfiche files, found dozens of relevant journals, photocopied, read and summarised, typed reports listing everything under theme, topic, keyword or author? She sat behind him on the stage.

His large hands gripped either side of the podium. He leaned forward and intoned, 'Today we focus on the life habits of the...'

No need to listen or take notes. She researched the paper. Typed it. Hank pulled himself up to his full six foot five and tightened his buns. Great buns. Maggie laughs at the memory of adoring faces, leather patched elbows on desks, chins resting on hands clasping pens raised ready to preserve every word the Great Man uttered. What would they have thought if they knew the night before, Hank, their prestigious professor wearing only socks, was in her bed?

Maggie enjoys the fringe benefits of being married to someone famous and accompanying him on his university-funded research trips.

I love to travel. Imagine having three great trips in one twelve-month period. In Peru, we visited the fantastic ruins of Machu Picchu. I'm sure you have heard of it. It is hard to believe that without modern machinery...

They were retired, but funded research still takes them into the Arizona and Mexican deserts searching for rattlesnakes. A hessian bag in one hand and long hooked stick with a retractable rubber loop in the other. On hearing the familiar buzz identifying a rattler, Hank deftly slips the noose over its head then carefully drops the snake into the sack. Maggie pulls the drawstring tight. If it is a small specimen, guess who carries the bag? Later, Hank measures, weighs and bands the snake, then rejoices while it slithers across hot sand to freedom.

Local village children always gather around them begging

for sweets. Hank grins wickedly and shakes a discarded snake rattle in a small clear plastic box. They scream, eyes scanning the ground, until he opens his hand. They say he is loco.

'*Para que los amigos,*' he says, handing out chocolate. A month later, we are off again, this time carefully imprisoning scorpions in screw-top jars.

On the bottom bookshelf in her study she searches past Africa, Canada and Easter Island until she has Peru in her hands. She opens the journal at random and reads.

Huge blocks of stone were so perfectly fitted that even now, you can't put a knife blade between them. Machu Picchu is 7000 feet above sea level, about the same elevation as Santa Fe. The pointed peak behind the ruins seems impossible to climb, but....

On top of the world, she flings her arms wide and embrace the glory of mountain peaks. A wild wind presses her clothes tight against what she calls her fubsy frame. Stones, covered in moss, long tumbled over precipices, rest on vivid green grass far below. The porters smile at her rapturous joy. Sitting on their haunches, they husk corn and boil herb flavoured rice. Such strong men: rugged and vital with the timeless features of the ancients. Their colourful serapes the same as the singing shepherds herding llamas past huge boulders. Feathery tussocks curl like lighted incense sticks in large brass cauldrons in smoke-drowsy temples.

'Maggie,' Hank calls. 'Where are my glasses?'

'In your duffle bag.' Hank is on his knees, bending over a small green fern half-hidden by a moss-covered rock. He counts the fronds. Without looking up, he snaps his fingers and stretches out his hand, palm up. Maggie rummages amongst shirts and shorts until she clasps the firm cylinder of the glasses case then slaps it into his open hand.

'We may have a new species here,' he says, voice trembling. Maggie drops down beside him and peers at the tiny fragile fern.

'It resembles Cyathea concordia. Look,' he says in awe, pointing to a leaf. 'The hairs are restricted to the veins and,' he takes a deep breath, 'Are those coloured stem scales?'

'Has it been recorded?'

He doesn't answer, already mentally writing his paper, etching his name forever into refereed scientific journals. Maggie's excitement dies. Over thirty years ago, he discovered a new species of snake. All this discovery means is more work for her. More research and pages and pages of typing.

What will you name it? she inquires. Hank grabs her hand. She can't believe it when he says, 'I'm naming it *Maggie Meum Concordiae.*'

Maggie faithfully records everything and imagines Diane's delight when she finds a photo copy of the journal in her next letter.

From La Paz, Bolivia, to Santiago in Chile and then on to Easter Island with its strange stone figures. There are more horses than people. The friendly islanders gallop madly everywhere. This is one of the remotest spots on earth. The air is pure and clean, and so is the ocean. On the map, Easter Island is almost due south of Albuquerque...

Thirty hours straight to get home. Thirty hours. Two thousand miles east to Chile, north to Miami and then west to Albuquerque. How ridiculous.

'Damn airplanes,' Hank moans. 'Noisy, crowded and once they git you in, you can't git out.' He refuses to be crammed into what he calls the sheep section. At the boarding gate in Miami, every seat is full. Tired toddlers run endlessly up and down luggage-laden aisles.

'Attention all passengers on American Airways flight 507 travelling from Miami to Albuquerque. Due to mechanical problems, your flight has been delayed' booms over the loud speaker. Maggie puts her hand on Hank's knee to stop the drumming of his foot.

'Flight 507 will now depart at eleven p.m.'

Hank pushes her hand aside and strides over to the newspaper stand. He angrily flicks pages of several books without buying one. With the Financial Times tucked under his arm, Hank makes his way to the counter then hands the sales clerk the exact change.

'Have a nice day,' the girl says. Hank looks around the crowded airport. 'I have other plans,' he replies and strides off.

Maggie worries that there is no way of getting word to Barb. She left Santa Fe hours ago on the long trip to the Albuquerque airport.

Dear Maggie, I hope you didn't mind me asking for a copy of your travel journal. It sounds like a wonderful trip, and I don't think we'll ever get to Peru. I've always dreamt of travelling to exotic places, but with Kerry to educate...

The back door bangs.
'Kerry, I've told you a thousand times not to slam the door.'
'But Mum...'
'It will soon be off its hinges.'
'But Mum.'
'Don't but Mum me.'
'But Mum, I've got a letter from Miss Finlay. She says to tell you I won that scholarship to Hallston College.'

Diane hugs Kerry and blesses her teacher in year-six at Kubunji Beach State School for suggesting Kerry sit for the entry exam.

Kerry thrives on a blend of academic classes, basketball and music. Soaking in the bath is what looks like an upturned cow's-bladder. Kilted in green-and-gold Gordon tartan, Kerry looks every bit a Highland lassie. After several noise-induced headaches, Diane bans practising in the family room; the wail of bagpipes not so ear-shattering in the backyard. Not so for Sally. Sitting on the back step, head at a pathetic angle, the dog howls. Many a Greendale golfer misses a putt on the seventh green.

It is a struggle to pay for school fees, books, uniforms, sporting activities and excursions. Diane shops at the local market for specials, forgets the new lounge suite and replaces the worn-out welsh plugs in her 1965 XP Ford Falcon. When she hears the newly constructed Riverside Retirement Village wants a hairdresser one day a week, she feels it is the answer to her prayers.

No matter how early she arrives at the salon, there are always several elderly clients sitting in chairs waiting for her to open the door.

'Don't hurry, Dear.' They patiently watch Diane fumble for the salon keys in her bag.

'We have all day. No rush.'

The clients are mainly women in their seventies and eighties who grab the broom and sweep up hair, pop chocolates in Diane's mouth to keep her going, bring her coffee in bone china teacups with sugar lumps on the side.

'How wonderful to be so young,' they say on days when she drags her feet. They chat, tell jokes and laugh until tears run down wizened cheeks.

'Do everything while you can. Life is so short.' They have so many stories to tell. Lifetimes of experiences. Diane starts keeping a journal.

After Kerry and Ron are in bed, exercise book on her knee, warmed by the Coonara heater, she scribbles long into the night. Her pen skims across the page capturing stories.

Ninety-three-year-old Violet remembering collecting wood for the outside copper where her mother boiled and scrubbed other peoples' clothes.

Danny, a World War Two fighter pilot with a severed nerve in his leg who drags his right foot, whispering of the horror of being a prisoner of war.

Eighty-nine-year-old Thelma, blue-rinsed hair bobbing,

hurrying into the salon requesting, 'Please fit me in. I'm off to hospital today for an autopsy.'

Diane laughs, remembering her shocked reaction. Autopsy/biopsy. Similar words, but such different meanings. Thelma always mixes up her words. She told Diane about a visit to a local Italian restaurant and asking for a small serving of gnocchi.

'I love a bit of nookie,' she said.

Thelma was the reason Diane bought a journal in the first place. She had to jot it down. Had to share it with Maggie.

*

Maggie turns on the TV for the CNN news. Images flash across the screen. Pelicans struggle and die in a black oil slick oozing over the beaches of Brittany. A turban-headed Ayatollah sits cross-legged in the grass, waiting, watching, hoping. Isaac Bashevis Singer wins the Nobel Prize for Literature. Bodies beside a Red Cross truck announce the death throes of Rhodesia. Such trouble in the world and it is with relief that she returns to her half-finished letter.

> *Diane, I've just re-read Ernest Hemmingway's 'The Old Man and the Sea'. It stood out from all the others on the return shelf of the library. This is one of the main advantages of being a volunteer. I get first pick. It is great story of an epic battle between an old, experienced fisherman and a large marlin, and won the Pulitzer Prize in 1952. I'm sure your library will have a copy.*
>
> *Thank you for your kind offer, and we are still thinking of coming to Australia. But not this year. Have I told you how glorious it is to go hiking in the Jemez Mountains at this time of the year?*

Maggie's thoughts are filled with majestic pine forests, colourful leaves and the whispering winds of Valle Grande. It only takes her a day to hike the Coyote trail but she sets a snappy pace. Many in her hiking group, much younger than her, have trouble keeping up.

I often wonder at the time it takes for a letter to travel from Australia to here and vice versa. Your last letter finally arrived, but I don't know when you mailed it. You wrote 'Fri' but no date and there was no postmark.

I've been meaning to tell you that when you write 'America' on my address that it should be 'USA'. It's easier and it tells which 'America'. Canada and Mexico are America, as are all the various countries in Central America, not to mention all those in South America. Your letters do get here, but better that they don't confuse anyone, no?

*

Diane's journal 2018

You never made that mistake again. Maggie, via her letters, informed, reprimanded and educated. Tucked between observations on her family and the weather was always something educational or a comment on the ineptitude of the current political administration. Never afraid to voice her concerns, she later bought a bumper sticker 'Bush shit'. Environmental issues were also included. The East African Wildlife Journal of Ecology arrived in your letterbox and you learnt about the plight of the African Elephant. You sent a small donation. You read about the World Conservation Union and the Environmental Liaison Centre International. Organisations and Societies you had never heard of before. Slipped between recipes of green chilli and beans, you discover a world outside of family, work, and Australia.

*

Diane glances again at Maggie's letter, tries to write, scrubs the ball point pen on paper, but still no ink, throws it in the bin, grabs another and carefully prints in the top left-hand corner,

Thursday, 25th July 1980.
   Dear Maggie, I can't wait—

The phone rings. Thelma wants a permanent wave. Tomorrow. Diane stretches the phone cord as far as she can, drags her bag towards her with her foot and reaches inside for the appointment book. She glances at an already full day. Where she can find two hours for a perm?

'Would eight o'clock be too early?' Diane smiles and jots down the name. She'll have to be quick off the mark tomorrow.

She stuffs the appointment book back in her bag and dumps it beside the front door. Walking back to the kitchen via the lounge, she stops at the bookcase. It is a little off centre. Strategically placed to hide a watermark on the wall from the last wild storm. Thinking of Maggie, she runs her fingers across the spines of the Dymo labelled books Kerry is studying. Dickens, Bernard Shaw, Jane Austen. Diane yearns to have the time to read at least some of the stories. She stops at *The Complete Works of Shakespeare*. Kerry constantly quotes the Elizabethan bard. It sounds like another language. Opening the book to *The Tragedy of Macbeth*, she glances down the page.

Act 1—Scene 1. A desert place.

Propped on the arm of the couch, Diane imagines the rolling sand hills and hot wind of Coopers Creek.

> *When shall we three meet again.*
> *In thunder, lightening, or in rain?*
> *When the hurlyburly's done,*
> *When the battle's lost and won.*

Not bad so far. She skips to the next page.

*As two spent swimmers do cling together
and choke their art—.*

The shrieking whistle of the kettle has her shoving
Macbeth back into the bookcase and running to turn off the
gas. Diane promises herself she will read it one day. As soon
as she has time.

*We can't believe that we both managed to get the time off
work, Maggie. Kerry will be fine. She's going to stay with
my Mum and Dad. I'm so sorry we won't be able to meet
Anna. Alaska is such a long way from Santa Fe. You must
miss her. Do you think we'll get to see Barb? I'm busy
packing our cases and learning as much as I can about
New Mexico. My Lonely Planet book says the light
switches are upside down, and the water goes down the
plughole backwards? Is that true? Another difference I've
noticed is that I write my birth date as the third of
August and then the month and year 3/8/1941 and you
put August first, 8/5/1917. Did you realise we are both
Leos, both lions? Do you believe in astrology? Should I
pack thick jackets?*

Plump pink and white blossoms cover the weeping crab-
apple tree outside Diane's bedroom window. Her mum
refuses to call it a crab-apple. Too common. Isn't the
Betchel's Ioensis gorgeous this year, she says. Fallen petals
decorate a newborn lawn. Diane tries to imprint a detailed
memory picture to sustain her over the hot summer months
ahead. Freesias are blooming and a delicious, delicate scent
of spring wafts through the open window. Diane tosses and
turns. Clutching the sheet up to her neck, she holds her
breath and listens. Outside is a rasping sound, like deep-
throated heavy breathing. A burglar searching for the best
place to enter? A perverted prowler? She punches Ron's
arm. He snorts and turns over, dragging the doona with him.
She thumps him again.

'What?' Ron rubs bleary eyes.

'There's someone outside.'

'What do you want me to do?' He pulls the doona over his head.

'Go and look.'

'At two in the morning? You've got to be kidding.'

She pulls back the doona. One glance at her face, and he stumbles towards the kitchen, checking Kerry's room on the way. Drawers slam. Ron mumbles obscenities. Diane drags the doona up under her chin. Not daring to move, the raspy breathing conjures visions of a leering Peeping Tom only two feet away.

Ron plods back to the bedroom. 'Found it,' he says.

Diane shields her eyes from a dazzling beam of light. Ron puts down the torch and struggles into his dressing gown

She gestures dramatically towards the door.

'Okay.' He rummages in the bottom of the wardrobe searching for his slippers.

She points again.

'Okay. I'm going.' The front door creaks open, footsteps disappear down the drive, torch light flashes through leafy trees.

'Piss off,' Ron shouts. 'Get out of here, you bastard.' A scuffle. He may need help.

Leaping out of bed, she grabs the beside lamp: yanks the cord out of the plug, runs through the front doorway then down the path.

Ron is shining the torch into the branches of a tall pyramid tree. He directs the beam on Diane, flimsy nightie flapping in the breeze. 'Not bad,' he says.

She brandishes the lamp with trailing cord. Ron points the beam of light into the crab-apple.

'Bloody possum.' He wraps his arm around Diane's waist and gives her a squeeze. 'He's as big as a boarding house pudding. You won't get any more flowers this year. He's eaten all the buds.'

Diane neatly folds the heavy duffle coat, an out-of-season bargain from Aussie Disposals. How will it fit into the already full suitcase? Wear it? In this heat? Impossible. Carry it over her arm? She places it on the floor beside the case. She'll worry about it later. She must pack the three t-shirts, their 'made in China' tags carefully removed. Diane admires the bright aboriginal designs under a bold AUSTRALIA emblazoned across the chest. Ochre for Maggie, Navy blue for Barb and dark green for Anna. Maggie can post it to her later. Hank's fuzzy little koala on a key ring will slip into her pocket. But twenty-one kilos? And winter in Santa Fe. Maybe even snow. Diane studies the ever growing pile of 'must have' clothes. Boots. She needs winter boots. She glances at her bare legs and flip flops. Packing summer clothes would have been easier.

After reading every book on New Mexico she can find at the Kubunji Beach library, Diane still expects nothing will prepare her for the actual experience, reminding her of their first 'out of Australia' family adventure.

They watch the Norwegian cargo ship the Samos berth at Appleton dock.

Kerry runs up the gangplank while Ron and Diane trail behind, struggling with two suitcases plus Kerry's backpack and the outsized pink teddy bear Grandma insisted on giving Kerry just before they left. Their forward cabin is spacious with a view of a huge packing case. An acrid smell, accentuated by the over-eighty-five degree heat, reveals it holds a horse.

Sailing down the Yarra River, they lean on the deck rail and watch dock lights disappear. A summer breeze ruffles hair, noses twitch at the smell of hay and fresh horse dung, but nothing can mar their pleasure. They pass underneath the flying buttress of the Westgate bridge, framed by stars. Sail past the shadowy hump of Point Nepean, the beacon of the

Queenscliff lighthouse a thin shaft of light in the night sky.

Sweat stains Diane's shirt, but Kerry, oblivious to the heat, jigs beside the roped off lowered gangplank. Diane and Ron patiently wait, eager to feel dry land under their feet. She gazes at the denuded hills and scattered township of Port Moresby. This is not Maggie's Africa. Too humid, no flame trees and no elephants, but it's the next best thing. Certainly cheaper. Two days on a cargo ship, a week bunking with friends, and an economy flight home. Travelling on a shoestring means meeting ordinary people and having unplanned adventures.

On the wharf far below, New Guinea nationals squat on boxes and squabble over card games. One stands, cups his hands around his mouth and shouts 'You bringum newspaper?'

Ron throws down a *Melbourne Sun*. A black hand waves, a page torn out, large tobacco leaf added and the whole lot deftly rolled, lit and smoked.

The man on the dock, carefully snuffs the end of his newspaper cigarette with his fingers and hurries down the wharf. The *Samos'* siren blasts three times. Seagulls wheel in fright. Crewmen hurry past, secure cargo and shout commands. The gangplank creaks and cranks back into sailing position, while propellers thrash foam. The *Samos* slowly sails from the dock.

Diane grabs Kerry. Sits her on the rail while a large ocean liner sails towards their recently vacated berth. White paint gleams, a line of flags flutter from bow to stern, three rows of portholes indicate multiple decks. Kerry points to a nuggetty tug shepherding the huge liner. FAIRSTAR in bold black letters on her prow.

A straw-covered semitrailer, complete with thatched hut and palm tree, is pushed onto the wharf. Grass-skirted girls writhe and dance, men in bird-of-paradise plumed headdresses beat drums, stamp and chant tribal songs.

'What's that?' Kerry sniggers and points to long tasselled

tubes covering penises bouncing up and down to the drumbeats. Diane grabs Kerry's finger and folds it under.

'And that,' Kerry says, pointing with her fist to the bunch of arse grass swaying behind. Diane laughs. Before she can explain the custom, a group of chanting, swaying women distract Kerry. She slips to the deck, holds up both arms, wriggles her hips, stamps her feet and imitates their hypnotic stomping dance.

Street vendors swarm. Passengers scurry like an army of scavenging soldier-ants up the hill to the waiting town.

*

Diane's journal: Australia

> *You re-read what you have written, checking for
> mistakes and the odd strange word. Suddenly you laugh.
> A hearty uplifting laugh. You have the cargo ship Samos
> birthing at the dock. You imagine baby ships bobbing in
> the watery swell. The automatic spell checker confused,
> deceived. Once again, you marvel at the difference one
> letter can make.*

*

When the Samos docks stern to bow behind the Fairstar, engines thrum underfoot. Diane feels for the captain having to give up his place for high paying tourists on a strict schedule. Only half of their ship fits on the wharf. Diane peeks over the side, making sure to hang onto the rails. It's a long drop from the deck to the water.

Captain Largos, shaking his head, points to the only crane out of three working. Bundles of cargo in a large wire cage are winched overboard and onto the wharf below. Kerry jumps up and down, crying, 'Let's go. All the way. Okay?'

Diane vigorously shakes her head and points to the secured gangplank. She picks up her backpack, grabs Kerry's hand,

50

insists they return to the cabin with an offer of chocolate and games, but braces herself for Kerry's inevitable question.

'Why?' Kerry asks. There it is. Always the why. Why go to the cabin? Why can't they go ashore? Diane points to the gangway. 'It can't reach the wharf.'

Kerry shows her a rope ladder over the side. Diane shakes her head, and mouths a silent no.

'I'd be careful. I'd—'

'If you put one foot—'

Captain Largos sees Kerry's pouting lips and tear-filled eyes. 'Would you like to go ashore in the cargo cage?'

Kerry beams. Diane feels the colour drain from her face. Heights not her strong point, especially from the deck of a large ship.

'Thank you, but—'

'Please, pleeeese.'

Diane stares with horror at the empty cage swinging high in the sky and vigorously shakes her head. 'You're not getting me in that thing.'

Looking up with big blue eyes Kerry grabs her father's hand. 'You'll take me, won't you, Daddy.'

The cage swings back onto the deck, wire door open. Diane taps the wooden pallet floor with her toe. It seems firm enough. Two small hands push against her bottom and she stumbles in. Ron follows and clamps both arms protectively around Kerry. Diane grabs his bicep with one hand and the wire cage with the other. The door secured, she feels like a captured animal heading for the zoo. With the speed of a lift accelerating to the fortieth floor, they are hoisted high, only to stop with a jolt. They sway in midair, the sky and sea a blur of blue.

'Shit, shit, shit.' Diane's fingernails dig into Ron's arm. Fear prickles her armpits. The swaying eases. Sweat stings her eyes. She wants to close them tight, to shut out the image of eye-level wheeling seagulls and tiny figures on the wharf below.

'Again. Do it again.' Kerry tries to break free from her father's arms.

'Stand still,' Diane cries. The crane moves and they swing like a pendulum. Kerry screams in delight.

'Oh, my God, Oh, my God.' The chain above scrapes and creaks.

'Look at Mum's face.' Kerry laughs. 'She's losing it.' The fingers of Diane's left hand tighten their grip on wire, her other hand cuts off the circulation in Ron's arm. Slowly, the cage is lowered and lands with a thud on the wharf below.

'Wow,' Kerry says. 'Better than Luna Park.'

Diane hurries home from the Lakeside Book Club, clutching Thomas Hardy's *Tess of the d'Urbervilles*. Maggie will be pleased to hear she has joined a Council of Adult Education reading group. Secretary by default. No-one wanted the job, and it's no big deal. The twelve members range in age from nineteen to eighty-four. This month, each member will have selected a title from the designated reading list. Once a month, a box arrives with twelve copies of the book, plus discussion notes. Diane must look up who chose Tess. It must be Merl. She loves nothing better than what Diane calls an intellectual doorstop. She snuggles into bed, props open the book and reads, A pure woman faithfully presented...

In the morning, the book, open at page three, is on the floor. Next month, once again she'll guiltily blow the dust off the cover before slipping it back in the box. With the trip to America coming up fast, there isn't a minute to spare.

*

8/20/1989

> *Dear Diane, Tess of the d'Urbervilles is an interesting*
> *read. What did you think of it? Such a tragic tale of loss*
> *of innocence. The ultimate destruction of such a young*
> *gal overwhelmed me. Thomas Hardy's writing is good,*

*but there are several authors I enjoy more. The one I like
most is John D. McDonald. He has two main characters,
Travis McGee and Myer Myers. The good guys always
win, and McDonald cares about the environment. So do I.
I have several of McDonald's books waiting for your
arrival. I hope you leave enough room in your suitcase
for them. Three days is too short a visit, but my beloved
mother-in-law always said, fish and visitors spoil after
three days. I'm sure that doesn't apply....*

Maggie strides down Camino Ranchitos, Diane's letter in her pocket. What if the old saying is true and their friendship begins to stink after three days?

Sixty-six and set in her ways. She'll have to give them the main bedroom and make up the spare beds. Maggie pumps her arms and power walks in time to her thoughts. Where will she take them? What will she feed them? What if Diane asks about Anna?

In her letters, she need reveal only what she wants to reveal. Present any persona she desires. Make out life is perfect. She absentmindedly waves to Nancy Garcia, their nearest neighbour. Hank's first Santa Fe conquest. The first of many. Nancy soon learned that he quickly tires when it's free and easy. She walks even faster. Will Hank behave himself? Keep his cruel wit under control? Maggie tries not to think about the headache forming at the base of her skull. She knows her family is like a broken cup, glued together, but the crack forever visible. A twig cracks under her foot, the sharp noise reminding her of Anna's tenth birthday.

Hank is working in his study and Maggie is busy in the kitchen when Anna runs past waving an object above her head. Barb's favourite doll? Maggie braces herself for the conflict to come and sighs. This scenario repeated often before. But this time, when she recognises Hank's irreplaceable ancient Aztec statue, she freezes. The pride of his collection.

'Put that down.'

Anna turns and laughs. Maggie runs towards her. Anna ducks.

'Right now,' Maggie shouts hysterically, pointing to the coffee table. Anna ignores her. Waves the statue in front of her face. Maggie tries to snatch it out of her hand. Anna smirks and runs back into the living room. Barb is transfixed, her face twisted in horror. Anna holds the statue high above her head. Barb jumps up and down, trying to reach it, pleading, 'Give it to me. Please, please give it to me.'

'What's all that hollerin',' Hank bellows from his study. 'I'm trying to work.'

'Nothing,' Maggie calls back and stabs her outstretched hand towards Anna, soundlessly demanding she hand over the statue. Anna laughs, makes as if she is going to give the statue to her mother, then throws it with all her strength onto the floor. Shards of ochre pottery litter the room. Barb screams.

Hank rushes from his office. The three of them stand motionless in the middle of the room.

What happened? He bends on one knee, turns a piece over and over in his hand, shakes his head like an old lion, and they wait for the roar. Instead, his eyes narrow like a rattlesnake ready to strike. An icy shiver runs down Maggie's spine as he slowly rises to his feet. Towering over them, he coldly says, 'Someone's responsible'.

Silence. Barb and Maggie watch Anna. She looks Hank straight in the face, tears well in her eyes, bottom lip quivers.

'Barb didn't mean it, Dad. It was an accident.'

'It wasn't Barb, Hank. It was Anna' gasps Maggie. Hank ignores her, wraps a protective arm around Anna's shoulders and glares at Barb. Eyes wide in disbelief, she shakes her head from side to side, her breath rasps in her throat; another asthma attack imminent. She rushes to her mother who gathers her in her arms. Hank snorts his disapproval. Once again, Hank believes Anna. Always believes Anna, the smart one. Anna the magnificent. Bright as a button. Top of her class. Who would believe that Hank Jackson's brilliant creative child could be flawed? Born without a moral compass?

The headache throbbing at the back of Maggie's neck expands to her temples. Anna. Why does everything in her life come back to Anna. Such simple things can bring waves of grief. A flower. A song on the radio, writing a letter, and the words, How are your children? Best to quickly put it all aside. Ignore it all. Bury it all beneath a hard-won feisty exterior.

Friends are understanding, but when they see red-rimmed eyes, they shuffle their feet, cough, look away, talk about the weather or the price of eggs. They no longer talk about their children. When they ask how she is coping, she wants to scream at them, *How the Hell do you think*, but instead she smiles and says a brisk 'Fine'.

She can always talk about books; biographies, novels, non-fiction, you name it. To read and talk about other people's lives is her salvation. She has always been an obsessive reader. Often women addicted to being perfect wives and mothers accuse her of neglecting her husband, children and domestic chores. Goddamnit. Three days...

*

Dear Maggie, I've bought a long singlet type, skivvy thing to wear under my jumpers. My mother insists I keep my nether regions warm. To her, the nether regions are your lower back, especially the kidney area. To achieve this you must tuck your garment right under your bottom. So I'll arrive in Santa Fe with my nether regions protected. It won't be long before we are talking our heads off. How fortunate that you can take us to Jack Master's tiffin, (you'll have to let me know what a tiffin is). He sounds like an amazing man. Seven books? Incredible, and I'm not surprised you have the entire collection.

Diane folds the letter, placing it on the kitchen bench. What will it be like to meet again? Maggie is cultured, well-read. And wealthy. The country she lives in is the Land of the Free: of star-spangled banners and Cape Canaveral. Glittering literary festivals and poetry readings. To Diane's extended family, students performing a Gilbert and Sullivan light opera in the local hall is the pinnacle of artistic outings. Religiously, every Saturday, the family follow Australian Rules football and barrack for the Footscray Bulldogs, shouting, 'Chewy on your boots' and 'Moz, moz, moz' to upset the opposing team. *Up There Cazaly* sung at the top of their voices. Does Maggie like football? Will their differences add spice, or be a barrier to friendship? What if they don't like each other?

Diane busies herself baking a fruitcake to remind them of their first meeting. The two hours at the Dig Tree still vivid in her mind, and there have been years of letters in between. This meeting could break the friendship or bind them closer. It is a risk worth taking. Her mental picture of Maggie is an educated, artistic, world traveller not afraid to speak her mind. She is everything Diane wants to be. But Maggie is her mother's age. Will that make a difference? Will she live up to Diane's expectations? What expectations does Maggie have of their friendship? Either way, three days under the one roof will be enough—for both of them.

*

After Diane and Ron finally get through customs, Diane searches the crowd for Maggie and Hank. Diane waves, but how should she greet Maggie? Cheek kiss? Shake hands? Hug? Diane doesn't know the boundaries. Throwing protocol to the wind, Diane stoops and wraps her arms around Maggie in a bear hug.

Maggie seems smaller and has no spare fat on her frame. Diane's duffle coat hides her love handles.

*

Your memory of being a bulky teenager surfaces. You were always the tall girl marked for a succession of male roles in school plays. Maggie's strong features beneath a crop of wayward hair reassures you that neither of you would be selected to play cutesy girlie parts.

*

Hank's greeting is easy. A firm handshake. Straightforward. Men are like that. He seems even larger than before. A bear of a man at least six foot five with only the slightest sign of a paunch.

'What is the population of Australia?' Hank asks. 'How much is the national debt?' On the drive home, neither Diane nor Ron can answer his rapid-fire questions. Hank pounces when they don't know. After half an hour, Ron says, 'Fiscal policies? Don't ask me. I just live there, mate.'

The Chevy Blazer's wheels crunch to a stop in the gravel drive in front of a house. It is just like the photo of Maggie's home pinned to Diane's kitchen corkboard. Ropes of bright red chilli line the doorway. On the step, a hedgehog-shaped boot scraper. Inside, is a landing with steps down to the living room. Maggie leads them past a study with endless shelves stacked to overflowing with books, to a bright sunny room with narrow floor to ceiling windows. She pulls back wooden shutters.

Two single beds, pushed together, face the windows, providing a view of the natural desert garden. A silver clock sits on a bedside table, and in one corner is a wardrobe, probably full of clothes.

'We can't take your room.

Maggie laughs. 'See you downstairs for dinner.'

Maggie shells peas into a bowl.

'Can I help?'

'Out of my kitchen, wench.'

Diane wanders into the living room. Mellow, wooden

coffee tables, laden with books, squat on patterned Indian rugs scattered over the reddish-brown brick floor. She picks up an intricately woven basket, noting the fine close weave. A variety of small clay statues, rock specimens and carved wooden figures cover a wide display shelf. Barbed wire twisted into crucifixes and clay masks cling to the walls. A small, stone statue of a dancing, humpbacked flute player with feather antenna catches her eye, but she doesn't know where to look when closer inspection reveals a huge phallus.

Maggie emerges from the kitchen. Diane quickly points to a clay figure further along the shelf. 'What a fascinating statue. I like the sloping forehead and thick lips.'

'Hank had one even older than that.' Maggie quickly adds, 'But I like this statue. It has the face of the ancient Mayans.'

Diane nods, and stares at the statue.

Maggie takes a large book from the bookcase. 'Read this. It has everything you need to know about the Central American tribe.'

Ensconced beside Ron on the body-weathered leather couch, Diane gazes in admiration at Hank. Surrounded by Indian art and craft, he stands, hands clasped behind his back, feet apart in front of the fireplace. He picks up a rectangular metal plate with a steel handle on the side and another at the top.

'What do you think this is used for?' He holds up the object. 'I found it in Mexico.'

Diane and Ron gaze at the old iron contraption. Maggie fidgets in her chair, crossing and uncrossing her legs. Hank watches them squirm like two ants under a magnifying glass. Diane breaks the silence. 'Two handles? Why two?'

'Make a guess'

'A lid for a box?'

'No.'

Hank looks at Ron. 'A handle for...something?' Ron says.

Maggie picks up a *National Geographic* and flips pages.

Ron turns the object round and round. 'Some sort of farm implement?'

Hank shakes his head and turns his gaze to Diane. She looks across to Maggie, but she is focused on Hank.

'I give up.' Diane throws up her hands.

Maggie covers her ears. Hank holds the contraption by the top handle and vigorously twists. The metallic clanging reverberates around the room.

'What the hell is it?' Ron shakes his head. 'It blew the wax out of my ears.'

'It's a Metraca.'

They wait to hear the rest. Hank straightens his moustache with his forefinger and continues. 'Mexicans are not allowed to ring the church bells during lent, so they use this instead. God awful sound, don't you think?'

Diane and Ron nod.

'When those hombres hear this, they sprint to church—'

'And I'm calling you all to dinner.' Maggie points to the dining room table. 'I hope you like your steak rare.'

'Well done for me,' Ron says.

'You'll get it rare. I'm not drying out good steak for anyone.'

Ron rolls his eyes at Diane.

*

Maggie fills the right side of the double-sink with hot soapy water then throws in dishes. Hank and his mind games. She calls this one, 'guess the artefact'. He never misses an opportunity. Show off. How would Diane and Ron know about a Metraca? Seeing Hank play with them is like watching a rattlesnake before it eats its prey, only he doesn't give any warning before he strikes. He sprinkles his conversation with Spanish, knowing they don't understand. He calls Ron *blanco hijo de puta* and smiles when Ron asks what it means. Tells him it's Spanish for friend. Not true. It's actually white sonofabitch, meaning an arsehole. The bastard. Maggie wants to tell him to go to hell.

She wants to relax, to discuss what Diane and Ron would like to see, to do, but as always, Hank holds the floor. Now, he's moved into phase three. He shows them his hand-crafted woodwork. This will take at least two hours. Maggie will never get a chance to talk to Diane on her own. Just women's talk, or idle prattle as Hank calls it. Instead he has them fixed in his mesmeric gaze, showing them an intricate box faceted out of small pieces of different species of wood from around the world. He turns it around and around so they can view it from every angle. Points out the mitred corners, the inlaid colours. Next step? There he goes. He's lifted the lid. Revels in Ron and Diane's exclamations of delight at the snakeskin lining and small pieces of black obsidian called Apache tears.

Maggie twists the faucet harder, but the goddamn thing still drips.

Hank's woodwork is beautiful, like crafting a scientific essay. All the separate parts fit together and produce a significant article. At least woodworking keeps him out of her hair. Especially since he retired. All their friends have innumerable spun bowls, knick-knack boxes, square blocks for pencil holders and every form of salt and pepper shaker imaginable. Maggie's cupboards are jam-packed with the stuff.

Thank God he's currently co-writing a scientific book, titled *Venomous Reptiles of South America*, with an ambitious forty-year-old colleague. A younger replica of Hank. Rebellious black hair bent over a stack of typed pages. Beside it, an unruly mass of grey. They work well together. Hank's red ballpoint pen slashes and burns, but apart from proofreading, he's not really involved. The collaboration works well. The young researcher will have the name of an eminent herpetologist to add veracity to his project, and Hank will have his name on a current publication. To prove he is still working, still alive. At least this time, he is not travelling to some far-flung desert. Someone at the

University of Arizona will do the typing, and Maggie's fingers get a rest.

'Thanks for a delicious tea.' Diane grabs a tea towel and lifts a well-rinsed dish from the drainer.

Tea? Goddamnit. Maggie knocks herself out fixing a large dinner and Diane thanks her for tea. Does she mean afternoon tea?

'Do you usually have dinner later?'

Diane looks bemused, and they realise there has been cross communication. They search for other examples of language differences. She says petrol instead of gas. She calls biscuits, scones. Cookies are biscuits. Swimming costumes are togs or bathers. She has breakfast, lunch/dinner and tea. Why? Because that's what her mother calls the main meals. Everyone knows dinner is at night. And the weirdest of all? The herb oregano. Diane pronounces it or-e-**ga**-no. I call it **oreg**-ano.

'Diane,' I say. 'You put the wrong em-**pha**-sis on the wrong syl-**a**-ble. '

*

The fire in Maggie's eyes, and the quickness to state her point of view and stick to it against all opposition, fascinates Diane. If only she had the courage to be the same. To make outrageous statements. To be taken seriously and have the unshakable belief that she is right. But, aside from the domestic ties of motherhood and meals, where is their common ground? Their conversation is like her grandfather's word games.

'The English language is crazy,' Diane says. 'There is no egg in eggplant, ham in hamburger, apple or pine in pineapple.'

Maggie leans forward, her broad smile encouraging. Diane warms to the game. 'English muffins were not invented in England or French fries in France.'

Maggie laughs and joins in. 'If a vegetarian eats vegetables

—'Maggie's smile is wicked— 'What does a humanitarian eat?'

Diane finally relaxes. Laughing, they make their way upstairs to the room off the landing. When Diane steps into Maggie's study, her eyes widen. Apart from a thin vertical window, the walls are lined with books. Rows and rows of spines, trumpeting titles, advertising contents, announcing authors, with names emblazoned in gold, red or bold black: Dickens, Austen, William H Prescott. Authors her teachers at State School mentioned, but whom she never read. There's a complete shelf of dictionaries. Others hold travel, non-fiction and novels. Overall, the sharp smell of old leather and new ink takes her breath away.

'This is a first edition.' Maggie reverently hands Diane a gilt-edged, leather-bound copy of Tennyson's Poetical Works. She admires the plush red-and-gold cover page and the bewhiskered portrait of the man himself. Opening the book at random, she reads,

> *thick leaved ambrosial*
> *With an ancient melody*
> *of inward agony...*

Inward agony is right. She will need a dictionary beside her to make sense of these poems.

'Amazing.' Diane carefully returns Tennyson to his rightful place. 'But I'd need a month to read it.'

Maggie beckons her to a shelf crammed with travel journals. Handwritten titles and dates neatly inscribed on each spine.

> *Mexico: Oaxaca 1971.*
> *Arizona: Nogales 1972.*
> *Africa: Nairobi 1973.*

Taking a well-thumbed journal from the bookcase, Maggie eases into her favourite chair. Patting a seat beside her, she passes the journal to Diane.

'My favourite trip.'

Diane turns page after page of meticulously typed words and intricately designed graphs and tables. 'And you say you're not a writer?'

'I wouldn't call a record of dates and species, coupled with a few personal observations, good writing.' Maggie points to a page. Diane reads out loud:

'Nairobi 1973. Of all African countries, I love Kenya. When I'm here, I constantly smile. I find the people naturally exuberant and quick to laugh. However, today I felt old and affronted when a middle-aged African man called me 'Mama'. I was not his mother. My reaction seemed to bemuse him. Later, our tour leader, Jock, explained that in Africa 'Mama' is a title of respect....'

They share a smile. Language differences yet again.

'I often wonder where my love of Africa comes from.' Maggie rubs her chin. 'I think it dates back to the mid fifties. Someone unearthed a huge talking drum in the American Museum of Natural History.'

Diane settles into her chair, happy to hear one of Maggie's stories. How different they are to the stories back home about the 'goings on' next door, or the strange habits of the postmaster's dog.

Maggie's eyes half close. 'Sometimes long forgotten ancient collected items are found in the basement.'

Diane imagines a dark dungeon, clouded in mystery, packed with archaeological treasures.

'A Nigerian drummer, Babatunde Olantunji was in New York City. I don't recall how we and our colleagues, Pete and Angie, were invited to join a small group one night to hear the old drum come to life.' Maggie laughs. 'Why would they think two herpetologists would care about anthropology?'

Her voice has a dream-like quality. Diane can't take her eyes off Maggie's face.

'Few of us had ever been in the basement of the museum.

Olantunji's long fingers reverently caressed the enormous, carved, hollow, log.' Maggie's fingers unconsciously stroke the air in front of her.

'He softly explained that before a tree was cut down to make a drum, it was necessary to speak to the tree's spirit. Ask permission for its use.' Maggie looks at Diane and smiles.

'First, he struck the drum lightly, and then he began to make it talk.' Maggie shivers. 'When something moves me, music, art or poetry, I get chills.' Her finger waggles at Diane. 'Believe me, that man nearly froze me. Especially when he stopped sending messages and began to play complicated sounds, one rhythm on top of another until it seemed as if at least four hands were at work.'

Diane imagines the blur of hands, like the calypso drummers on TV that Ron admires, who create sounds that defy description.

Maggie points to the journal. 'In spite of this experience, I was still conditioned by all the books I'd read.'

Diane raises an eyebrow.

'You know, Tarzan and the apes: noble tribes, vine-festooned trees and grinning chimpanzees.'

'I loved The Jungle Book and Riki Tiki Tavi,' Diane says, remembering her favourite childhood book.

'Africa,' Maggie says dreamily. 'I felt as if I was home.' She takes the journal from Diane and closes it. 'Maybe it's genetic.'

Diane doesn't reply. She knows nothing about genetics.

'I heard that Richard Leakey, Professor of Anthropology at Stony Brook University in New York, thinks so.' Leaning forward in her chair, Maggie takes a deep breath before adding, 'Maybe we do all go back to the three-and-a-half-million-year-old Ethiopian Lucy.'

Diane is fascinated, but also feels as if she's back in school. This is going to be a long couple of days. She wriggles in her seat, rubs her knees.

'Do you know that Lucy is the first almost complete

skeleton found of early woman?'

Diane nods. She does now, so it's not a lie.

'You must read Donald Johanson and Maitland Edey's *Lucy: The Beginnings of Humankind*.'

The back door slams, heavy footsteps enter the downstairs living room. Maggie struggles to her feet. She hands the journal to Diane and indicates the shelf.

'Frankly, I'm not crazy about the book.' Maggie walks towards the stairs. 'But Lucy provides a good hook to hang one's ideas on. You can almost visualize the little creature being the mama of all who came later.'

Later, in bed, Diane toys with the idea of a genetic link from Lucy, through her mother to her. Memories surface of her mother's stories of how Diane's grandfather had crushed her mother's dream of a singing career. Forbidden to take singing lessons, she cooked, cleaned and sewed for five younger brothers and chafed at the injustice.

Diane tosses her schoolbag onto the chair by the back door and sits on the step to wait. She soon hears the staccato clack of high heels hurrying down the cracked concrete sideway.

'Sorry to be late, Love.' Her mum pulls out the long hat pin that secures her latest handmade creation of felt and flowers to her greying curls.

'Come on in. I'll get you a slice of bread.' She twists the key in the lock then hurries inside. Placing her handbag and coat on a chair in her bedroom, she closes the door. Ties a cobbler apron firmly around her ample waist then runs fingers through greying hair.

'Hurry up and set the table, Love. Your dad will be in any minute.' Diane and her mother are used to this ritual.

Ever since her mum joined the Uniting Church Choir, she often forgets the time.

'Years ago, I wanted to enter the Sun Aria Competition, but my father... The choir master says I'm the best soprano they've ever had.'

Diane's mum pours boiling water from the kettle into two pots on the stove. She sings, *One alone, to be my own, I alone, to know her caresses. One to be, eternally, the one my worshipping soul possesses*, each word a treasured diamond. When the pot lids rattle from the steam, her mum looks around. A neat pile of ironing, done before leaving, sits on the ironing table. Physical evidence of a day's hard work. Table set. Pots bubbling. Her mum nods with satisfaction.

The back door opens and Diane's dad steps into a warm, steamy kitchen to be greeted by her mum with an armful of folded ironing. Putting it down, she takes his jacket, hangs it on a hook behind the door. Diane takes the kitbag out of calloused fingers. Her dad inhales deeply. 'Smells good. Dinner ready?'

'Won't be long, Love. By the time you change out of your overalls, it'll be on the table.' As soon as he leaves, her mum starts peeling potatoes.

Diane sips a cup of percolated coffee, listening intently as Maggie outlines the plans for the next day.

'We're all going to Jack Masters' seventieth birthday celebration.'

'Jack who?'

Maggie looks startled. 'Masters. Jack Masters. His real name is John, but all his friends call him Jack.' She waits for the name to register. 'I wrote to you about him.' Diane waits for her to continue.

'The world famous English author of *Bhowani Junction*?'

Diane helps herself to carrot cake, brushing crumbs off her lap. She vaguely remembers an old black-and-white film, but can't recall the story.

Maggie hurries to the bookcase beside the fireplace. 'I have a signed copy.' She lifts down a small, dark brown book and flicks open the cover. Diane reads, To Maggie, Best wishes, Jack Masters, 1955.

'He lives in Santa Fe, so I wrote to him. Told him how

involved I became in the story and how much I respected his research.' She reverently strokes the cover. 'I was shocked and delighted when he replied.'

Diane stares at Maggie's animated face and wonders how anyone could be so enthusiastic about an author and his books.

'Jack is the leader of our Santa Fe Chilli and Marching Society.'

Diane glances to see if Maggie is serious. Elderly people practicing drill, or training to be marching girls? The thought of Maggie in a short, pleated skirt, barely covering her bottom, makes Diane giggle.

'It is an excellent hiking group, but any hike with Jack is like a forced march.

He's a lieutenant-colonel. DSO and OBE. Treats us like foot soldiers training for a campaign.'

Diane has a vision of the famous author striding out in front with his gaggle of followers marching behind. She manages to maintain a serious expression. Maggie picks up the empty mugs and heads for the kitchen...

'You should read his war trilogy *Loss of Eden*,' she calls over her shoulder.

Diane makes a mental note of yet another book, three in fact, she'll have to look up when she gets home. She wants to run a mile. Feels like a dumb Australian.

That night in bed, Diane pummels her pillow. Famous authors. Poets. Playwrights. She's never heard of Jack Masters, or whatever his name is. Does she call him Jack? Mr. Masters? What of the others? At least twenty, according to Maggie, including Ned Colbert, who worked with Hank at the New York Museum. Apparently, Ned discovered the first complete skeleton of a *Coelophysis*: She can't even pronounce that, let alone knows what it is. She has no idea who these people are, yet she has this uncomfortable feeling that she should know, should be impressed. Well, too late now and no use pretending. Let them take her as she is.

Heavy, antique, wooden doors swing open to reveal an indoor floor-to-ceiling waterfall. Water trickles over delicate ferns clinging to the ceiling-high rock-face. It swirls around blue water lilies thriving in a large pool. Four steps lead down to a huge open bedroom/lounge with a stunning view of mountains and valleys. Plate glass windows make up the entire back wall. The entrance is at street level, but Jack and Barbara Masters' adobe home is cantilevered over a canyon.

Maggie, eyes sparkling like an infatuated schoolgirl, tugs Diane's arm.

'This is our world famous author.'

Diane can't take her eyes off his leathery, brown face, overshadowed by an outsized, canary yellow, Stetson hat with an eagle feather stuck in the band. Jack crushes her hand. Pumps it up and down.

'Any friend of Maggie's is a friend of mine.' He leads Diane over to the bar.

'Name your poison.' He holds up his half-full whisky glass. Diane points to the water jug. She wants to keep her mind clear.

'You can't drink that.' He grins at her. 'Fish piss in it.' He pours her a glass of red wine.

As soon as Jack walks away, Maggie hurries over, grabs Diane's wine and replaces it with a glass of water. 'Fish might piss in it,' she says, 'but that other stuff will give you problems.'

Jack taps his whisky glass with a knife and shouts in his ex-Indian Army voice: 'Let the competition begin.'

People scatter to find seats. Everyone takes a turn reciting poems, reading short stories or reporting the successes of authors Diane has never heard of. Maggie walks to the front and announces: 'An ode to Ned and his Tyrannosaurus Rex.'

The crowd laughs. Ned stands, takes a bow, and is hooted down.

A fossil hunter named Ned
Went looking for critters long dead
Imagine his glee, at the uncovery
Of Coelophysis in bed

Maggie hesitates, glances around the room. With a flourish, she bows low, accepting the applause. Hank grabs Jack's hat and in a western-movie-actor's drawl asks, 'What is the difference between a buffalo and a bison?'

The audience shouts back, 'You can wash your hands in a bison.'

Jack presents Hank with a blue winner's sash.

Diane feels like one of Jack's pissing fish helplessly flapping out of water, until she notices gnarled hands and lined faces. Everyone is the age of her parents. Retirees enthusiastically reliving past glories. Santa Fe is full of them. Is it for the weather? In Australia, Grey Nomads flock in the thousands to sunny Queensland — beautiful one day, perfect the next — to avoid the extreme heat of the far north and cold of the south. Or is it for Santa Fe's easy-going lifestyle? It's reputation of being a centre of art and culture?

'Diane writes wonderful letters,' Maggie announces. She hands Diane an envelope. It was in the mailbox when we got home. 'Read it to us.'

Diane recognises her own handwriting. 'But it's for you, Maggie.'

She hands it back. Maggie rips open the envelope then extracts the neatly folded pages. She holds them out to Diane.

'Come on. Share the news.'

'Out loud?' Her stomach churns. Her mind races. She wrote this two weeks ago. Had she said anything negative about Ron, who sat beside her? Personal thoughts to be shared only with Maggie?

Diane slowly opens the page. She looks at Maggie, who nods.

'Dear Maggie,' Diane begins, her eyes trying to read ahead before she speaks. She swallows, her face red.

'Dear Maggie, it won't be long before we...' She edits as she reads, adding pieces about the weather, Kerry at school. Innocent, general conversational pieces she never committed to this page. Her ad libbing covers the sections she omits. Personal observations about Ron's health and a growing feeling that that she wants more out of life than the nurturing roles of dutiful daughter, wife and mother coupled with full-time work. None of it meant for an audience. Diane finally finishes with, 'Much love, Diane. Kiss. Kiss.'

With a sigh of relief, she stuffs the letter into her pocket.

'Come on, you lazy barracudas,' Jack says. 'Time for some musical entertainment.' Imaginary lines divide them into three groups. Jack extravagantly conducts their enthusiastic singing. *Row, row, row your boat.* At last, here is something Diane knows. The song triggers memories of pre-television family nights.

Diane's Grandma and Grandpa are staying overnight. Her family sits on straight-backed, wooden chairs around the Laminex table in the pearl-grey and woodland-green kitchen. Her dad takes a harmonica from his pocket, taps it several times on the palm of his hand. Cupping his left hand around the silver shaft, he plays a couple of riffs, before the family lustily sings Kookaburra sits in the old gum tree. Merry, merry king of the bush is he.... Later, it is card games or Scrabble. Some nights, her dad brings out the Novelty Evenings, Parlour Games book.

'Who's going to play the Ring Contest?'

'What's that again?' Diane's mum's chair scrapes closer and she grabs a pencil.

'The answer to these questions must end with Ring. The ring of an acrobat...Daring. The ring of a doctor...Curing. 'Her dad looks around the table at unenthusiastic faces.

'No? Maybe Twisted Animals? Each word represents an animal. Let's see.' He checks the book.

'Peesh? Too easy. Sheep.' He runs his finger down the page.

'Gooakanr. Kangaroo.'

Diane has *My Own Colouring Book* and a box of crayons, but in front of the adults are pencils and notepads. On the first page of the notepads is a list of sixteen sentences.

> *Worth Studying*
> *Extravagant and Peculiar*
> *Makes Travesties etc.*

Her dad, book open at page nine reads, 'Can you name the author? The initials are the capital letters in the describing sentence. You have fifteen minutes to see how many you can get.' He waves a block of Cadbury dairy milk chocolate, 'First prize.'

All eyes are on the kitchen clock. He raises his hand. Pencil points are licked. When the second hand hits twelve, he drops his arm: 'Go.'

The only sound is the ticking clock and the occasional 'Could you have picked anything harder, Len?' Answers scribbled.

> *William Shakespeare*
> *Edgar Allan Poe*
> *Mark Twain*

When her grandma wins, Diane shares the chocolate. Usually her grandpa wins, but tonight he says the English language is daft.

'Just because you won tonight, Minnie, Don't get any big idees.'

'You're supposed to say ide-er, Grandpa.' Diane ignores her mum's stare. She's used to what she calls The Double Whammy.

'Show me the R in idea and I'll say it.' He looks like a bantam rooster. Feathers ruffled, ready for a fight.

'Don't encourage him, Diane,' her grandma whispers.

Grandpa looks around the room. Her grandma sighs.

'English is an impossible language.' He sits up straight and crosses his arms. 'How can I tear my shirt and shed a tear?'

No one answers.

'And we have noses that run and feet that smell.' Grandpa makes a lot of sense, but he argues about everything.

*

Diane's Journal: Australia

> *Did you learn English by osmosis? Sitting in a chair pushed up against the kitchen table, a fountain pen placed in your hand? Your mum stands over you while you scrawl a thank you letter on pink paper to Aunt Mildred for the birthday present. Was this more than a lesson in good manners?*
>
> *Christmas cards and get-well notes to aunts and uncles, holiday postcards to friends and family, parlour games. The gift of a pink leather-covered diary and primary school teachers who praised your script and cared. All part of your basic training, the beginning of your writing apprenticeship. In later years, Maggie's letters introduced you to a world of literature. Pricked your curiosity. You made lists of authors and books that even when dipped into, made you lift your head for a moment to a place far beyond the busyness of life.*

*

Maggie opens the bedroom shutters to a world of white. A glitz blitz of powdery snow.

'Damnit, Hank. And it's only October. Maybe we should skip Bandelier and take Diane straight to the airport?'

He peers out the window. 'Poe key toe snow'.

'It may be a little bit, but it's still Goddamn cold.'

She wanders around mindlessly, tidying the living room. Why go? It's years since she's been there, but at the gathering yesterday, Jack grabbed her arm and took her aside.

'Take Diane to Bandelier'.

72

'They're leaving tomorrow.' Jack raised his glass.

'We'll only have a couple of hours to get them to Albuquerque.' The eyebrow lifted higher.' And...' Jack raised his whisky glass and waggled his finger. 'Do it,' he said and walked away.

But why? Why stir up old memories?

Her mind drifts back to four of them climbing narrow, two storey-high, wooden ladders. Anchored against the sheer cliff walls, they lead to abandoned Native Indian cliff dwellings and sacred caves. She can almost see the dust that rises like fairies riding a shaft of sunlight. Smell the smoke that used to drift from the narrow hole in the domed ceiling of the ancient ceremonial kiva.

They sit around the remains of a central fire and become part of the circle of life. The spirits of past ceremonies wrap Maggie in their embrace, like an old Indian warrior, his children hugged to his chest, all enfolded lovingly in a large blanket draped around his shoulders. The ancient tribes always protected their young. They taught their children their mythology, providing emotional and mental strengths. What did her children learn from a father cursed with *laissez-faire* arrogance? What did she and Hank give to their children? He was only interested in teaching brilliant students. Only interested in Anna.

Maggie glances at her watch. Time to round up everyone and get going. Grabbing several extra snow jackets, she hurries to Ron and Diane patiently waiting in the living room.

*

Hank's spare snow jacket reaches below Diane's knees. The sleeves cover her hands, but she is grateful for the extra warmth. At her feet is a pair of state-of-the-art hiking boots. 'Try them on,' Maggie says. 'I bought them in a hurry, and they're far too big for me.'

Diane has never seen such superbly crafted boots. Leather

uppers, solid sole, two rows of stitching and a cushy innersole. 'Are you sure?'

Maggie nods.

Diane unzips then kicks off her cheap vinyl boots. With fumbling fingers, she criss-crosses long laces through metal eyelets across a soft leather tongue.

'Stand up, gal. Wiggle your toes.'

Diane lifts one foot after the other, marches across the room, shoulders back, walking tall. 'Perfect.' She gives Maggie a grateful hug. 'I could walk to China in these.'

Diane's boots plough through powdery snow. She glances at Ron, his smile as broad as Kerry's on Christmas morning. It never snows at Kubunji Beach.

The towering cliffs of Bandelier National Monument look like a movie set. Hank and Maggie lead the way along pristine paths to promised Indian dwellings carved high into the cliff face. Eagles wheel and soar high above cliff-top pines. She shivers; their plaintive call captures the spiritual essence of the place.

Maggie strides ahead, shoulders hunched as if her backpack is full of bricks. Diane hurries to join her, wants to share her load, but they march in silence. It's a struggle to keep up. There is no breath to talk. Maggie, sweat glistening on her forehead, finally presses a hand against the cliff face and gazes at the cobalt blue sky.

Something about the stiff line of Maggie's back makes Diane leave her alone. After several minutes she asks, 'You okay?'

Maggie nods.

On the trek back, walking side by side, she whispers to Diane, 'My heart is in this place.'

Wedged into Qantas' economy class, Diane looks at her snow-wet boots to remind herself it is not a dream. It is so hard to believe that in twenty-four hours they will travel from the first fall of winter snow to the leafy crab-apple of an Australian spring. They left Australia on Tuesday, the twenty-first and arrived in America on Tuesday, the twenty-first. On their return they will get back their lost day. She would like to ask Maggie, Why is this so? She would like to ask Maggie about her heart and Bandelier.

*

Diane's Journal

You knew not to ask. Maggie had her own demons to struggle with and you knew your place. Your letters were about books, work and local news. This was a new and different world of back to front seasons, books you had never heard of and chillies around the front door. You did not want to upset anyone so did not delve or instigate a deeper communication. It was a supportive pen-friendship and you were delighted to have a Margery of your own.

*

11/2/1989

Dear Diane, I'm amazed your fruitcake made it through customs. In some strange way, it has become a symbol of our friendship. Rich and satisfying. Your letters nourish my soul in the same way a good book feeds my mind. Although, I am appalled that so many good books contain spelling mistakes and misused words. One exception was 'The Great Gatsby'. Whoever edited it did an excellent job. And it was a great read.

I don't suppose you will have time to read it now that you have your own hairdressing salon. Do you still get up at 5:00 a.m. like me? I don't know what I'd do without my early morning walk.

The din of Maggie's alarm clock jump-starts her. Five a.m. Hank is lumped under a heap of bedclothes. It's hard to get him into bed. Even harder to get him out. She considers throwing a frozen bag of peas under the cover but the thought of his red-faced bellowing stops her. He's not an early morning fitness freak. Soon, the coffee percolator burps. Half an hour of push-ups and body-curls, plus a two mile walk, always gets her going for the day. At least Barb and Elizabeth follow in her footsteps.

The island of Arran bus is filled with Scots. Maggie squeezes next to a hardy little woman, plaid skirt wrapped warmly around her legs and fastened with a thistle brooch. A silk scarf tied under her chin. She reminds Maggie of Queen Elizabeth taking her corgis for a romp.

'This is my granddaughter.' Maggie points to Elizabeth.

'Aye. I ken see the likeness.'

Apart from the dark red hair, Elizabeth does look like Maggie. Same brown eyes, same short sturdy figure.

From a worn, leather handbag, the woman produces a picture of two teenage girls sitting on a photographer's stool, legs crossed.

'I hae twae,' she says with a smile. She points with a work-worn finger. 'We both be hags.'

Maggie feels like an old hag.

She wants to moan and wail her discomfort as the bus bounces along the winding road towards their hostel. She can't believe she's staying in youth hostels and travelling on public transport. It's uncomfortable, cold and sparse. So different from the usual plush hotels, private suites and bevy of attendants and silver service. But Hank is not here to pander, protect and domineer. She's spending precious time with her daughter and grandchild. Three generations. Maggie clings to that. But dark, damp Scotland when she's a desert rat? This is not Africa. Yet the scenery out the window is spectacular. Beautiful, windswept beaches and wild sea. Mossy mountains, their summit obscured by mist, walls of stones, and an art colony.

She wishes they had time to stop, but Barb is on a budget.

She's always watching her dollars and this cheap Brit rail pass gives them seven days unlimited travel on every type of conveyance: ferry boats, buses, railroads and yesterday, a postal van. Maggie wishes Barb would lighten up. Maggie's paying for Elizabeth, and she is worth every penny. Her sunny smile and sense of humour keep her going. The bus lurches around a steep corner, revealing a majestic castle silhouetted against a misty grey sky. She takes out her map. 'What castle is that?' she asks the local woman who turns and looks out of the window.

'Ooh. That be the modern one.'

'When was it built?'

'Sometime in the seventeen or eighteen hundreds. I'm nae sure of the date.' She taps her finger on her cheek. 'You be better visiting the old ruin on the peak.' She points to a spot on Maggie's map who promises it will top her list. But not today. Later, much later. After miles and miles of bouncing over pot-holed roads, she too is old and ruined.

The bus driver pulls to the curb and points to John O' Groats Hostel high on top of a steep hill. Maggie rubs her aching bottom, ignores the twinge in her neck and humps her large travel case onto her back. The daypack hangs on her front. Elizabeth wants to take the daypack, but Maggie won't allow it. Elizabeth calls her a feisty little old lady, in hiking boots. Maggie taps the driver's shoulder, point up the hill and asks if there is any transport.

'Ooh. It's nae verra far,' he says, giving her a wink. 'Especially for a strapping lassie like yerself.'

*

14/4/1991

*Dear Maggie, The hairdressing salon is going well. I have
two excellent girls and an apprentice. They look after
things when I go to the retirement village. I still care for*

When the village residents talk about Daniel, the old soldier standing before the automatic teller machine shouting, 'I've won. I've won,' Diane turns away to hide her sadness. The residents laugh and smile, but when one dies, suffers a stroke or loses their faculties, or as Thelma says, facilities, a collective shiver runs through the village. They close ranks, deliver casseroles, sit and listen. The solitude of the bush, without the need for glamorous makeup, and no electricity for hairdryers, clippers or curling tongs, becomes irresistible to Diane.

The trip to Bandelier and the ancient cliff dwellings plants the desire to learn more about Australian indigenous culture and country. What better way than first hand? Diane organises a camping trip to Ayer's Rock. Maybe Outback travel will encourage Kerry to prod, question and explore.

Heat, soul-searing heat. Dirt, dust, scrub and mice, hundreds and hundreds of mice, scuttle under tent flaps, copulate in sleeping bags and feast on their food cache. Diane moves a box, and they scamper and scurry. Ron copes with chewed ropes, nibbled hessian bags and threatens to shoot the lot. Kerry chases them with the broom.

There are at least ten other camps nearby. A new arrival hurries past with her jeans soaked from the knees down: first time to the camp toilet. She will learn to stand to one side, press the button and run like hell to avoid the tidal wave erupting from the bowl.

Diane waves. Smug in her dry-legged jeans, she turns the camp oven just one twist on hot coals to evenly cook the beer-bread. One stubby of beer poured into self-rising flour and some sugar, lots of sugar, ensures they will not starve tonight. Ron calls it sacrilege, but two hungry adults and a growing girl take some filling.

An elderly aboriginal woman, her loose frock tugged by hot wind, sits on hot sand. She clicks two message sticks, smiles, then points to the ground. Diane and Kerry squat in the bull-dust, and are instantly besieged by millions of affectionate bush flies undeterred by the swish of leafy fly-swatters. Momentarily, the flies rise, only to settle again onto backs, cluster around eyes and buzz in ears.

'Uluru.' The woman points to the rock.

'Ayer's Rock?' Diane asks. The woman nods. 'Uluru.'

The sound rolls off Diane's tongue, the Pitjinjara word flowing and musical when compared to clipped colonial speech.

The woman clicks intricately patterned message sticks. Her rhythmic, mournful chant communicates more clearly than any words her timeless relationship to the land. With nods, gestures and a smile, the woman hands Kerry two seed grinding stones. Kerry finds some seeds to grind and puts her back into the task, wiping imaginary sweat from her brow. The childish antics make the woman and Diane laugh, but Kerry's grinding and the woman's stick clapping reveal an ancient culture stretching back thousands of years.

Diane breaks open a paddy melon, exposing soft white flesh and pink seeds. She points to her mouth.

The woman violently shakes her head.

A flock of wild budgerigars wheels and swoops across a limitless sky. Their wings flash iridescent green before they disappear into a blue deeper than any sea. Kerry points: talks about her Billy Budgie back home in his cage. Confined, content, secure. If only he could fly free above the small waterhole surrounded by palms teeming with raucous life. The pool is protected by towering ochre cliffs blocking out a thirsty sun. Cool, clear, a place to nourish body and soul. Diane drinks deeply of the water and the peace and vows this will not be the last time.

The lingering last rays of sun tease and caress the rock as it shimmers and preens under a darkening sky. Outside their camper, Diane sits on warm sand and cuddles Kerry while they watch the rock transform from wanton scarlet to consecrated purple. Rocking Kerry, Diane murmurs, '*Uluru, Uluru.*'

Gazing at the monolith rising out of miles and miles of flat scrubby ground reminds Diane of Gulliver, a captured giant who, with a bellow, could rise at any moment from a century's long sleep. This may not be Maggie's Kilimanjaro, but it is just as breathtaking. Hunkered in the earth, it allows mice-like people to scamper, climb, and nibble at its edges.

Following the Malu trail, they view the womb-shaped Fertility Cave, sacred to aboriginal women. Creep into dark, dank recesses to see where the fruits of that fertility were initiated. Shiver at the sight of the black, blood-soaked rock where boys were turned into men.

Holding Kerry's hand, Diane helps her over rough sections, and hesitates when Kerry points to the dark stain, wanting to know the cause. Diane's explanation of ore-stained water seeping through the rock is accepted.

They climb. Oh, how they climb, past Chicken Point where the safety chain finishes, to scramble hand over hand, often down on their knees as wild wind whips their hair.

'Come on, Mum, you can do it.'

Diane's legs are like two weak elastic bands, but Kerry won't let her stop. She tugs and pulls Diane until finally they reach the top and gaze in awe at...nothing. Miles and miles of flat nothing. Apart from the distant Olgas and the rocky outcrop of the Dome of the Dying Kangaroo their view is unhindered to the horizon.

Diane hugs her trembling knees. Her mind drifts to everyday concerns. Is everything all right back in Melbourne? Will the two-wheel-drive truck and old pick-up camper survive the corrugations and dust of this long trip? Will their meagre supply of flour be adequate? She tugs at her jumper. Does it cover the broken zip of her jeans? Was her life like one of those camp-ground mice, always scrabbling and scampering, consumed by the petty problems of everyday living? If only she could remember to lift her head long enough to see the magnificence around her. Kerry snuggles beside her. Diane smiles at the happy upturned face. She pushes a stray curl back from her daughter's forehead. Here, on top of the world, the wind picks up her puny troubles and scatters them harmlessly over the vast landscape.

*

Diane's Journal: Australia.

> *You love the sound and feel of tapping keys, seeing words skim across the screen. But where are you going with this novel? One minute you're confident, bubbling over with enthusiasm. But words often fail you. The visions are there, dancing in dark places. Scenes, characters and settings float past in an endless procession and, like the fairies in Lady Cottington's Pressed Fairy Book, you try to trap them.*
>
> *Sometimes when you're asleep, your dream catcher captures perfect words flowing out of your subconscious. You jump out of bed and grab your pen. Squish, snap, trap. Unfettered, unedited sentences that sing when read, but completely unrelated to the writing in hand, destined with great regret for the cutting room floor.*

*

The pot of red chillies on the bench droops in spite of copious amounts of water and tender loving care. The kitchen corkboard is covered in pictures of Maggie and Santa Fe. Diane glances longingly at them and yearns for something beyond doing the dishes and making money to pay the bills. Something to nourish her soul. She wants to learn, to understand, to be like Maggie.

*...so, Maggie, I've gone back to school as a mature-aged
student —I sound like a piece of old cheese—studying for
my year twelve certificate at our local Tertiary And
Further Education (TAFE) College. It was a sudden
decision. One I hope I won't live to regret. Sorry. I know it
sounds crazy, but I must run. I have homework to do.*

Like a novice skier hurtling down a black run, icy exhilaration lashes Diane's face, sharpens her mind, but it's just as scary.

A month ago, sitting in the balcony of the Robert Blackwood hall, only Kerry existed amongst the capped and gowned graduates. She walked to the stage and Diane suddenly saw a huge educational gap widening between them. Kerry's Bachelor of Arts Degree ensuring she already talks in a language Diane cannot understand. Maggie's letters constantly nudge her. Has she read anything new lately? What did she think of Douglas Preston's latest book? The yearning is there, but never the time. Kerry is beginning to map her own journey. The Whitlam government introduced free education for anyone deprived through financial hardship or lack of opportunity. TAFE College, only ten minutes away, has VCE classes for mature aged students.

'Write about anything you like,' the teacher, who looks the same age as Kerry, says to Diane. Opening the three-hundred-and-twenty-page exercise book, Diane stares at the blank paper. Her body is fertile, but what if her mind is barren? The other students begin scribbling. Diane's hand shakes, cannot hold the pen. Wrapping her bulky cardigan around her, she forces herself to write her name at the top of the page. At least it isn't blank.

But what can she write about? What does she want to say? Nothing. Zilch, zero. Her nose an inch from the paper, pen in a white knuckled grip she begins writing about why she sits in this classroom, her hopes and fears, her sick dog and the two snails crawling across the dew-drenched path this morning. A dove calling from the roof of the old tenement house in Footscray. Grandpa bent over, tending his beloved potted plants, nurturing them more than his eight children and ten grandchildren. Potted plants don't answer back. Black pants held up by braces, the seat, shiny with wear. White shirtsleeves rolled back, held by silver elasticised grips below bulging biceps, the result of working in a soap factory eighty hours a week. The studded, Sunday shirt, detachable collar removed. A small, nuggetty man with a shock of white hair on top of which is perched a jaunty, black hat, thumb marks imprinted in the front point of the crown.

'Cats on the roof.' He looks at Diane. She looks up, but can't see any.

'Where?'

'Those doves are telling us. See?' He points to a group of doves perched on the ridge, calling to each other. 'Listen.' In a singsong voice he chants—'There's cats on the roof, There's cats on the roof.'

'I hear them, Grandpa.'

'Now listen for the reply. Hear it?'

She shakes her head.

'Can't you hear, Well chase em off? Well chase em off?' Grandpa also thinks they say, The fruit salad's crook.

Diane is small and in Grandpa's bedroom, her shoulder blades pressed hard against the side of the bed. He rubs against her, rasping his unshaven bristles across her face—

'Stop...'

Diane doesn't hear the word 'stop' until the teacher's hand takes the pen out of hers. At the end of the class, she collects their writing. Diane prays she will be able to read her scrawl, but please God, never let her read her writing aloud in front of other students. She bruises easily.

*

Long buried memories flood your mind. Like a boiling pot, images spill out from under the lid and sprawl across the stove. Images of her in her little girl pink party dress running to climb on grandpa's knee. Wanting to be special, the favourite grandchild, liking the forbidden attention paid for by the secret fingering while he pretended to read her stories. You don't want to remember the bedroom and you quickly slam the lid of the pot on your leaking memories.

*

7/11/1992

Dear Diane, I'm afraid I'm not much good with plants and have managed to kill my fair share. Have you tried leaving your chillies outside in the sun?

I'm so pleased you have decided to further your education. You can do it. A woman has more brains than two men put together but it will not be easy juggling family life, full time work plus study. However, you are studying two of my favorite subjects, English Literature and Biology. I love anything to do with the natural world and was a whizz at biology and you know how much I love to read. I always have my nose stuck in a book. Keep me informed about your progress.

Hank's mother is old enough to be Maggie's grandmother. On their wedding day, Hank's mother grabs her shoulders. 'Why are you marrying him?' Kind eyes gaze into hers. 'You've got yourself a real handful there, gal, but since you've made up your mind...' She unclasps the twisted gold and silver chain from around her neck. It sits neatly above the scallop of ivory lace of her future daughter-in-law's gown.

'Good luck.' She kisses Maggie's cheek before wrapping her arms around her and hugging her tight. 'You're going to need it.'

Maggie soon understands she has hitched her wagon to a roller coaster. The slow ratchet pull of research, the magnificent view of knowledge from the top and the stomach churning drop into the rigour of publishing. Brilliance and paranoia. The steel trap of his mind. But amongst all the chaos of research started and abandoned, abrupt manner and self absorption, of papers littering the floor, Hank and Maggie are the perfect team. The magnificent Lone Ranger and his clever sidekick, Tonto, government funded, travelling the country and eventually the world.

A year later and six months pregnant Maggie is having a horror of a day. If Hank's article is to be published in the next research journal, it must be on the editor's desk by the end of the week. The bibliography is a nightmare. So many obscure references to check and change. She wonders why he doesn't keep detailed accounts of the books he reads instead of piling them up on his desk? Surely he would know what to do by now. All footnotes must be verified, and he has dozens of them. How does he expect her to get it done in such a short time? She's already taken several headache tablets. Time for a break.

Reaching up on tiptoe to their kitchen cupboards, obviously designed for a giant, she grapples for a mug. Coffee black and strong will help. Rolling her head around, listening to the grisly cracks of stiff muscle and bone, she doesn't hear Hank sneak up behind her. His arms around her waist, warm and comforting, until he presses his groin and the hardness she knows only too well against her buttocks.

'Not tonight,' she groans.

'Forget the essay.' He nuzzles her neck.

'You have to take more care with your references.' She tries to push him away. 'If you'd only follow the Harvard style—'

'Have you finished talking, Maggie, or are you going to enlighten me some more?' She becomes rigid in his embrace as the words hit home. He presses harder, grinds against her, his arms pinning hers to her side. The more she struggles, the more aroused he becomes.

'No Hank. Not now.' Her refusal angers him. Lifting her off her feet, he marches into the bedroom and throws her on the bed. She struggles, pinned down, his face two inches from hers.

Spit sprays when he shouts, 'If I want to fuck you, I will.'

Wham. Bam. Not even a Thank you, Mam. Being pregnant was no protection. She could eat an apple while he had her and he wouldn't care.

Maybe she could run away. Slam the door. Instead, Maggie decides to take her father's advice. She made her bed now she had to lie in it. But how was she going to live with this man, who expects her to respond enthusiastically to the constant thrust in the dark.

With Hank constantly in the bedroom, Maggie worries she will end up with fourteen children.

A month later, Maggie's mother-in-law pulled her chair up close. Talked about the coming baby, the weather, future family outings and the blood-cleansing properties of spinach before saying, 'Are you serious about having only two children?

Maggie nods.

'You realise you're safest straight after your period, and most fertile in the middle of the month?' She can tell by Maggie's vacant look that she has no idea of what she is talking about. She tut tuts in frustration.

'You must learn all you can about natural methods to avoid becoming pregnant.' She looks straight at her. 'Surely you've heard of the Billings Ovulation Method of contraception.'

With her mother-in-law's knowledge and assistance, and tolerating, even encouraging Hank's infidelities Maggie manages to limit babies to two. If only her mother-in-law could have helped her raise them.

The colors of the large cliffs guarding the entrance to
Cave Creek Canyon change almost every hour. This year
the rains are late and the leaves of the large sycamore,
oak and juniper trees are brilliant orange, red and gold.
But what good is that to me when...

'Hold on tight', Hank shouts as the four wheel drive slides and grinds along the slippery Canyon Creek road. Black clouds rumble, lightning crackles above mountain tors. Torrential rain lashes the windscreen and at, Turkey Creek, they have to pull over to wait out the worst of the thunderstorm. A bedraggled black-throated desert sparrow, outside Maggie's side window, shelters on the lowest branch against the trunk of a mesquite bush. Water drips off his beak and, every now and again he pathetically peeps.

'Hang the microphone out of the window,' Hank shouts.

Maggie reaches into the back seat, searching amongst anoraks, spare boots, and piles of books and papers. Hank's fingers drum the steering wheel in time with the rain.

'Hurry up.'

'It's here somewhere—'

'Hijo de puta, Maggie. The storm will be over.' Dragging up the mike by its cord, she hangs it out the window. The running tape captures the syncopated boom of thunder, crack of lightening, and drumming rain interspersed with the sparrow's peeps. An unforgettable opus to nature.

They aquaplane home on the flooded gravel track, arriving back in camp just in time to record the perfect climactic roar of a flash flood. Added to this, within hours, the spade-foot toads start their mating calls.

A cluster of primitive cabins is this year's research base. Compliments of the American Museum of Natural History. Pete, Angie and family have to use the amenities block. Hank and Maggie have the only building with indoor plumbing and roomy, shelved closets.

'How's this?' Hank leans back in his chair, legs crossed, looking directly at the camera. He wiggles his bushy eyebrows, jiggles an imaginary cigar—a plausible imitation of Groucho Marks. Julie laughs, tossing back blonde hair, leans over and grabs his chin, turning his face to the light. An intimate look passes between them. Their laughter, jagged fingernails raking the blackboard of Maggie's heart. Do they have to flaunt the affair. Do they think she is blind, cannot see what is going on between them, or do they simply not care.

Hank touches Julie's arm, leans forward. Another lingering look. Snap. Snap. Snap. How many photos does she need for her damn article?

'Coffee?' Maggie clears a spot amongst the deluge of papers littering the table.

He jokes and laughs. She clasps her hands behind her head. Fiddles with her hair, piles the long locks high on top of her head, tendrils curl bewitchingly around her face. Breasts thrust invitingly forward, she leans well back in her chair to reveal long limbs. He sits legs spread apart, hands on hips. Body language. She sees Maggie watching and flashes a grin. Bitch.

'I've read your husband's article in the *American Museum of Natural History Bulletin*' she says, as if genuinely interested in only his mind. 'It's fascinating.' White teeth flash.

'Julie needs to photograph rattlesnakes for her article,' Hank adds. 'I'll take her up into the canyon. We'll only be gone a week.'

With the laundry door closed, Maggie gropes for and finds the half-full cranberry juice bottle filled with port in the bottom of the soiled linen bin. Listening for the sound of approaching footsteps, she unscrews the cap and doesn't put the container down until it is nearly empty. Her breathing steadies as alcohol eases the tightness in her chest.

'Go,' she says out loud knowing no one will hear. 'Don't worry about me. I'll look after the children.' Maggie upends the bottle again. 'And type your latest article.' Bottle in hand, she salutes the laundry door. 'Good luck to you. At least you won't be pawing me for a while.' Wiping away tears with the back of her hand, she drains the bottle and then hides it at the back of the shelf. With a smile firmly planted on her face, she returns to an empty room.

With Hank away, the house is quiet. The girls lie on their stomachs on the sitting room floor, drawing in their exercise books, crayons spread out in front of them. Maggie digs her fingers into the base of her skull to ease the pain. The last thing she needs is a migraine. Checking the girls are okay, she finds the cranberry juice container she tucked behind the Cheerios box in the pantry. With shaking fingers she unscrews the cap and takes a hasty drink. Sucking an extra strong peppermint, she goes back into the sitting room and flops down beside Barb, adding a sun here, a moon there, and playfully tugs her long hair.

'Can I have a candy,' she asks. She loves her mommy's peppermints. Everyone thinks they are Maggie's favourite. She hates the things, but the stronger the better. Taking the packet out of her sweat pants pocket, she gives one to Barb and offers the packet to Anna. With a disgusted look she screws up her nose, shakes her head, packs up book and crayons, stomps to her room and slams the door.

The whispering sounds of birds settling for the night drifts in the open window. Walking around the silent house, Maggie picks up a stray crayon. Pops a sock into a sneaker, before tucking the girls in for the night. Barb wraps thin arms around her neck and hugs her tight. 'Nighty night. Don't let the bed bugs bite.' She leans over to kiss Anna. She turns her face to the wall.

In the sitting room, Maggie picks up her latest book. Flips the pages. Throws it onto the couch and ponders how an author can write such trash? Predictable plot. Unbelievable characters happily humming love songs as they live in domestic bliss. Songs of copulation more like it. The pain in her head spreads to her temples. In the kitchen, she grabs the cranberry juice bottle filled with port, bought from The Grand Hotel, no questions asked, pours herself a large glass, drains it and sighs.

'What are you doing, Mummy?'

Maggie jumps. Anna stares at the glass in her hand.

'What are you looking at?' Maggie rinses her glass until it is squeaky clean.

'Can I have a drink?' She points to the cranberry bottle on the draining board.

'You're supposed to be in bed, my lady.' Maggie pats her on the bottom. She pulls a face, drops her bottom lip. Puts her hands on her hips and stares.

'Off you go. To your bedroom.'

'But I want cranberry juice.'

Maggie mouths the word No.

'Why can't I?' She pushes past Maggie and reaches for the bottle. Turning quickly, Maggie knocks it into the sink, the contents gurgle down the drain. She grabs Anna's shoulders and shakes her. 'Now look what you've made me do.'

The next day, keys in hand, Maggie dashes out the front door and jumps into the car. She is half an hour late and the kids will be waiting. Where had the time gone? One minute it was two o'clock and the next four. Had she been asleep? Upright at the kitchen table? It must have been another blackout. Two hours this time. Maggie screeches to the curb where the gals are sitting on the low brick wall surrounding the school.

'Where have you been, Mommy?' Barb flings her arms around her.

'So sorry, Honey. I was working for Daddy and fell asleep.' Anna looks at her with penetrating eyes, and walks away.

'Come back, Miss.' Reluctantly, she climbs into the car. Maggie starts driving down the road.

'Where are you going, Mommy?' Barb asks.

'Home.'

'You're going the wrong way,' Anna shouts. Maggie makes a U turn and heads off in the right direction.

The girls leave for camp the next day.

Alone in the cabin, tears prick Maggie's eyes. Trickle down her cheeks. Hurrying into the kitchen, she reaches for the bottle. Her hand freezes in mid air. Anna's lunch is on the bench, Barb's backpack beside it.

Maggie sits on the side of the bed, curtains drawn against the morning sun, wet wash-cloth draped across the back of her aching neck. Her head spins. She checks the box of painkillers to see how many are missing, wondering if she has already taken two. Maybe four? She pops another two into the palm of her hand, stares at them and decides it is not enough to ease her pain. Dragging open the bedside table drawer she searches through boxes of medication, finally placing a selection on the bedside table. Such pretty colours. The blue sleeping ones are her favourites but maybe Valium will help. Maggie swallows two, plus the painkillers, washing down with a glass of port. Tosses from side to side. Imagines Hank flirting with his new flame, helping her over streams, carrying her pack. Julie laughing at his lame jokes.

'What rock is that?' she asks.

'Intercoursite.'

'Intercoursite? I've never heard of it.'

'Just another fuckin' rock.'

She reaches for the half empty bottle.

Sunlight floods the room. Covering her eyes with her hand, she is confused. It should be dark. Maggie checks the bedside clock. 10:00 a.m. The next morning. Out of it for twenty-four hours. She sees the empty 2-litre juice bottle on the floor. The world spins. Bed rocks. Trying to stand, she falls backwards. She stares at the ceiling, horrified by the distorted faces in the shadows, hordes of spiders swarming up the walls. There are blank places in her head. She tries to remember what is missing. Pushing back a lank lock of hair, Maggie catches a glimpse of herself in the dressing table mirror. Not yet forty and she looks a hundred. What if Hank walks in? Finds her like this. Eyes red, stinking of port. The overpowering rank smell seeps through her skin, permeates her clothes. Lush. Lush. Lush keeps circling through her mind. Maggies mouth is dry, every cell screaming for a drink. Anna. Barb. She could lose her children. Her eyes fill with tears. She reaches for a tissue. Is surprised how much it hurts to blow her nose. Somehow she must stop this agonizing pain. Make it go away.

Maggies eyes won't focus. Books don't help. They haven't done it for her for years. Painkillers? Hallucinogenic mushrooms? The Oaxaca Indians use those. Not strong enough. She dreams of holding an electric drill to her skull. Boring into the black spot, the source of the pain. That would kill it. Instead, she fills her palm with pills and brings them to her lips. Searches for a bottle to wash them down but only finds empties. Maggie stares at the handful of pretty pills. So easy to simply toss back her head and swallow. Blackness. Oblivion. They'd be better off without her. The kids? Who will take care of the kids? Hank? His latest floosy? No way. Pills fly across the room, pepper the wall'

'Help'. She cries flopping forward, her hands clasping her knees. 'Help me!'But who? Who can help? Not God. Not Allah. Not some fictitious omniscient deity. She closes her eyes. Rocks back and forwards. Asks, Why? Why should she live?

A cougar coughs a warning. Maggie grabs pen and paper. Scribbles memories of baby kisses, first footsteps, her mother and father, aunts, friends and all the people who have ever loved her. Wraps all the love in the world around her. Promises never to drink again. Cries out to the universe, 'Help. Help me.'

Eight hours later, pouring every last dreg of hidden port

down the sink, she hides empty bottles in the middle of a bag of trash then pours a long glass of water. For four days Maggie shakes and shivers, sipping at a glass of water that never leaves her hand. She feels as if she's drunk a dam dry.

Hank and Julie walk in. They don't look at each other. Julie, water running off her hiking jacket, hair lank, finger by finger drags off wet gloves. Dumps her bag on the floor by the settee.

'Did you get the photos?'

'It poured nonstop.' Hank replies. ' And we didn't find one friggin' rattlesnake.' He throws his wet jacket on the floor. 'We'll have to do the interview using caged snakes.'

With shaking hands, Maggie pours another long glass of water.

*

Diane's Journal: Australia.

> *The nights belong to the novelist. You burn the midnight*
> *oil and commit words to text. It becomes an addiction.*
> *Floors are left unswept, dishes pile high in the sink, bills*
> *languish unopened. Life revolves around the story. When*
> *you wash dishes, sweep floors and pay bills and are*
> *trapped by the busyness of life, the novel nags for words.*
> *Should you include Maggie's addiction? It was only told*
> *to you when last you talked to her.' It was never written*
> *down and an unanswered letter on the kitchen bench*
> *begs for a reply.*

*

Diane searches for something to write that isn't doom and gloom. She must keep the letter bright and cheerful. She yawns and straightens her back. Her spine creaks.

How are you, Maggie? I've just scoffed a whole block of rich dark chocolate. You'd love it. It's a new variety full of hazel nuts. Delicious, but probably the worst thing in the world for me.

I seem to have gained an extra kilo and it's clinging tenaciously to my hips. Maybe that is why my left knee keeps seizing. I'm sorry it has taken me so long to reply to your welcome letter, but Mum hasn't been well, hairdressing has been crazy.

I know, excuses, excuses.

Leaving the barely started letter on the kitchen table, Diane ventures outside. Moonlight outlines tall gums and highlights scarlet Canna lilies. The softness of night wraps around her, and she breathes crisp air. Facing the full moon, eyes closed, she bows three times. If only her wish could come true.

A constant ringing. Diane rolls over and grabs the bedside phone. 'Hello?' Listens to the urgent voice. 'I'll be there as fast as I can.'

On the edge of the bed knuckling sleep out of her eyes, she reaches for the folded track suit on the floor. Ron's head appears above the covers. 'Off again,' he murmurs, gently rubbing her back.

She touches her lips to his forehead. He smiles, mutters something, pulls the continental quilt up to his neck and rolls over. She wishes she could curl up beside him. Be there when he wakes and sleepily gathers her in his arms for an early morning cuddle. It will be at least five hours before she returns.

She grabs the bag, hanging on the bedroom doorknob. It contains her mum's medical details, doctor's phone number, correct money for the telephone, several tissues and an old *Woman's Weekly* in case her mum wants to read. Sally Morgan's *My Place* will help Diane. She'll need Sally's down-to-earth sense of humour. Bright light spills out the Emergency entry. White ambulances unload trolleys supporting anonymous blanketed forms. Diane's shoes squeak along the shiny hall. Doors swing open to a babble of noise. 'Code grey. Code grey.'

'You fuckin' idiot.' An addict, high on drugs, berates the triage nurse, shaking a fist in her face. 'Code grey. Code grey.' Security guards instantly appear and the man, still screaming abuse, is dragged away. Crying children in dressing gowns and slippers cuddle into concerned parents. A drunk holds a bloody cloth to his forehead. An elderly woman doubled over in pain, her husband patting her hand.

Diane approaches the desk. 'Can I see Valerie Gilbert?'

The nurse checks her admittance form. 'Take a seat, we'll let you know as soon as doctor has seen her.'

'She's eighty-three, and I need to be with her.'

The weary nurse sighs.

'I've been before. I know to keep out of the way.' Diane is waved through.

Groans and cries come from behind blue-curtained beds. White-coated doctors and nurses hurry past. Diane wants to chant, I'm late, I'm late for a very important date, and expects to see the mad hatter and Cheshire cat appear. In the last bed in a long row of cubicles, a small figure struggles for breath, oxygen mask clamped to her face. She takes her mother's bony hand, gently squeezes and smiles.

'Sorry to trouble you, Love,' her mother whispers.

'No worries, Mum. I wasn't doing anything anyway.' Her mother's smile extends to her eyes. Diane drags up a chair and sits beside her. It is always a long, long night.

*

11/9/1992

*Dear Diane, I'll be so glad when summer is over. I hate
hot weather. Of course, knowing me, I'll be bitching
about cold weather all too soon.*

*I was sorry to hear about your mother. It is so hard
when a loved one is ill. I know I've mentioned this before,
but have you talked with your mother about the future?
Maybe it is a good time now that she is feeling a bit
better. Hank and I both belong to what we call the
Hemlock Society.*

Maggie stops writing. Should she mention this? Is it too harsh? Maybe, but these things have to be faced. Both she and Hank decided many years ago that they did not want to be kept alive if there was no hope of a full recovery. Many of their friends agreed. Maggie is often plagued by the fear of becoming a drooling fool in a nursing home.

*To cheer you up, I've sent you a subscription to SWARA
magazine. The last issue focused on the culture and art of
the Wabenzi tribe. This inspired me to write a limerick.
Why don't you try one? They are great fun and will help
you forget your troubles. You'll find the rules in Baring-
Gould's book 'The Lure of the Limerick'.*

Maggie remembers the rollicking rhyme written for her own amusement.

*There once was a man named Mwenzie,
Who worked himself into a frenzy
He got filthy rich, that son-of-a-bitch,
And joined the tribe of Wabenzi*

She decides not to send it to Diane, but vows that when she returns from Rwanda, she'll send Diane a heap of travel stories to take her mind off nursing homes and the Hemlock Society.

Maggie can't wait to leave Santa Fe. But first there are suitcases to pack, both hers and Hank's. She doesn't want to begin to think about being crammed into an airline seat for twenty-four hours. Especially when Hank insists on taking the window seat and she's squashed next to someone she doesn't know. They invariably try to engage her in inane, trivial conversation.

Maggie has contacted East Africa Wildlife Safaris and insisted that Jock Anderson once again be their guide. Just his name sends a delightful shiver down her spine. That Kenyan-born big braw Scot is built for tossing the caber. And he tells such hair-raising tales. Four years in the mountains fighting the Mau Mau.

Last trip, he strode along, never once looking back to see how she fared at crossing streams and getting through the bush. Finally, she had to say, 'Do you always leave little ladies to fend for themselves, or are you paying me a compliment?'

He pondered a minute. 'Paying a compliment, I guess. And besides, you wouldn't accept help anyway. '

She hopes Jock doesn't find out that she turns sixty-eight on this trip. His legendary speciality is a birthday cake made out of a big, dry elephant turd decorated with icing. Diane's fruitcake is more to her taste.

Fierce tsetse flies swarm around her, but one quick spray and she's surrounded by corpses. Hank grumbles and snorts his disapproval. Their guides speak only French. Fortunately, Jock hands them a list of instructions on how to behave when they meet the gorillas.

Walk quietly without speaking.

Stay with the group.

Crouch down when approaching gorillas.

Sit still.

Do not make eye contact.

Do not make any quick or aggressive movements.

The mountain slope is steep and slippery, and they are soon in a murky, cloud-filled forest. Sweat pours down their faces. They bushwhack their way through dense vegetation and clumped bamboo, until she is exhausted. Sitting on a log, Maggie can't stop rubbing the welts and itchy rash from stinging nettles. All forgotten when their guides make low, guttural, grunting noises and point to the first gorilla signs: fasces, uprooted bamboo and flattened places where they made beds for the night.

Crawling under a branch, she sees two young gorillas. A little distance away, their mothers placidly munch leaves. One mother has a tiny baby. Maggie crouches and slowly moves forward to get a good look at its sad, little, wrinkled face as it peeks out from its mother's arms. The other young ones are rambunctious and devilish. They obviously want to play and swing overhead on bamboo stalks. Sneaking up behind her, they touch her arm and scamper away. Before long, the young gorillas move on and she follows.

Reaching a ridge, she realises she has wandered off on her own. Something Jock always warned them against. He will be furious. She listens to hear if he and the others are bashing through the bush below but can't hear a thing. Even the birds are silent. Maggie's heart thumps in her chest, and she pushes her way through the undergrowth. A crashing sound makes her look up the slope. A Big Daddy silverback gorilla ambles towards her. She freezes. Forgets to crouch. Forgets Jock's warning lecture.

Directly opposite her, the silverback rises to his full height. He is magnificent. Majestic. Black shaggy fur, leathery bearded face, thick hairy arms, his hands the size of a dinner plate. He clutches a piece of bamboo like a conductor about to instruct the orchestra. Every inch the dominant male. Maggie defies all the rules, takes the chance and snaps a hasty photo. He is so regal. His power tangible.

A deep-throated bellow makes her instinctively fold her

hands across her chest and submissively bow her head. He grunts, drops down and continues down the slope. Maggie sinks to the ground, her back against the base of a huge bamboo, euphoric, dizzily silly and grinning like a hyena. A gentle pat on her head. It is a young gorilla. The experience far outweighs the lecture she will get from Jock for wandering away from the group.

Back at the hotel, begging children surround them, tug at their clothes, hound them for money or treats. Drinking lemon squash in the bar, her ears assaulted by disco music, and nauseated by the feeding frenzy of the buffet, Maggie writes in her journal,

Best birthday present ever, but if the human race keeps procreating at this rate, there will be no room left for majestic gorillas, not to mention all the other African animals. Already their habitat is dwindling at a colossal rate due to the greed and necessities of man. Here, human habitation is as dangerous a threat to the survival of the gorillas as the poacher's snare.

She wants to run away. Back into the forest. To sit with the gorilla our guides call Ndume. 'Goddammit,' Maggie swears under her breath. She has always considered gorillas to be mankind's cousins and closest living relatives after chimpanzees. There are scientific papers proving that their DNA is ninety-nine percent identical to that of humans. Anger rises, bringing bile to her throat. How dare mankind destroy the forest. How dare people destroy what is rightly theirs. Missionaries should teach birth control. Offer a transistor radio for a vasectomy.

Back in Santa Fe, Maggie has the photo of Ndume enlarged and framed. In his honour, she attempts to create a double dactyl. She has to fudge a bit on the extent of her travels, but the result is:

Honkety tonkety,
Maggie's a naturalist
Veteran traveller
Cairo to Cape
USA to Australia
Zaire to Zambia
Anthropomorphizing
Every large ape.

*

12/12/1992

Dear Maggie, So that's a double dactyl. I looked up the rules. How on earth did you manage to construct one?. They are nearly impossible. I gave up after the first line. Maybe we could try one when you are here, but I can't guarantee I'll be any help.

According to Diane's Webster's *Third New International Dictionary* (unabridged), a double dactyl is a witty verse form, also known as higgledy-piggledy with a history as a parlour word game. Like a Limerick it is rigid in structure and is usually humorous.

True, it was fun to write her first limerick. Not that she would show it to Maggie. But this is beyond her. And there is more. The entire poem is a single sentence and...Diane needs another dictionary to look up what parthenogenesis and choriamb mean. She slams the dictionary closed and shoves it back on the shelf. Forget it. She's not like Maggie. Diane has a full-time job and heaps of study. Maggie can travel to Africa and write the double dactyls.

We are envious of your constant travels, Maggie, especially your trips to Africa, but at the moment Asia is the best travel option for us. It is closer, warmer (but not as warm as Kenya) and certainly much cheaper.

*Hairdressing cannot be called a high-paying job, and I
have to make every penny count. Barb and I would get
along just fine. Qantas advertised incredibly cheap
airfares to Penang, and Kerry is happy to look after the
house. I haven't been there since 1965 and can't wait.*

For Diane, Penang feels like home. After twenty-nine
years, apart from one or two big resort hotels, it still has the
same old-world Portuguese and colonial Malayan charm.
People smile and the sun shines. Ron hails a taxi.

Stepping inside is like sitting on the couch in her mother-
in-law's living room. Hand-crocheted doilies drape over
plump, embroidered cushions. But this driver carries his
comfortable domesticity theme to a higher level. A bright
floral lining, called Contact, designed to cover kitchen
shelves, sticks to every panel. Tiny, pink roses on a blue
background. On the dashboard is a miniature red shrine. The
pièce de rèsistance is a vase of artificial flowers wired to the
back of the driver's seat.

Ron raises his eyebrows at the decor.

'You stay?' The taxi-driver's grin reveals large yellow teeth.

'The Casuarina Hotel on Batu Ferringi.' Passing the
upmarket resort boasting royal patronage in domestic
splendour, they sweep into the palm-lined drive of an old
refurbished hotel. Cheap, clean and close to a bus stop.

Diane tosses her suitcase onto the bed and drags out a
lightweight t-shirt. Ron looks for an air conditioner. Diane
laughs. Points to the overhead fan lazily circulating hot air.
She pulls back heavy drapes and sighs with delight at the
view. Tall palms line a crescent of golden sand leading to
manicured green lawns dotted with La-Z-Boy loungers.

Soon loud snores reverberate around the room. Diane
hurries downstairs and books a morning tour of Georgetown.

'Welcome to our shitty tour' the coach driver announces,
wiping his sweaty face with a not-too-clean cloth.

'What did you say?' Ron tries not to laugh.

'Welcome to the shitty of Georgetown.' The coach driver's brown, shiny face and white teeth grins at them from the rear-view mirror. Diane and Ron, hands over their mouths, try to smother their chuckles.

It reminds Diane of her first trip to Penang. Arriving late at night, she put both hands together in prayer position saying *Selamat pagi* and wondered why everyone laughed. Apparently, she was wishing everyone good morning with a heavy Australian accent. And she never did get her tongue around surnames starting with Ng.

At Glutton's Lane, they eat curried prawns, lean elbows on the table, drop food and loudly burp to show appreciation of a good meal. It is easy to slip into the gin-sling, joss stick and trishaw travelling, Asian culture experienced by foreigners.

*

Diane's journal: Australia

> *Maggie was always trying to get you to travel in Africa,*
> *but you simply didn't have the money. And did you really*
> *want to go glamping in Africa? Maggie and Hank were*
> *government funded in the early days. They could afford*
> *to have chocolate mousse and be served by African's on*
> *their later, self funded personal tours. They had contacts*
> *and were given access to private tours. But the message*
> *was there in Maggie's letters. See the world as much as*
> *you can, while you can. You chose to travel in Asia.*

*

Diane rubs her aching lower back. Camping for a week on a blow-up mattress is not the best way to sleep, but she needs to be beside her mum to give her painkillers or help her onto the commode during the night.

Her mum's bed is in the large front room of the Retirement Village Unit, and Diane's dad constantly moans about being 'kicked out' into the smaller bedroom. Her mum blames the crippling arthritis that caused many restless nights, but Diane suspects that it is her mother's attempt to find some small haven to call her own in the close confinement of a small unit. At least, she could shut the bedroom door and leave her husband's political ranting and raving behind.

'Are you sure?'

Her mother nods.

Planting a kiss on the wrinkled face, Diane feels the paper-thin skin. The doctor says her mother's condition is brittle. What does he mean exactly? Fragile? Delicate? Frail? Ready to shatter? But that was a week ago and nothing much seems to have changed. Would one morning make any difference?

'It's our exam today.' Diane holds her mother's hand, feeling the fragile bones give under the gentle pressure. Osteoporosis. Osteoarthritis. Silent killers.

'I won't be long. Are you sure you'll be okay?'

'I'll be all right.' Her mother swallows hard. 'Don't worry about me,' she whispers, but her eyes plead for Diane to stay. Fingers curl around hers and hold on. Diane hesitates. It will only be for three hours.

'See you soon, Mum,' she says, withdrawing her hand with difficulty from her mother's grasp. A cheery wave, and she is out the door. Her mum will be okay. Once she gets her appetite back, she'll improve. They have been through this so many times before. Diane is in for the long haul, spacing herself to last the distance. Once she would have been nervous about sitting for an exam, but after a week of commodes, plumping pillows and listening to fluttering life struggle through old veins, Technical And Further Education classes are an excuse to get in the car and escape for a couple of hours. Her dad is left in charge.

Sitting at a desk, folded exam paper in front of her, pen poised, Diane watches the hands on the clock tick to 9:00 a.m. A bell rings. She opens the paper and begins to read.

Machiavelli and *The Prince*. Power and politics.

Question One: Who wrote, Power corrupts, and absolute power corrupts absolutely? She smiles, Maggie would love this one and quickly writes, Lord Acton in a letter to Bishop Creighton in 1817. One down, twenty-nine to go.

Question Two.

Diane continues answering the multiple choices, but underneath the veneer of the dedicated, mature-aged student, is the image of her mother's face. As soon as she finishes this exam, she can hurry home. She shouldn't be here. She should be rubbing cooling ointment into an angry bedsore. Positioning pillows to buffer aching bones. She forces herself to focus. Back to Machiavelli. Back to *The Prince*.

'Diane Simpson,' someone calls. Diane raises her hand. A teacher hurries over. Diane see the urgency in the teacher's face, hears it in her voice.

'Your mother is gravely ill.' She shakes Diane's arm. 'It's taken half an hour to find you.' Giving Diane a push, she shouts, 'Go,' and points to the door.

Grabbing car keys and leaving the half-finished exam and her bag on the floor, Diane races to her car. She must get back. Must be there. Her mother needs her. Is waiting for her. White-knuckled, she grips the steering wheel, plants the accelerator to the floor. A heart attack? Stroke? Pain? Struggling to breathe? The speedometer reads one hundred and ten kilometres. How many times had they sat together in this car? The flying flea her mum calls it, but today it can't go fast enough. Faster. She must go faster. Presses metal to the floor. One hundred and twenty. Diane feels her mother's presence beside her. She turns to look. The car veers to the side of the road. Wheels skid on gravel. Diane slams on the brakes and unconsciously flings back a protective arm. The seat beside her is empty. Diane's voice echoes in the car.

'Mum, if it's time, don't wait for me.'

Peace fills the car. Diane's knuckles regain colour. The speedometer climbs to one hundred kilometres and stays there. She yearns to see her mum, hold her, be there for her, but—No. Not if it means more pain. No more suffering.

An ambulance blocks the drive. Diane's car skids to a stop, and she runs into her mother's room. Her mum lies on the bed, the village nurse's hand cups the drooping chin. An ambulance attendant, head turned to one side, eyes half closed, stethoscope hooked into his ears. Hollow cup pressed on her mum's bony chest, he searches for the music of life. On his young face is the same rapt attention as a teenager plugged into CD player headphones. Fingers drumming to a heartbeat rhythm no one else can hear.

He removes the earplugs.

There's the slightest pulse. He looks at Diane. 'We can bring her back.'

Diane stares at him. She shivers with hope. More time. To be together. Hold her. Love her. She looks at her mother, as if to ask permission. The skeletal face is serene, forehead no longer wrinkled with pain. Hands calm on the covers. Bring her back? To what? The ambulance officer is filling a syringe.

'Let her go,' Diane hears herself saying. 'Let her go.' She takes her mother in her arms and cradles her. Gently rocking, she strokes the fine grey hair and croons.

*

Three a.m.

> *Dear Maggie: I'm sorry about the delay, but I've had the rug pulled out from under me. Mum died. For several weeks her condition was described as brittle, but it still caught me by surprise. I can't sleep. All I want to do is write.*

Diane folds the front of her dressing gown over her chest. Her feet in fluffy slippers. She shivers. Stretches weary arms and sighs. Jumbled thoughts cover pages of an exercise book.

What compels her to sit here, night after night, recording her mother's stories? Some funny, but most sadly reliving the pain of parting. Time for a break.

*

Diane's Journal: Australia.

> *Coffee mug in hand, you open the door and walk out into the night. Across the newly mown lawn wafts the heady perfume of ginger plants. Sounds carry in the crisp, dry air. The bark of a dog, caw of a crow and the rustle of gum leaves.*
>
> *A full moon sends a silvery ladder to earth inviting all who dare to climb. Is this why you are so restless? Are you, like many others, affected by the full moon? It's deeper than that, a primordial urge to not only record your mother's story. Why this compulsion to write? To preserve your mother's, and Maggies life within the pages of a book. At first, you don't know where to start. Now, every time a memory pops into your mind, you grab a pen. The feel of a fine biro skimming across the page seems to bring with it some relief. A coming to terms with loss.*

*

Diane sifts through a shoebox of certificates and comes across several photos. Her mum smiling proudly in her new winter coat with the treasured fox fur stole draped around her shoulders. The immortalised fox head with glittering marble eyes grips in its teeth its own leg, holding the stole in place. It seems macabre to see the art of the taxidermist displayed upon your mother's shoulders when she wouldn't have hurt a fly. A photo of Diane's mum wearing a rakish brown hat to Aunty Mary's wedding. She must show the photos to Kerry. Tell her about the young woman her grandmother was before either of them arrived on the scene. But Kerry's eyes will glaze. She'll pretend to be interested. She is too young, too busy making a life of her own to delve into the past. To discover the woman behind the remembered elderly grandmother. Later, much later, she will want to know her roots.

The stories Diane is now typing onto her computer will reveal to Kerry her grandmother's life.

Diane hopes that one day her mother's stories will become a book. But who would want to read an ordinary story of an everyday woman? What could be interesting in that? Most books are of famous people or contain dramatic events. Nathaniel Hawthorne wrote about religious frenzy and Puritanical fanaticism in *The Scarlet Letter*. Hester was an ordinary woman, who had a child outside of marriage. This sin resulted in expulsion from her community and incredible suffering.

Angela's Ashes is a memoir of Frank McCourt's Irish childhood and a mother courageously coping with sub-standard housing, an alcoholic husband and a family on the brink of disaster. But Sally Morgan's *My Place* is a down-to-earth story of everyday life where Curly the dog bites the Health Inspector's bottom. Hidden beneath the humour and personal anecdotes the story reveals what it is like to be aboriginal in a society that ostracises them. The ease of the story and the humour helped Diane through many a dark hospital night.

Maybe her mother's story will do the same. Show what it was like for her mother's generation of Australian women. Show her mother's hopes and dreams in contrast to the reality. So what if it doesn't get published. At least the family will have a record. Valerie Dulcie Gilbert will not be forgotten

But the fear is there. Can she write this story? She opens the fridge. She'd kill for cheesecake. Searches the shelves. Apparently His Roundness has discovered the last slice left over from the night before. With a sigh, Diane opens the sweet biscuit tin.

*

Diane's Journal: Australia.

> *The night belongs to the writer but you struggle with what appears to be pages of useless drivel. Writing a book is like trying to drive a bulky four-wheel drive with a flat tyre. It won't do what you want it to. You struggle with what appears to be pages of useless drivel. At least you won't be upset if you once again click some vague computer key and lose two hours of work. Good riddance.*
>
> *Your last computer program was much friendlier. It had a little paper clip with big eyes that blinked and Clippy would tap, tap if you hesitated too long over the keyboard. This new word processing is more sophisticated, but you miss your tiny computer friend. Maybe a cup of espresso, strong and black with just a touch of milk, will help you concentrate.*

*

1993: Kubunji Beach, Victoria, Australia

> *Dear Diane, I've enclosed a copy of our Australian International Expeditions itinerary so you'll have some idea where and what we're doing. I must admit to being excited. We fly directly from Cairns to you.*

A quick sip of coffee is enough to make Maggie grimace, but the long buffet has a plentiful supply of cookies, dried fruit and nuts. Hank, feet planted well apart, The Sun newspaper spread wide, expertly skims the page. Quickly capturing the essence of an article, he grunts disapproval. Maggie leans back into plush upholstery and crosses her legs. The Qantas First, or the platinum level lounge, is a quiet oasis amongst the bustle and clatter of Cairns Airways terminal. One benefit of travelling with a world-renowned scientist, even one that has retired is to not have to mingle with the hoi polloi.

A sombre customer service attendant approaches. This can't be good. She's seen that look before and it has always meant trouble. Hank keeps reading, oblivious to what is happening. The attendant glances at him and decides Maggie is her best option. Good choice.

'I'm sorry, Mrs. Jackson,' she says, 'but your flight has been delayed.'

Maggie taps Hank's knee.

'What?' he shouts, reluctantly taking his eyes off the page.

She motions for him to turn on his hearing aids. 'We've been delayed.' She waits for the explosion.

'Again? Can't we ever catch a plane without it being delayed?' Glowering at the attendant, he demands, 'How long?'

'Approximately two hours.'

'Two hours.' He whacks the newspaper against his leg. 'What am I expected to do for two hours? I—'

Maggie grips his thigh and squeezes.

'Get us on another flight,' Hank orders.

'There are no other flights, Sir. I'll keep you informed.' The attendant is already backing away.

'I can't be hanging around a godforsaken—'

Maggie squeezes again. He glares at her.

'Snafus and stuffups are par for the course these days.'

'But—'

She passes him a bowl from the buffet. 'Want a nut?' He glares at the cashews, shakes out the paper and continues reading.

Three and a half hours later, they board the plane.

Diane's tight blonde curls stand out amongst a crowd of bobbing heads.

'Maggie,' she calls, waving both arms.

Hank pushes their cart loaded with three large suitcases and some duty free. He may be over eighty, but in his Texas hat, bolo tie, denim shirt, faded jeans and brown leather boots, he looks the quintessential American male. What must she look like in her Gore-Tex pants, shirt and multi-pocketed jacket? Ready for the next African safari?

Before she knows it, Diane engulfs her in a bear hug. Maggie notices that Diane hasn't any lumpy love handles this time. The five years have been kind to her. Maggie wishes it was the same for her. It will take a lot of trekking and many push-ups to shed her extra ten pounds.

'God awful trip.' Hank pumps Ron's hand up and down.

'What about coffee? It's an hour's journey home.' Diane guides them to a coffee shop that sells organic, gluten-free bread, cakes and muffins.

'Damn stupid term.' Hank points to the sign. 'I haven't seen any inorganic food, have you?'

Maggie sighs with delight as she sips a steaming mug of Kenya and mocha blend, with a twist of lemon.

Diane insists that Hank sit in the front of the RV with Ron so 'the girls', as she puts it, can chat on the trip home. they talk about the vagaries of air travel, inclement weather and possible sights to see before Diane launches into a detailed report of what she calls 'The Kerry Capers'. Maggie squirms in her seat.

'How's Barb?' Diane asks.

Maggie explains that she is looking after their home in Santa Fe.

'And Anna? Still in Alaska?'

Maggie lifts her backpack onto her knee, drags out a tissue and blows her nose. 'She'll be there for a while.' Diane leans forward, expectantly waiting for more. Maggie continues. 'She's married you know.'

'When? What's he like?' Diane is eager for news. Maggie takes off her glasses, wipes them with a clean tissue and puts them back on again.

'Recently. A great guy. Works as a lumberjack up in the Yukon.'

'Tell me about him.'

Maggie hesitates. 'We had a falling out.' She sighs. 'It's a touchy subject.' When the car pulls into the driveway of a cream-brick house, Maggie is limp with relief.

'We're here,' Ron calls. 'Hacienda Kubunji. Welcome, amigos.' With a flourish, he gallantly opens the car door.

Amber glass flanks a strong wooden door. Ron and Hank put their cases onto two single beds in the front room while Diane gives Maggie a quick tour through the funky house. There are some large rooms, some small ones and a big family room, off which is Kerry's bedroom. A wood-burning stove glows in a corner. After three weeks sweltering in the tropics Maggie needs heat and stands in front of it rubbing her hands. Beside the stove is a large packing case stacked with what Ron calls Mallee roots. They come from up north and burn with a clear, bright flame that gives out a lot of heat.

Maggie is dismayed to discover there is only one bathroom and wonders how the hell they cope with one. And how will she manage sharing with four other people for a week? On the most primitive safaris in Africa, she always had her own bathroom and worries that she will end up constipated.

The next morning, there is hoar frost on the lawn, and most of Maggie's clothing is for the tropics. A pair of Hank's socks and a one of Diane's sweaters helps, even if she has to roll up the sleeves three times and the band is under her buttocks. She makes straight for the wood burner.

There is more food than she can believe. It feels as if they never stop eating. Eggs and bacon for breakfast, cookies at morning tea, huge lunch, fruitcake for afternoon tea, and a full dinner at night. Maggie revels in the variety but by the end of the day is so stuffed she can hardly move. She hopes she won't put on too much weight.

'Would you like to go for a walk before it gets dark?' Ron shoves his arms into a navy-blue jacket and opens the back door. Maggie is used to trekking in tree-covered mountains or kicking up dust on a desert trail. Pounding pavement past rows of suburban homes is not on her list of things to do.

Diane sees her disinterested look and quickly adds, 'We'll go through the back gate to the golf course.'

Warm and cosy inside one of Diane's winter jackets, Maggie follows Ron, Hank and Diane through the wire back gate into the golf course. A setting sun casts long shadows across the undulating fairway.

Several golfballs dot the back yard. She hopes all the golfers have gone and can imagine a golf ball bouncing off her skull. Most golfers have a wicked left hook. Diane assures her that even the most fanatical golfer has left the course for the day, drawn home by the thought of a hot meal or they are drowning their sorrows at the eighteenth hole.

They stroll past a row of tall, ancient pines planted when their housing estate was a dairy farm. Hank points. 'Do you know what they are?'

'Pine trees,' Ron replies.

'I know they're pines trees. There are seven hundred different species of pine. What are these?'

'The species that grow here.'

Hank hoots with laughter.

The following morning, Diane braces against the strong wind that sweeps the cliffs at The Nobbies. They are at the topmost point of Phillip Island, and the wind brings with it, in gusty blasts, the stinging smell of seal pee. Public binoculars are hard to adjust. Past the breaking waves, Diane can barely make out Seal Island and what appears to be a mass of brown rocks. She twists the knob one more turn and the rocks become a seething throng of seals, barking, flapping flippers, skimming off rocks into foaming blue water below.

Gripping windswept parkas they walk along the boardwalk. A fine misty spray dampens their hair. Maggie's grey, wavy tresses twist into curls, but Diane's perm begins to frizz. She pulls on a beanie.

Hank and Ron stroll ahead. White feathers twist and twirl in the air. Overhead, seagulls scream and squabble looking for a place to roost on crowded cliff ledges. Nests, containing head-waggling chicks, occupy every spare inch. Maggie and Hank have their own binoculars slung around their necks. They handle them with the ease of long familiarity.

A seagull swoops low. A long stream of shit hits Hank on the side of his head and dribbles onto his left shoulder.

'Blanco hijo de puta,' he swears.

'I wouldn't call that gull a friend,' Ron laughs and glances at Hank. He is too busy dragging out a large handkerchief and ineffectively wiping bird shit out of his hair and eye to answer. Maggie doubles over with laughter.

'Goddamn pesky critter.' Hank flaps the useless handkerchief. 'Maggie!' Hank is red faced, the left side of his grey hair plastered to his head.

'Not a happy camper,' Diane whispers to Maggie. They giggle like two school girls, smothering laughter with their scarves.

'Maggie!'

She recovers enough to hurry to his side to pat and wipe with the end of her scarf.

Let's get back to the motel. Ron walks towards the car. 'This bunch of *blancos hijos de putia*,' he says mockingly, 'have to leave before dusk if we are to catch the penguin parade.'

Buses. Rows and rows of tourist buses. On the walk to the visitor's Information Centre, they pass an obscenely expensive, state-of-the-art, silver Porsche.

'Look at that.' Ron gives a long, low appreciative whistle.

Maggie glances at the car. 'Why would anyone want something like that?' She sniffs loudly. 'It's just a big, silver suppository.'

Ron chuckles and hurries ahead. Diane's eyes open wide, and she laughs. Only Maggie could get away with something so outrageous, but she glances around to see if anyone else has heard. 'Do you always speak out like that?'

In her best Texas drawl, Maggie replies, 'Darlin', I cain't do nothin' else.'

Floodlights lead them down a concrete path into a cluttered shop. The shelves are packed with every tawdry souvenir imaginable, penguins on rulers, rubbers, t-shirts and aprons. Bookmark koalas, kangaroos in glass snow globes. Diane turns over a toy kangaroo. Made in China. A book on Australian animals? Printed in China. It becomes a game between Maggie and Diane to see who can discover something made in Australia.

'I win.' Diane waves a bunch of everlasting daisies.

Sitting on concrete steps with busloads of tourists, they watch a high tide swell onto a flood-lit beach. Soon, Fairy Penguins will return home to their burrows after a day at sea. The public address system constantly tells them, in seven different languages, what to do.

Stay on the steps.

Do not go onto the beach.

Do not use a flash light. You will permanently damage the penguins' eyes.

Do not...

The light slowly fades and the wind strengthens.

'Look.' The collective cry ripples through the crowd. Fingers point to a single penguin emerging from the dark sea, stomach full of krill for waiting chicks hidden deep in dark places. Its throat contracting, ready to regurgitate into demanding beaks. Everyone jumps to their feet, pointing and shouting in different accents. Ja, Ja, See. Look. Hai. Kawii. The voices sound like those issuing from the biblical tower of Babel.

The penguin waddles a couple of paces up the beach. Flash, flash, flash. It hesitates, shakes its head, waddles a couple more inches. Flash, flash.

Diane glares at several tourists, but they are oblivious to anything that isn't framed by a camera lens.

'Stop!' Maggie shouts at a young Asian couple. 'Do you

want to blind them?' The couple look at her uncomprehending. She is an angry foreigner speaking in an unintelligible tongue, but her violent gestures and tone of voice unmistakable. They move away.

'Goddamn tourists,' Maggie says loudly.

Diane pulls her beanie over her ears, presses the scarf against her cheeks and pretends not to hear. Her thoughts race back to another time. Same island.

*

Diane's journal: Australia

> *The night is crisp and clear as you type your story.*
> *Memories of an earlier time when you are very young are*
> *triggered by your writing.*
>
> *'Quiet,' your mum shushes. 'Don't make a noise.' Cold*
> *sand tickles bare feet. The path leads through scrubby*
> *tea trees and tussocky grass covers penguin burrows.*
> *Hopeful peeps greet them as they pass. Your dad's torch*
> *beams the way while you slip and slide the last couple of*
> *yards down a steep sand dune to Mutton Bird Beach. A*
> *click extinguishes the light and the night wraps around*
> *you like the blankets draped around your shoulders. You*
> *sit like Geronimo and his braves smoking a pipe of peace.*
> *The only sound are the waves sizzling on the shore and*
> *the odd call of a hungry penguin chick.*

'Here they come,' your dad whispers. Your gaze focuses on the black sea. 'Not there,' he says. 'Look up.'

High in the sky are flocks of mutton birds, swooping, soaring, squabbling and fighting. The cries fill your ears. On the sand, heading for their burrows, the mutton birds chatter amongst themselves. Harsh words are said, unwanted guests rejected to search for another boarding house for the night.

'Look.' Your mum points to the ocean. A single penguin glides in on a swirl of water. Momentarily, it rests on its belly then stands, shakes and stretches. For a brief instant, the body and outstretched flippers are a shining white cross against a blue-black sky. The penguin quickly waddles past and disappears into a burrow to the joyous cries of its chicks.

Soon, two more Fairy Penguins appear, then more and more. Every new wave beaches a line of penguins. They huddle together, reassuring each other, before making a dash up the beach. The sand is soon covered with indigo shapes. The chorus of hungry chicks grows louder and louder. They seem to call 'Me, me, don't forget me.'

*

'Look, Maggie.' Diane gently holds back a bent tuft of grass. Maggie hurries over, drops to her knees in the sand and peers down the well-concealed penguin burrow.

'Cute chicks.' Maggie places the tuft gently back across the hole.

Why didn't she think to bring them to Mutton Bird Beach last night? Why go the tourist route? Instead of seeing a multitude of birds waddling up the beach to feed their young, they witnessed thirty dazed and bedraggled, genetically programmed birds running a gauntlet.

They slip and slide the last couple of yards down the steep sand dune to the beach. Ron and Hank trail behind, while Maggie and Diane walk in companionable silence along the shore. Salt-laden air stings Diane's nostrils. Waves leave white lacy patterns on wet sand. She feels ten again, and joyously collects a gleaming alabaster cowry shell. Maggie holds it in the palm of her hand.

'What a perfect specimen of a *Notocypraea*.'

When Maggie doesn't know the biological name for strands of black seaweed, Diane expels a sigh of relief.

Running along the water's edge, she pops seaweed bubbles with her heel. A lone mutton bird rests on the sand, its beak open, eyes staring. The tiny chest heaves, every breath

116

laboured. The men catch up.

'What can we do?' Diane kneels. 'If we leave it here, the crabs will get it.' She looks at Ron, who shrugs his shoulders. The bird flutters a wing.

Maggie and Hank exchange a long look. Maggie nods. Hank scoops the bird into his large hand. He carefully pulls out each wing, studies it and gently folds it back. He feels its breast and...squeezes. The bird's beak flies open. The thin liquorice strip of a tongue protrudes in a soundless scream. Hank squeezes harder and holds tight until the tiny head drops forward and the bird lies still. He gently places the body back onto the sand and walks away. Wind ruffles lifeless feathers.

Come on, Diane. Maggie grabs her arm and starts to walk away. Be happy it didn't suffer.

*

Diane's Journal: Australia.

> *You need a break. Time to let the memory settle. And you typed penguin chip instead of chick. A Freudian slip? You are hungry. You've been tapping here for hours, lost in another time, another world. Your shoulders ache, your neck hurts. What did Ken say during that health and safety lecture at Chisholm TAFE? Every hour, get up and walk around your chair, stretch and bend. At least you have an appointment with the physiotherapist tomorrow. Hopefully he can manage to sort out your kinks. You ask yourself why you are doing this. Why put yourself through so many hours of typing and learning. You worry about the family. Are they coping?*

*

Maggie wonders how many are coming; she's never seen so much food. The savoury smell of party pies whets her appetite, but her favourite is what Diane calls a crock-pot curry. She must get the recipe. Her job is to cut mountains of fruit for the fruit salad.

'This should be enough.' Maggie puts down the knife.

'Keep chopping,' Diane says, adding a large can of peaches. 'You don't know this mob. They eat as if there is no tomorrow.'

Maggie glances at the overloaded table set up in the family room and shakes her head.

Quiches cool on the kitchen counter. Cutlery, plates and napkins are on the sideboard. Diane checks a huge, silver clock on the kitchen wall. It's large enough to challenge Big Ben.

'Ron's parents and my dad should be here any minute.' Diane wipes her hands on a tea towel. 'And you'll meet Kerry's boyfriend.' Imitating Kerry's voice, Diane adoringly says, 'He's so gorgeous. You love him, don't you, Mum?' Winking, she hands her a huge pineapple and a large carving knife.

Maggie gazes in amazement. Where to start? She wonders why Diane doesn't use the symmetrical rings of pineapple in a can. 'Surely you won't need this as well?'

Diane points to the bowl and keeps her eye on Maggie's valiant attempts to rid the pineapple of its skin.

'I'd better hurry and get the cake done.' Diane slathers whipped cream over a large sponge cake, then decorates it with strawberries.

'Have you seen the sparklers?' She searches under the clutter on the counter. 'We must have a couple of sparklers.' Finding two she jabs them into the centre of the cake.

'Imagine. Ron's Ma and Pop married fifty-nine years. What a milestone.' Diane stands back and admires her handiwork.

'Pop says you get less than that for murder.'

Diane, her mother-in-law, Elsie, and Kerry genuinely hug and kiss as if they haven't seen each other in years. Warm smiles are reflected in their eyes, and their light-hearted banter ranges from flab and fat to old age. Maggie never knows what to say to Barb. One slip of the tongue, and she won't talk to her for weeks. It's like walking on eggshells, always careful, always anxious not to crush or destroy. She mentally edits her words before speaking, and still Barb isn't happy. She accuses Maggie of being withdrawn. Whereas Diane and her mother-in-law are friends. Maggie's wishes her mother-in-law was here. She would have joined in and talked for hours on any subject and always has a quick answer, especially for Hank. She instantly put him back in his box. Hank often accuses Maggie of only marrying him for his mother. She constantly reminds him that when she left college and flew to New York for their wedding, his mother wasn't on her mind.

Lara's Theme from *Dr Zhivago,* plays in the background. The men have retired to the living room. Kerry is up to her elbows in soap suds. Where will she rinse them? The sink only has one bowl. The plates go from the soapy sink to a dish drainer. Elsie dries and Diane puts away. Maggie is horrified when they don't rinse the dishes, but wisely walks away.

Outside in the garden, surrounded by lush greenery, Maggie remembers how her home is falling down around her ears. She's had the flat roof repaired several times, but it still leaks and in winter when it snows chill winds howl through cracks in the walls. Wardrobe doors swing askew and taps drip. In summer she has to put a pot beneath each one to save water.

Dishes clatter. A burst of laughter. Maggie wonders why she and Barb can't be as easy with each other; why it has to be so hard. She keeps telling Maggie to change her tune and not be so negative. When she gets home, she vows to try to be a better mother.

She wanders back inside and Elsie throws her a tea towel.

'You can't get out of it that easily,' she says. Diane dobs a speck of foam onto Elsie's nose. Wiping it away with the back of her hand, she dips her fingers into the suds and flicks Diane. Laughter and fun.

Hank tells Pop a gag. As per usual it's his favourite. The one about the inebriated customer sitting at a bar in a tiny Texas town. Maggie has heard it a thousand times before, but Pop listens to every word.

Hank leans forward, revelling in the rapt attention.

'...and the customer looks up at the barman and says, This town is the arsehole of creation.'

Pop and Ron are already laughing.

'The bartender ignores him. The customer repeats what he said. No response. The third time he hollers, this town is the arsehole of creation.'

Hank pauses for effect before delivering the punch line. 'And the bartender asks, Just passing through?'

Elsie's hand clamps her mouth to smother a giggle. Pop laughs so hard he falls off his chair. Hank hoots, hollers and slaps his knee.

The airport departure doors open and close, devouring passengers. Hank shakes Rob's hand. '*Muchas gracias, amigo,*' he says before enveloping Diane in a bear hug. On release, she clings to Maggie and hugs her tight. Maggie whispers in her ear, 'I'll never forget the party.'

*

Diane's journal: Australia.

When you talked to Maggie there was nothing better than face to face. Maggie's strong, opinionated voice, the way she shrugged her shoulders, the slight curl of her lip when she called Ronald Regan a washed up has been hick actor, gave extra life to the meaning of her words. Her eyes either pinned you to the wall or invited you into her literary world. But there was an invisible barrier beyond which you dared not go. Flashes of sarcasm covered fleeting sadness. Today, you want to write and tell Maggie about the early morning, raucous call of wattlebirds outside your bedroom window siphoning

*nectar from the crab-apple blossoms. Ron pulling the
continental quilt over his head threatening, 'If those
birds don't shut up, I'll cut down the bloody tree.'
Flipping through one of your favourite books, you find
your thoughts and feelings distilled in a fourteen-word
poem by Dominique Hecq. You send it to Maggie.*

> *The day breaks
> Into a ball of sounds that roll
> & knock you over*

*You wish you could be a poet and write eloquent,
inspirational words that concisely convey your thoughts
and feelings. You are in awe of the power of language.
Marvel at, but also cringe at how inadvertently omitting
one character can change the entire meaning of a
sentence. Like the email you sent to the Director of the
Melbourne Writers' Festival. Instead of typing, Dear
Louise, you put Dear Louse.*

*

10/27/1994

*Dear Diane, Your letter only took five days. That must be
some kind of a record. I wish I could have been with you
at Kerry and John's wedding. To see them walk into the
church to the skirl of bagpipes would bring tears to my
eyes. Just wait until your grandchildren marry. That's
when you feel old.*

A row of pictures line Maggie's desk. Elizabeth's first smile, first steps, first day at school, going to the prom and graduating from college. She's Barb's daughter, but there the likeness ends. It won't be long before she finds some guy she wants to marry. God help her. Maggie looks closer at the flaming red hair wondering what they have in common. She slowly smiles, they both love reading.

*I tried to ring you, Diane, but only got the goddamn
answering machine. I apologise for the long silence and hope
you understand. Hank has had a stroke, but he is home and
coping well. Barb insists I still go on the trip to Kenya.*

'Maggie!' Hank bellows from his armchair in the living room. She ignores him.

'Maggie,' he calls again. Ever since the stroke, he has become even more demanding.

'Coffee's percolating,' she says and looks again at the printed itinerary on the kitchen counter. Should she go? Hank's walking with a cane, and his speech is not affected, but will Barb be able to manage her father, especially if he gets in one of his moods? He keeps telling her to go. Says he will be all right. It's only for two weeks, and she can do with the break. What if Diane can join her instead of going to the Himalayas? She should experience Africa. Before it's too late.

*I know you like eastern countries, Diane, but please don't
spend your money on the Himalayas. I think they'll be
there for a while yet, but I can't guarantee that the
African animals will.*

*I hate what mankind is doing to our beautiful planet
and dread seeing the destruction of the forest. Jock
Anderson is our guide and the Kenya safari still has
vacancies. It would be marvellous if you could join our
group. It is much too short, only thirteen days, but it
goes to my favorite places and is all private camping. To
give you some idea, here is part of a write up from the
Nairobi Times.*

*For sheer abundance of wildlife the Masai Mara game
reserve is the tops in Kenya. The golden plains, which
seem to stretch forever, teem with hundreds of thousands
of wildebeest. To see twelve lions in one hour's game-
viewing is the norm. Herds of giraffe, gallop away like
painted rocking horses. Beautiful topi stand sentinel on*

*

Diane looks up from reading Maggie's letter. Outside the kitchen window, a honeyeater, clinging to an overhanging Grevillea branch thrusts its tongue deep into drooping red flowers. Diane runs tired fingers through her hair. Africa. Maggie is raving about it again. The multitude of animals: lions, tigers, and her beloved elephants. For the past twelve years, they have trumpeted from photos stuck to the corkboard on the kitchen wall. Even from this letter. At the bottom of each page is a line drawing of seven African elephants against a backdrop of Mt. Kilimanjaro. Maggie's handwriting finishes well before the frieze.

Tempted? Of course. Diane turns the letter over and rereads the second page. Thirteen days. Six thousand dollars. Four hundred dollars per person, per day-not including airfare. And that's American dollars. Even more when converted to Australian. Double that amount if Ron wants to go. With that sort of money, Diane could pay off the mortgage. Maggie may be, as she puts it, in a *carpe diem* frame of mind. It's all right for her to say to hell with expense. She can afford to have chocolate mousse for dessert while sitting in a deckchair watching an African sunset. Has she ever lived from wage to wage and bought her clothes at the local opportunity shop? Has Maggie seen her older cousin in a pretty dress, knowing it will be two years before it is passed on to her? Folding the letter, Diane slips it back into the envelope. She'll write and tell Maggie why she hasn't a hope in hell of going.

*

Maggie forces herself to sit and write. The lounge needs dusting, pantry stores replenishing and another volunteer is ill so the library wants her to do an extra day.

2/19/1995

Dear Diane,

You nearly got a typewritten letter from me. I thought I had lost my old, faithful typewriter years ago during our move from New York. Today, I unexpectedly unearthed it from behind a pile of furniture stored in the basement.

I'm overjoyed to have my old friend back. However, it is like me, a bit worse for wear. Some keys stick. So I have abandoned my old friend because this letter must be written. Must be sent. I need to shed a letter's worth of guilt.

Rereading her last paragraph, she feels better already.

I fervently hope that this will break my inability to get to the huge pile of unanswered correspondence that grows every day. The more I procrastinate the harder it is to get started. I don't think I answered your last letter dated Oct. 1st. Horrors. My profound apologies. One reason is that I arrived home from Kenya to some horrible news. Please keep this in confidence. I tell you because you are part of our family.

Barb hurries over to gate six of the Albuquerque airport, pecks her mother's cheek and grabs the backpack.

'How is everything?'

'Fine.'

'Your father's okay?' She nods and strides ahead. Maggie has trouble keeping up.

The drive through Albuquerque is silent. It's 6am and Barb's already driven an hour to get to the airport. Maggie wonders if Barb resents the early rise. If so, has she forgotten already all the times Maggie has got up early for her? All the dirty diapers and midnight feeds? They reach open grasslands. Storm clouds, heavy with rain smother the *Sangre de Cristo* Mountains. Lightning flashes.

'Did your father give you any trouble?'

'A bit.'

'What do you mean?'

'The bastard tried to kill himself.'

Maggie's hand clamps over her mouth. She's afraid of what will come out.

Scattering gravel, the car skids to a halt on the side of the road. Barb leans her forehead on the steering wheel.

Maggie's voice wavers. 'Are you sure?' 'He's doubled up on his medication before.' Barb sits defiantly upright.

'You never told me he had to be watched twenty-four hours a day. Anyway,' she glares at Maggie, 'It was no mistake. It was more than pills.' Barb's fingers pinch her lips. She looks as if she is twelve again and defending herself against Anna's accusations.

'What do you mean, more than pills?'

'I got there at seven-thirty in the morning.'

Maggie's mind is racing. She blurts out, 'I hid his gun, and he can't get around with that useless —'

'Do you want to hear?' Barb shouts. 'This is not one of your shitty novels.'

'I'm sorry...' She squeezes her daughter's arm, takes a deep breath and grits her teeth, preparing to hear the worst.

Barb's tone is matter of fact.

'He took a bunch of pills.' She cocks her head to one side. 'But the added touch was a plastic bag tied over his head.'

'What?' Maggie's thoughts imagine auto-erotic asphyxiation. Is this something else Hank has hidden from her?

Barb takes a deep breath, turns her head away and continues speaking as if Maggie is not there. 'The house was too quiet. The porch light still on. I kept calling his name. The living room smelled like a bad nursing home. Stank of urine. His face was purple. I ripped off the plastic bag—'

Maggie catches her breath. Barb turns. 'He was still breathing, Moth-er.'

Maggie opens her mouth to speak, but Barb holds up her hand. 'You weren't there. I didn't know what to do.'

A sudden shower of rain drenches the car. Water streams down the windshield, obliterating the outside world. Tears glisten and Maggie's own unshed tears burn her eyes. 'If I'd been there, the misery would be over.'

'Would it? You didn't see him,' Barb shouts, her back pressed against the driver's door. 'Didn't see the agony on his face.' She closes her eyes at the memory.

Maggie keeps her mouth shut.

'When Dr. Shultz took a look, he asked me what I wanted to do. Father's vital signs showed his life was in the balance. I decided to wait and see.'

Maggie's mind whirls. The pain and confusion in Barb's eyes a reminder of how much Hank hurt them all, especially Anna. Threw Anna out of their home. Refused to talk to her ever again. Why didn't he die?

Through the cascading veil of water Maggie sees clearly for the first time. It was an attempted suicide. His way of destroying both of them. Did he think Barb would ring Maggie and she would come home? How dare he plan this for after she'd gone. Typical. Selfish bastard. Up to his usual tricks. Heaping the responsibility onto Barb. Again. And she has failed. Again.

'I'm so sorry.' Maggie doesn't know what to say, how to comfort her daughter. She reaches out to her but her hand is brushed aside.

'Father slept for twelve hours. Then he started talking nonsense. Real gibberish. I couldn't understand a word. I didn't want to be on my own. I needed someone to put their arms around me. Tell me it was going to be all right.'

'I'm sorry, Barb. I haven't been much of a mother to you, have I? We're certainly not a family that does relation -ships well.'

Barb glares at her mother. 'I had no one I could ring. Father woke up in a rage. He fought against the restraints. Called me pathetic. Useless. A selfish bitch. Abused me the whole night for tying him to the bed. For not helping him to die.'

Barb rolls up her sleeve to show yellowing bruises. Familiar marks, identical to those Maggie hid under her long-sleeved sweater after nights resisting Hank's nocturnal advances.

'I told him next time I'd tie the bag tight around his sad arsed neck.'

'Where is he now?'

'The psych ward.'

Maggie tries to put her arms around Barb, but she pushes her away.

'You know what he's like, Moth-er. They diagnosed clinical depression. He told them to fuck off, and the restraints there are leather belts, not his goddamn necktie collection.'

'Barb, when my time comes, I hope you make sure I don't mess it up.' Barb stares at her with wide eyes. 'I refuse to be a burden.' She turns her head away.

'But I won't choose something as horrific as a plastic bag.' Maggie grabs Barb's chin in her hand and looks her squarely in the eyes. 'Do it for me. Promise?'

She nods.

'Slide over,' Maggie says then walks through rain to the driver's door.

*

Diane checks the appointment book. Today is Millie's hairdo day. A retired volunteer worker, she has adopted Diane's hairdressing salon as her latest project and happily sweeps up hair, makes tea and takes out hair-rollers. She bustles over to a client, lifts the hairdryer and asks, 'Can I take you out?'

'Where?' the surprised client replies.

'Just your rollers, dear.' Millie carefully removes the hair net.

Like many women in the village she is on her own and the residents have become her surrogate family. She fusses and worries over them as if they are the children she never had. She tells Diane about a male resident driving the village bus to the shops and not knowing which way to turn. Worries he might have the beginnings of Alzheimer's.

Diane glances at her watch. Maybe with a bit of luck and Millie's help, she will finish early today.

She has to hurry home and pack.

15/6/1995

*Dear Maggie, Last night, I watched Joan and Alan Root's
TV program and found it fascinating. I've always been
interested in the life of a baobab tree.*

Diane smiles. The thought hadn't entered her head until she read Maggie's letter.

*I can't wait to see their balloon flight over Mt.
Kilimanjaro, but it will make me envious. There is no way
we can ever afford to travel in Africa, but I have found
the cheapest deal for flights to Nepal. I've read so much
about the Himalayas, especially the first successful
ascent of Mt. Everest by Sir Edmund Hillary and Tenzing
Norgay that I can't wait to go...*

Arriving at the Kathmandu airport, Diane's lei of wilting marigolds sticks to her sweaty neck. She fans her face with an old newspaper. The sign, Foreigners with visa please wait here before passing out, seems appropriate.

Diane and Ron, transplanted from a cold Melbourne winter into the blistering heat of Nepal, struggle onto a minibus. Holding on tight, they bounce down crooked streets, narrowly avoiding overloaded bikes, trishaws, small dented taxis and *tuk-tuks*. People push, dogs scrounge and sacred cows, high on diesel fumes, lie in the middle of the road chewing discarded paper. Traffic weaves around them. Diane mentally records the sights and smells to write up later. At last, she will have a travel journal to share with Maggie.

The Harati Hotel blends with the local decay. Its doors open directly onto a narrow pot-holed street, but the interior is neat and clean. Large foyer windows give the illusion of a glasshouse protecting delicate blossoms from a polluted world.

Horns blow, cymbals clang and a body, covered by red cloth and marigolds, bounces past on a stretcher carried by monks. Diane leaves Ron resting in the hotel. Stepping into the street, she squints in the harsh sunlight. The smells of urine, cow dung and hot dust sting her nose. A shopkeeper wipes dust off a bottle of water before handing it to her. She checks to see if the top is still sealed. She doesn't want to get Bali Belly, or The Pharaoh's Curse. Back home, they call it The Trots. She hopes there isn't a Nepalese version. Local biscuits look nice, but a funeral pyre of dead flies squashed against grubby glass ensures she hurries past.

A thin mother dressed in rags, nursing a tiny baby, pleads with outstretched hand alongside thin dogs and shrewd monkeys. A young boy smiles and asks—'How much you pay for night?'

'The night?'

He raises his eyebrows and a quick gesture makes his meaning clear. Diane laughs, shakes her head and hurries on. He follows.

'Only one hundred Rupee,' he emphasises. 'Two Ossie dollar.'

Placing the back of her hand dramatically against her forehead, Diane sighs loud and long. In her best theatrical voice, she says. 'Headache.'

'The whole night,' he insists, flashing a winning smile.

Diane pushes some rupee into his hand and hopes he has a good night's sleep.

Maggie, I'm writing this to the beat of an Oklahoma tune. At Chitwan National Park, I finally rode an elephant.

*

Diane's Journal: Australia

The tunes of Oklahoma rattle through your brain. You're typing to the beat of Oh what a beautiful morning, Oh what a beautiful day, remembering grass as high as an elephant's eye and hidden tigers. A mahout with a broom scrubs his elephant's back. Other elephants bathe, trumpet and squirt fountains of water. Push, pull and roll trimmed tree trunks into a pile. One lumbers down a riverbank, the mahout standing on its neck, holding an umbrella to keep off the beating sun. The elephant is soon submerged, only the tip of the trunk visible. The mahout appears to be walking on water. The elephant slowly emerges from the deep. Baptised.

A trunk taps your arm. A baby elephant nearly knocks you over to grab the bunch of bananas out of your hand. The hair on his head as stiff as a straw broom, his trunk snotty. You fall in love with him. Stroke his side, scratch under his chin. He leans on you, and you almost topple. His mother hurries to him. Majestic, maternal, magnificent.

You pretend you're on Maggie's Kenya safari, minus Kuku Paka chicken in silver tureens and white-coated African waiters.

Climbing a tower, you clamber onto what looks like a seat made from an upturned table tied to a matriarch elephant's back. Clinging to one of the four 'table' legs, you lumber off in search of rhino. Hump de humpety, hump de hump. Along an open section of the track, a mahout on another elephant cheerily waves. Holding on tightly with one hand you enthusiastically wave back. People are so friendly. He waves again. You wave even

*harder, until you realise he is pointing at your leg.
A huge, fat grub crawls up the leg of your jeans. You
freeze, then whip off your bush hat and quickly send it
flying. Your elephant lumbers on. Will this memory go
into your story? You know you must remain focused. You
will decide later.*

*

Back home at Kubunji Beach, Diane opens the front door then throws a bag of used hairdressing towels into the laundry. She can't wait to make a cup of coffee and get stuck into her studies. She should be able to fit at least an hour in before the six o'clock news.

Walking into the kitchen, she finds the floor awash with water and Ron working on the back of the dishwasher.

'Mice,' he says at her startled look. 'They've eaten through the pipes.' He holds up two pieces of PVC pipe with serrated edges. 'I'm not sure if I can fix it.'

Diane races to the laundry, grabs the bag of hairdressing towels and upends it onto the floor. The towels are soon soaked.

'Where has all this water come from?'

'The fridge.' Ron concentrates on meticulously measuring pipes.

'What's wrong with the fridge?'

'I think it's carked it.'

Diane opens the freezer door. Meat, chicken and pizza slices are slowly defrosting. She starts unpacking it onto the bench, wondering what she can cook before it spoils. She drags out the electric frypan.

'You may want to put a pot on the stove.'

Diane stares at him.

'I forgot to tell you. The electric frypan doesn't work.'

Later, the hardware store rises from the land like an Egyptian pyramid. Men are drawn to it eager to discover the treasures inside. Ron loves to meander down the aisles fossicking for screws, hoses or whatever takes his eye, convinced whatever he buys will 'come in handy one day'.

He picks up a multipurpose, fully adjusted ratchet. Turns it over, feels the weight, and twiddles the adjustable screw. A slow smile steals across his face.

'Perfect.' He nods approval and wanders farther down the aisle.

An electric hedge trimmer. 'Only fifty-five dollars, ninety-five cents.'

'But we don't have a hedge.'

He reluctantly puts it back on the stand and moves on.

'Duct tape. Two meters by 3 centimetres. Only five dollars, fifty cents.' He puts it in Diane's basket beside the electric frypan. Next is a jigsaw that will cut holes in anything.

Diane doesn't mind, especially when she has shelves in all the wardrobes, a rod to hold winter coats in the laundry cupboard and a slow-drip system to turn on once a week to keep the lavender alive until the winter rains come.

At least Ron isn't like his father. In his parent's home, the new, extra large refrigerator was crammed into the tiny kitchen. Ron's dad worked out that directly behind the refrigerator was a laundry cupboard. One day, he sat having his breakfast when he jumped up and grabbed a hacksaw on the bench. He cut up the plaster wall beside the refrigerator, over the top and down the other side, just missing severing several live electrical wires. He then pushed the refrigerator back into the cupboard.

Beside the garage, he uncovered several long lengths of trellis strapping. Using 'liquid nails', he soon covered the jagged gaps framing the refrigerator. Ron's mum had nowhere to put her brooms, dustpan or vacuum cleaner, but the refrigerator door was now flush with the kitchen wall.

Ron considers every disaster a personal challenge. Diane wants to call a tradesperson, but knows it is futile to even suggest it before Ron has a go at repairing whatever is broken.

He spends hours in his garage, sitting on the floor like a
garden gnome, or at his bench, comfortably ensconced in the
large, black leather office chair gleaned from a neighbour's
hard rubbish. Rescued from their pile of discarded junk on the
nature strip waiting for council collection. Diane mutters,
Men are from Mars, Women from Venus, calls the garage the 'man
cave' and keeps well away.

*

Diane's Journal: Australia.

> *You trundle along together in a comfortable routine.*
> *When the first rays of the sun create dancing patterns on*
> *the bedroom wall and the raucous wattlebirds shatter*
> *the early morning peace, you get up. You make breakfast*
> *while he showers. You chat for a while about your*
> *daughter, or the day's list of things to do. He does the*
> *dishes. Then you part. He goes to his garage and projects*
> *and you to your study; the latest pile of readings as large*
> *as the Bible and twice as difficult to read.*
>
> *Your desk is lined with folders: you yearn to live the*
> *story. There will always be emails to file, passports to*
> *renew, bills to pay and there is always hairdressing. But*
> *today, you push the daily domestic clutter to one side,*
> *put on imaginary blinkers, boot up the computer and,*
> *with a smile, immerse yourself in a world of heat and*
> *dust. In your letter you share your life with Maggie.*

*

Maggie stands in front of Hank, sitting shoulders hunched, on
the side of the double bed. His hair's a mess. Most men his age
are bald, but the hair she has always loved is now a nuisance.
It takes her ages to tame the wreckage. And he needs shaving
again – not that anyone but her will care. It's a balancing act,
another one: which does she hate more? The unshaven face or
the act of shaving. That awful scrape, the pinching of the

nose, the tilting back of the head and shaving under the chin. The Gillette, not a cut-throat, too close to his jugular. To leave him unshaven for a day won't make any difference. There's always tomorrow.

He's not so fussy about his appearance these days. She holds up the blue checked shirt, the one he wore with the turquoise Bolo tie for their fiftieth anniversary.

'Left arm first,' she says, aware of the acrid smell of stale sweat when she lifts the useless arm and pushes it into the waiting sleeve.

'Now the other.'

His smile is sweet. Maggie buttons his shirt, and he asks, 'Did you ever get married?'

She laughs and holds her sides, hoots and hollers. Hank doesn't understand, but laughs with her. They cling to each other, tears of laughter streaming down their faces. Finally, she pulls herself together. 'Yes. To you. Over fifty years ago.'

Bubbles of laughter vanish. His eyes widen and his mouth forms a soundless scream. They have feared this moment. His brilliant mind finally destroyed by relentless mini strokes randomly killing parts of his brain.

'Is it time?' he asks.

How does one decide? How far does a mind have to deteriorate before it is time?

Hank takes Maggie's hand. Traces the lifeline stretching from thumb to wrist.

'Never a nursing home...'

She stares out the window, watching the wind bending the sycamore trees. There's the cry of a coyote on some far hill. If only she could throw back her head and howl. She tries to digest the situation, the awful realisation that everything is about to change. Hank squeezes her hand.

'We need to talk.'

She can't breathe.

Hank stares at the palms of his hands. 'I keep falling,' he

says, absentmindedly rubbing a scar on his forehead. 'And now this. It's time.'

Maggie cups his face in her hands and searches his eyes for doubt. He is calm. Sure. His good arm wraps around her, and she sinks against his chest and sobs.

The grandfather clock strikes the hour. What is time? Something she's had so little of with this new Hank. It took a series of strokes to kill his sarcasm, the belittling, the womanising; to destroy hatred in her heart and replace it with a sad compassion. A blood clot to tame the lion. Although he is not caged or cowed. The brilliant mind she fell in love with works some of the time. Last week, he wrote a page of an essay on the feeding habits of the Western Banded Gecko. At these moments, his mind transcends the damage and shines as bright as before. The world is still theirs.

When they navigate from bed to chair they soon come tumbling back to earth. His bulk and towering height leans on her short frame. They stagger, fall, struggle, laugh and cry. He reaches out to her with both arms. After many years, he is once again emotionally and physically hers.

Hank lounges in his father's leather chair. The only part of his inheritance left from the family home after the old man died. His right fingers drum the worn arm. Maggie busily prepares a tray of coffee before taking her seat next to him; the Lone Ranger and his faithful Tonto ready to support him to the end.

Their doctor leans forward. 'Are you sure?'

Hank nods.

Years ago, they joined the Hemlock Society to prepare for a dignified end. Maggie refuses to end up like her mother. She had to key in a code to open the door and push past a wiry resident in a pink dressing gown, hunched over like a sprinter on starting blocks.

'I must go. Must go. Must go,' the resident repeated over and over.

In spite of the flowers and room deodorant, the acrid smell of urine permeated the home. On good days, Maggie found Mother in the drawing room. Her wheelchair pushed close to a large, polished table.

Bent heads, twisted limbs, vacant eyes surrounded them. Still better than her lying stretched out on her nursing home cot, with the side-rails up, face twisted in pain. A shot of morphine brought relief. Aunt Nettie's crocheted rug the only colour in a grey room. Her mother never acknowledged the gaunt figure on the other bed. Both women believed they had a room of their own.

'Would you like to go to the garden,' she'd whisper in Mother's ear.

'Lovely, this is the dullest party I've ever been to. No one knows how to make conversation any more.'

Maggie wheeled her through glass doors into the terracotta brick courtyard. To what they called their wooden seat and the brass plaque. In memory of... When cut crystal champagne flutes and a bottle of Moët appeared from the depths of Maggie's tote bag she'd shiver with delight. Her mother, Hanna Maria Roydon, may have been addled, but she never lost her taste for good Champagne.

'What is this?' Her nose wrinkled if Maggie tried to pass off a cheaper bottle. She talked, Mother listened, until a butterfly flew past, a spot on her arm needed close inspection, or a white uniformed nurse hurried across the courtyard.

'The hired help is wonderful here,' she'd smile.

'Yesterday, they brought butterscotch pie, fresh from the bakery down the road.' Mother leans forward in a conspiratorial manner and, with a gracious wave of her hand towards the opposite ward, confides, 'You know the president lives there. Mamie Eisenhower's parties are elegant and impressive. She serves sweet tea with lemon and ice, corn on the cob, hushpuppies, and then steaming bowls of She-crab chowder and southern fried chicken hot from the pan.'

Maggie wiped saliva from her mother's chin.

Was mother still living in the rambling old Southern home of her youth surrounded by friends? Secure in the love of her family? Attending parties, being wooed by gallant beaux, the smell of honeysuckle heavy in the hot night air?

Maybe being addled was not so bad after all. Until rare moments of reality when tears streamed unchecked down her cheeks, her body wracked by spasms of pain. Then she asked, 'Why? Why? Why?' Why tie a large white bib around Mother's scrawny neck and call it a napkin? Feed her spoonful by torturous spoonful? Why leave her like this?

Maggie and Hank often have to give injured lizards a lethal injection to end pain. Society can call it euthanasia, right to die, any Goddamn thing it wants, but they believe it is their right to end their own lives when it becomes intolerable. But is it time? Only Hank can tell them that. Their doctor reaches for his coffee, and they discuss the options.

'Lethal injection,' Hank suggests. Doctor shakes his head.

'Tablets and a plastic bag over the head?'

Maggies mouth gapes. 'Have you forgotten already?' she shouts at Hank. 'How will you tighten the string?'

The doctor looks at Hank. He points at her.

'Forget it—'

'Maggie can't help you,' the doctor interrupts. 'It must be by your own hand.' They talk for over an hour and finally know what they must do.

*

1/10/1995

Dear Maggie, How is Hank? Is he any better? It must be such a blessing to have Barb living so close. Can Anna get away for a visit? I'm sure Hank would love to see her but I know it must be hard when they are trying to build up a new business.

Tomorrow is a very special day for me. One I never thought I'd see. But I've learnt that to survive this educational journey takes dedication, hard work and most of all enthusiasm. That's what gets you through more than anything.

I love the challenge but my friends think I'm crazy. They keep telling me I've studied enough and should give it away. Especially the men. Even Ron gets a glazed look in his eye when I mention further courses.

*

Diane's Journal: Australia.

Dust, driven by gale force winds, billows down from the drought-stricken Mallee and chokes the city of Melbourne. It is 4:00 p.m at Kubunji Beach. You have three hours before the graduation ceremony. In the car, you check the bag at your feet. Purse, glasses, hairspray and make-up. You want to look your best for the photos. You visualise walking up stairs. Reaching the dais. Shaking the chancellor's hand. Receiving your Bachelor of Arts degree and accepting the Golden Key for academic excellence. Will you stop at the top of the stairs and hold them aloft in glee? The music from The Stripper pops into your mind. Dah dah dah,de da da da. Gowned arms outstretched, doing a shimmy. Ron would have a fit. Your sedate walk down the stairs is more suitable for a woman in her late fifties.

Wetting the tip of your finger, you nervously rub a spot on the knee of your black slacks. The jacket is fine. Back from the cleaners that morning. The white blouse new. Ron turns into Punt Road. Traffic is banked up and over the hill.

'We've hit a slow-moving car park.' His fingers drum the steering wheel.

'It doesn't start until seven.' You look at your watch and

flick on the radio. Visibility zero. Westgate bridge closed. Roads blocked. Tornado force winds. Sheep blown across paddocks. City traffic in chaos. You move one hundred yards.

Five p.m. A rooster crows. You swear under your breath. You will kill Kerry for making that rooster your ring tone.

'Just letting you know we are here.' Kerry's voice is calm. 'Where are you?'

'On our way.'

'Ring when you get near.'

You checks your watch, look at the traffic jam and begin the moan. 'We're not going to make it.'

'Don't panic.' Ron says gripping the steering wheel.

Six p.m. The rooster crows.

'Still in Punt road.' your voice is tight and high.

'Don't worry if you don't make it, Mum,' Kerry says. 'We'll still take you out to dinner.'

The traffic moves another few feet and you reach the turn off, but it is six forty-five.

'Hang on,' Ron says. 'Gap ahead,' and drives like a maniac toward the university.

You slump in the seat.

Seven p.m. You've missed graduation. A hundred dollars gown hire fee down the drain.

The rooster crows. Kerry's voice is elated. 'Looks like a lot of people haven't made it yet. They're delaying the ceremony for fifteen minutes.'

'There's the gate.' Ron skids to the curb. 'Run for it. I'll park the car.'

You leap out of the barely stopped car, dodge traffic to cross the road, run past wrought iron gates, between buildings, beyond Burgan Hall to the student union block. Taking stairs two at a time, you sign in, a dresser throws a gown over your shoulders and jams a too small mortar board on your head. It slips rakishly over one eye.

'Go,' the dresser shouts, pointing back down the stairs.

Gown flying out behind you, you reach the hall. John holds open the door and Kerry pushes you through. You barely hear the processional march above the pounding of your heart.

*

The University pub is packed with rejoicing families. Conversation hums. Glasses chink and are raised to toast flower-clutching graduates. Diane, eager for the celebratory bubbles of champagne, beams at Ron, Kerry and John.

A young waiter bustles over, black apron tight around his youthful waist.

A bottle of Cordon Rouge Champagne, John orders.

The waiter brings the bottle, shows it to John for a nod of approval and asks,

'Celebration?'

'Bachelor of Arts,' John proudly announces.

The waiter, looking at Kerry, smiles and says, 'Congratulations.'

Kerry laughs. Points to Diane. 'Not me,' she says. 'Mum.'

With a shocked look on his face, the waiter turns to Diane 'How long did it take?'

Diane grins as she slips a photo into the envelope.

Can you believe it? I've finally graduated. It was a fabulous night. At uni they had photography booths set up in the student union building, and Kerry insisted I record the occasion. What a laugh. The photo says it all. Instead of proud parents standing behind the graduate, Ron, Kerry and John are behind me. Ron thinks this is the end of my study but I want to go further. There is still so much more for me to learn

*

12/3/1995

Dear Diane, Congratulations. I am so proud of you. I think these days I would be called a college dropout. I was twenty and in the middle of the college year when Hank transferred to the American Museum of Natural History New York city. I dropped everything, my degree, my academic dreams of becoming a biologist in my own right, and followed him. We married two months later. That was fifty years ago and I've been researching and typing his papers ever since.

'We can cope a bit longer,' Maggie tells Hank, but he's made up his mind.

She closes the door behind her and marches to the Santa Fe library.

Sleet slashes the public library, partly obscuring the old coach lamps on either side of the entrance. When lit, they show the way in. Everyone is welcome here. Every Tuesday and Friday, when she walks up the three wide steps and through the green-latticed doors and the ochre archway, her breathing slows and a weight shifts off her shoulders. Most people park their troubles by the door.

In this place of culture and learning she finds peace. She hesitates before pushing open the doors. Inside, people whisper and paper rustles. This is her church, her sanctuary. Especially today.

'Hi Maggie,' the librarian greets her. She smiles and nods, but does not dare to speak, afraid of what might tumble out if she unclenches her jaw.

'We can do with your help today.' The librarian gestures towards a genealogy group in front of microfiche machines. Old ladies in grey cardigans looking up death. Later, Maggie will sort out the messy pile of microfiche film, but now she hurries to her spot at the back of the library and files books. She greets familiar old friends, James Joyce, Margaret Atwood and Don Preston. She will need them all in the days ahead.

People speak, ask her questions, seek her advice. It's as if she is standing outside her body watching some other person sort, stack, tag and file.

She taps her watch. Two hours before she finishes. Barb always meets her at twelve for coffee. Maggie's stomach churns at the thought. There will be no coffee for her today. What will she say to Barb? She cannot come back to the house with her. Must not see her father. This is something Maggie must do alone.

She taps her watch again. Has it stopped?

The Dr. Seuss sessions finish in the reading room and happy children file past. Running the tips of her fingers along the line of spines, she randomly selects a book. Theodore Bernstein *The Careful Writer*. Her old friend Bernstein. The hands of her watch crawls towards the hour. Time to smile, greet, make small talk, be noticed. Bernstein falls off the table. She jumps. It sounds like a shot.

In the diner on Main Street, the meals are cheap and the coffee good and strong. Barb sits in her usual seat. The waitress delivers the obligatory coffee. She mentally counts four stirs clockwise and three anticlockwise. Barb would hate to hear, and would deny, that she is so like Hank. Before the stroke. One look at Maggie's face, and her smile disappears.

'Today?'

Maggie nods.

'I'll go back with you.'

'No!'

'Are you sure, Moth-er?' Maggie wants to lean on her, share the burden, but knows she will walk back up the hill, and Barb must wait at home for Maggie's call.

The juniper trees lining their driveway struggle in the wind, and her hiking boots scrunch on fresh snow. She shivers. Wet from the knees down. To walk close to the gutter, with cars whizzing past spraying water, is a dumb thing to do, but she doesn't care. New ropes of red chilli brighten their doorway. The groundhog boot scraper sits beside the welcome mat.

She pulls open the door and dumps her backpack. From the inside landing, everything looks the same. As usual at this time of day, Hank is asleep in his old man's chair, his mouth wide open. She'll walk down the stairs. He will greet her and the whole Goddamn nightmare of die now, die later, will start all over again.

But this time it is different. His eyes are open. She wants to close them, must close them until she remembers the doctor's adamant words. Do not touch him. Don't touch anything. Ring the police. Do you understand, Maggie? She understands, but cannot obey. The doctor is not here. A soft stroke of the eyelids is all it takes before she rings Barb. 'It's over.' She whispers. 'Come now.' Maggie's knees tremble but she steadies herself and breathes deeply before dialling again.

'Nine one one. What is your emergency?' the female voice asks.

Maggie hesitates.

'Your emergency?' the operator repeats.

What to say? She hasn't mentally rehearsed this part.

'My husband is dead,' she blurts out, quickly adding,' he suicided.'

'Have you tried CPR?'

'Are you mad? He shot himself.' She braces herself against the wall willing herself not to fall.

Barb's four wheel drive grinds to a halt. Maggie stands in front of the closed front door. Barb tries to push past.

'Remember your father the way he was,' Maggie says grabbing her arm. 'I need you here.' Maggie wants to protect her child, but needs Barb beside her, needs to draw on the strength of her daughter to be able to carry on.

Their street soon looks like a disaster zone. A fire engine arrives first, then an ambulance and several police cars. They stay outside. A man wearing jeans and a parka approaches from a sea of uniforms.

'Mrs Jackson, I'm a police chaplain.'

'I'm an atheist,' she quickly responds. The last thing she wants is some Bible-bashing cleric to tell her it's God's will.

The chaplain puts his hand on her arm. 'I'm not here in a religious capacity,' he says. 'I'll be a buffer between you and the police.' He takes them inside and they sit in Maggie's study.

She cannot look at the chaotic scene downstairs. A large policeman sits beside her. He flips open a notebook and clicks the top of his ballpoint pen several times.

'Where were you, Mrs. Jackson.'

'At the library.'

'Did anyone see you?' He wants names and addresses. Wants to know when I met Barb. Did they have coffee? When, how, and why Hank died? Did she know he was going to do it? Was he depressed, sad, aggressive? It is his manner, the tone of his voice, that makes her feel guilty. She is to blame. Her fault. She had not loved enough, given enough, been tolerant enough, had left Hank alone.

The chaplain intercedes. 'I think that's enough for today, Officer Gonzales.'

The policeman clicks his pen and puts it into his top pocket. He hands Maggie a card. 'I'll see you at the station tomorrow and we'll sort it out then.'

She nods, but all she can think about is Hank's body is downstairs. What is taking them so long? Why haven't they gone? It's a suicide for Christ's sake. Let the man rest in peace.

The kettle whistles on the stove. Barb pushes a chunk of her carrot cake across the table to me. 'Eat,' she commands. 'You get mean when you're hungry.'

Maggie takes a bite, but can't swallow.

'Are you listening, Moth-er?'

She nods.

'Who do you want me to call?' Barb grabs a pen and paper.

'Better they find out from us than the morning newspaper.'
She's right, but Maggie is still trying to swallow her cake.

'He asked me to go with him,' she says.

'You're free now, Moth-er. The bastard's gone'. Barb
sweeps up cake crumbs with a damp cloth. 'We must ring the
undertaker and let him know what's happening.'

How can she be so matter of fact? No shock, no dismay, or
why did he say that? No thank you, Mother, for staying.
Maggie zips her lips. Free? She's shaking. Her mind shattered.

As soon as Barb leaves Maggie picks up the phone. This
sort of news is better delivered personally. Diane will be
shocked, but will understand, will comfort and care. Maggie
hesitates. 'Goddammit,' she mutters. 'What time is it there?'

*

12/2/1996

> *Dear Maggie, What can I say. I wish I could jump on the
> next plane and be with you. I know you tell me that you
> will be all right, that you both planned it. My brain tells
> me that you have Barb and Anna even though she is far
> away. But my entire being screams to be with you. Ring
> me anytime day or night.*

For Diane, hairdressing is as busy as ever and manages to
take care of four days a week.

*

Diane's journal: Australia

> *To get one precious day of study you have to start work
> at 7:00 a.m. At least, you don't have to spend time on
> your hair. You've given up perms.*
>
> *Your hairdressing friends find your straight hair
> hard to accept and keep offering to fix it. 'You look so
> different,' they say. 'Would you like me to... do
> something?' Not a vote of confidence, but you are
> determined not to return to the Woody Allen curls.*

*

Diane is busy slipping into a jiffy bag three garage sale books. The covers are tattered, but it's the content that matters. When Maggie sees the copy of *Australian Short Stories*, featuring forty-eight authors from 1894 to 1996, she will be delighted to have a story a day for over a month. Hopefully that will take her mind off her troubles for a brief while at least.

Add to that a quirky collection by Elizabeth Jolley. The dog-eared copy of *Woman in a Lampshade* is full of fantastic characters, all of whom fail to achieve the expected. Diane has read each story several times and found them slyly comic, sometimes disturbing, but written with a delicacy and compassion as moving as the characters themselves. She has marked her favourites, *The Last Crop* and *The Pear Tree Dance*, with two Australian wildflower bookmarks, instead of putting an asterisk beside the titles or highlighting them with Texta. Diane marks anything significant in all her books.

Maggie would be appalled. She doesn't mind second-hand books as long as they are not, as she calls it, defaced. Thank goodness, she won't set eyes on any in Diane's bookcase. But if Maggie lived closer, they could browse together in a favourite second-hand bookshop called, of all things, *The Pigs Wings*. Later, they could swap books and discuss the stories. If only.

Her friends can't understand her passion to write, her commitment to study.

'Why do you do it?' they ask. 'Why lock yourself away? Get out and have some fun.' Diane translates that to eat more, drink more, gossip more. She is changing; she no longer wakes each morning feeling something is missing. She feels good. She has her own set of writing wings; as long as they don't fall off if she flies too high.

Diane can't wait to return to her computer, to her mother's story crowding her head. Away from dirty dishes and a shower recesses needing cleaning. Back to characters more alive, more vibrant and full of life than anything around her; until tomorrow. Tomorrow, real life takes over and, once again, she will pick up the threads.

Ron sticks his head through the study door. 'Do you want a cup of coffee? The jug's boiled and there's a great show on TV.'

Diane sighs. She dare not refuse. He will hang his head, shoulders slumped and say, 'Don't worry about me. I'll be all right,' which she interprets as I'm lonely. Please spend some time with me. For him, retrenchment/retirement is not what it is cracked up to be. Too much time, not enough energy, and not enough to do.

Three a.m. The phone rings. Diane drags the receiver to her ear.

'Did I wake you?' a familiar voice says. 'What time is it there?'

*

When Maggie slams her front door red chillies jiggle and dance. Dry, high-altitude air clears her head, fills her lungs. Hiking boots tightly laced, she shrugs her shoulders, adjusting the backpack, the dowager's hump an impediment these days. It is four miles to walk to the sheriff's office. She checks her watch. Nine a.m. A promise is a promise. Best get it over with. What can they do?

Barb's four wheel drive scatters gravel. She jumps out and grabs Maggie's arm. 'What are you doing, Moth-er?' she shouts. 'I told you to wait for me.' Her hand bruising Maggie's arm, she shakes her off.

'Why didn't you answer your phone?'

Maggie starts walking down the drive. Barb runs after her.

'Moth-er. Stop. Let's talk.'

'Keep out of this, Barb. It has nothing to do with you.'

Marching up the imposing steps of the Santa Fe Sherriff's Office, through the automatic sliding doors to the counter, Maggie feels like a suspect in a Mickey Spillane detective novel. Hopefully, the outcome will be the same. The innocent always walk free.

The officer on duty takes Gonzales' card and walks away. The wooden bench is hard on old bones. Her attorney hurries through the doors. Sits beside her.

'Remember what we said?'

Maggie nods.

The last time she was in this office was for a query about her driver's licence. A dishevelled young man, head hanging, is dragged in the front door, a burly officer on either side, but Maggie's eyes are on a young woman with wild eyes, slouched on a seat. Filthy overalls, cropped and matted red hair. Metal rings pierce her eyebrows, lips and ears. She cusses loudly at anyone who comes near. So familiar, so like Anna. Maggie wants to put her arms around her. Rock her, tell her it will be all right.

The sparse interview room smells of antiseptic. The plastic chair is hard and cold. Perched on the edge of the seat, elbows on the table, the comforting presence of the attorney next to her, Maggie waits. Gazing around the room, she tries unsuccessfully to spot the surveillance camera. She's focused on a suspicious section of the ceiling when Officer Gonzales, the name proudly emblazoned on a silver strip, strides in. Scraping a chair across the tiled floor, he sits in front of her. He looks more relaxed today in his navy shirt, corporal stripes, gold sheriff badge, Taser on his belt.

He flips open his notebook. Reads for a moment. There is accusation in his eyes. Disbelief on his face.

'You say your husband suicided.'

Maggie nods.

'You say you were at the library.'

She nods again. Gonzales is so arrogantly young. So sure of himself. So secure in what he thinks is right and wrong.

'What time did you arrive?'

How dare he judge. She grips the edge of the table. Unshed

tears sting her eyes. Goddamnit, man—

The attorney grips her arm. Pulls her back in her seat. She concentrates on a scratch on the table. Takes several deep breaths.

'What is the charge?' the attorney asks.

Gonzales ignores him. Leaning towards Maggie, he says, 'You understand, don't you Mrs. Jackson'—he pauses for full effect—'that the charge is murder.'

She doesn't hear anything after that, but her attorney's mouth moves. She sees him hand the officer a folded paper. Gonzales leans back in his chair. He reads Hank's suicide note aloud.

I, Charles Mathew Jackson, being of sound mind...

He thrusts the paper in front of Maggie's nose. Is this your husband's signature?

She nods.

He drums his fingers on the table. 'Looks shaky to me.'

Does he think she stood over Hank and made him sign? Held his hand on the pen and guided it across the page? That she pulled the trigger? He has no idea of who Hank was. No one could make Hank do anything he didn't want to do. This is ridiculous.

'What more do you want?' she asks.

'How did he get the gun? He was partially paralysed, I believe.'

'How the hell do I know?'

Question follows question. She answers them as best she can.

'He shot himself,' she keeps repeating like a broken record. 'Goddamnit, he died by his own hand.'

The interview over, her attorney shakes her hand and walks away, reassuring her that the case will be dropped. She'll ring him tomorrow and apologise for her temper.

Her mind reeling, she starts for home. Maggie will not leave Santa Fe County. He can call any damn well time he likes. And she will go home and bury her husband.

*

30/6/1996

> *Dear Maggie, Floral Waters. What a ridiculous name. I feel as if I should be skipping down the bank of the canal scattering petals out of a wicker basket, singing, Flowers that bloom in the spring tra la.*
>
> *We arrived here on Ron's birthday, and yes, even though it is a unit, it has the mandatory double garage. I often think of my mum. How she would have loved this place. She always dreamed of living on the water.*

A flock of black Cormorants gracefully glide onto the man-made canal. Through her study window, Diane catches a flash of wings and peers over the top of her computer monitor. She never tires of the daily feeding frenzy.

The cormorants work as a team, swimming, diving, herding an unseen shoal of fish towards the end of the two-meter-wide canal. Seagulls soar like white ballerinas above the black throng. Looking for easy pickings. And loping along behind is a lone grey crane. Diane hopes that one day he will catch up. She wants to pinch herself, to remind her of her good fortune to be here after searching for months for a home, not too big, not too small. Something just right.

It was a wrench to move after thirty years in the same place. She loved the old rambling home they had added to year after year. First the family room, then Kerry's bedroom and finally, the huge veranda across the front. Not to forget the extra large plate glass windows in the late eighties. On moving day, she walked through the house, thanked every room, said goodbye before turning the key in the door for the last time. But it was time to move. The Kubunji Beach house was too large for the two of them. And she couldn't face renovating. Not again. A modern unit, on a new estate built on a series of canals the answer.

'You haven't moved out of your comfort zone, have you,

Mum?' Kerry looks up from the street directory, her finger indicating the short distance between the old home and the new. 'The story of your life.' Kerry laughs. 'Born in Brighton you grew up ten minutes away in Parkdale, then married and moved ten minutes away to Kubunji Beach and now you are moving ten minutes away to Floral Waters.' Diane wants to explain that adventure for her was using her imagination and travelling to exotic destinations. She had looked further afield, possibly surrounded by two-thirds of an acre, but the peninsular was part of her heart, her soul. She was happy living by the bay. If only Maggie could see the jetty covered in cormorants, wings outstretched, facing the sun. How can she write the scene so Maggie will understand the joy it creates? See it through her eyes? Diane sighs. It is impossible to catch the contented ka, kar, karking cries of full bellies, or the whoosh of wings, or multitude of tiny splashes as cormorants rise high into the sky.

*

8/14/1996

> *Dear Diane, I wish we could communicate via telepathy. I
> really don't know why the news of your move bothered
> me. I suppose it's because now I can't visualize where you
> live. Please send me a floor plan, but especially a map of
> the area, and where it is relative to Melbourne. That
> really won't be enough, so I guess I'll just have to visit
> you to see for myself. Don't worry; it won't be for a while,
> I assure you.*

Barb straightens a rug, flicks a feather duster over the clay masks on the wall.

'You shouldn't be alone, Moth-er.' She straightens the sitting room cushions. Dad's gone and you're rattling around in this big house. 'Maybe I should come and live with you?'

Maggie stares out the window. The last thing she wants is

for Barb to live with her. For the first time in fifty-five years, she's free. But how to say no? Barb is disastrously divorced, living at a motel and cleaning the units to pay for her rent.

Sometimes Maggie misses the sound of Hank's voice. Misses the blood-stirring arguments. She'll have plenty of those if Barb lives with her, but Barb is a great cook. Maggie's stomach growls at the thought of moist carrot cake. Hot from the oven.

'You don't need this.' Barb moves a favourite chair into the basement.

'And why is this couch here? It would be much better by the window.'

Everything in the kitchen is different. Pots are where the juicer once lived, knives replace spoons in the cutlery draw and Maggie's treasured Aztec scatter cushions replaced by Barb's plain equivalent. The price of carrot cake is too high.

The worst part is the constant arguments over whether to use salt or pepper and the price of a loaf of bread. It's like living with Hank all over again. Two Bantam roosters in the one pen. Each fighting for its own space, only Barb is twenty-three years younger. Maggie wants her to leave, but she doesn't want to make a mistake with a daughter. Not again.

'Is that wise, Moth-er?' Barb flips through a stack of brochures. 'Travelling on your own to Australia when you're eighty? Maybe I should come with you?'

Maggie rattles off all her well-thought-out reasons in case Barb suggested this, ending with the word 'cost'. This time, she wants to be free to please herself. The thought of such freedom makes her giddy.

When Hank was alive, he told her when, where and who they had to see, but left it to her to make all the arrangements. It was her fault if planes did not connect. If baggage was lost. Or Hank caught a cold. Barb would be the same.

This trip is an eightieth birthday present to herself. For once, she'll be unhindered by the needs of others. A chance to visit friends before she is too old. A chance to catch up with Diane. This time, she will not invite Barb, or offer to pay her fare.

*

1997: Floral Waters, Victoria, Australia

Diane and Maggie relax on the outdoor close to the house to escape a keen wind rippling across Floral deck, chairs pulled Waters. Pelicans dip and fish along the edge of the canal. Plovers call to their mates. Gathering rain clouds hide the sun.

'Great coffee.' Maggie takes another sip. Diane is glad she bought the new percolator and some decent coffee beans. A mixture of Kenya and Mocha.

The wind freshens and sweeps up the canal. Diane shivers. 'We call this a lazy wind.' She pulls up the collar of her jacket. 'It cuts right through you.'

'You call this a wind?' Maggie laughs. 'It's nothing compared to the gales I put up with.'

They sit in comfortable silence. Diane leans forward. 'Did you hear that the peat fires are still raging in Indonesia?'

Maggie nods.

'What shall we do about our trip?'

'I hate to give up the idea of Kalimantan and the proboscis monkeys.'

'Me too.' Diane chuckles. 'Those monkeys remind me of a couple of rheumy-eyed old men I know at the village. But what can we do?'

Maggie sighs and shrugs her shoulders. 'Best to cancel.

'Sure?'

'I believe Kuala Lumpur airport is still closed. 'Maggie folds her arms. 'And the latest news has a cloud of orange smoke smothering everything and there's a threat of acid rain.'

Diane sighs.' I'm sorry it didn't work out, Maggie, but don't worry. We'll take you to a place you'll love.'

From her window seat, Maggie marvels at dozens of tiny islands strung like a necklace across Bass Straight: Flinders Island, an emerald in a sea of blue. The tiny AUS-Air plane flies low. The jacket Maggie borrowed from Diane keeps her body warm, but her feet are freezing. Sunny Australia? Trust her to arrive during the coldest snap in twenty-five years. Instead of flying to the warmth of Borneo, they're heading towards Antarctica. Damn the peat fires and god help those poor proboscis monkeys.

In the seat beside her, Diane studies promotional brochures gleaned from the Moorabbin Airport lounge. She looks up. 'Mount Strzelecki sounds good.' She holds up a picture of a lush, green mountain soaring into a clear blue sky.

Ron reads the airplane safety manual.

Diane smiles and points down. 'Not long now.' She continues reading. Maggie marvels at the ease of their relationship. The past week in Melbourne they have rolled along together, give and take. Comfortable companions. Maggie wishes she and Barb could be like this.

Above the drone of the engine come a series of staccato cracking sounds and Maggie glances at the wing. Metal fatigue? Is the plane falling apart? It looks well used with the torn seat pocket and dog-eared magazines. Rat a tat tat. Rat a tat tat. she crosses her arms and hold them tight against her chest. Murmurs her mantra against fear. 'No nursing home. No nursing home.'

Ron puts the safety manual back in the pocket. Diane licks her finger then turns another page. The other passengers chat or snooze and seem unconcerned. Maggie looks at the wing. Chunks of ice whip back from the edge and hit the fuselage. The only danger frostbite once they land. She wriggles numb feet. Maybe Diane has a spare pair of socks. If not, there should be at least one five-and-dime store at Whitemark.

The pretentiously named Flinders Interstate Hotel is the homeliest of places. Worn carpet, mismatched furniture and no elevator. Not quite up to Maggie's usual standards. Ron offers to carry her bag up the flight of stairs to my room, but she holds tight to the handle.

'I may be eighty, but I'm not decrepit. Hope you're not offended.'

'It's just that we have adjoining rooms.'

'Don't snore too loudly then.' Maggie shakes her finger at him. 'I remember your snores. It's a wonder you don't wake the dead.'

Diane laughs. 'Don't worry, Maggie. I've brought some of those strips to put across the bridge of his nose, and if that fails, I'll give him a swift dig in the ribs.'

Diane doesn't mind what unit she has, or where they go. This is her first chance to travel with Maggie. She wants it to be memorable, aware that at eighty years of age, this could be Maggie's last trip to Australia.

The rooms are sparse, with a basic en suite and a sink that gurgles. They have all lived in worse. Diane picks up an instruction manual for an old television high on a rack on the wall, but puts it back on the table. She stands at the window watching the sea pound against orange lichen-covered rocks. A fishing boat bobs and dips under a cloudless, blue sky. Who watches television with a view like that? Let the outside world look after itself. The worst that can happen here is bad coffee.

Diane checks her watch. Time to head to the restaurant. Diane stuffs her arm into a warm cardigan. Ron starts for the door.

'Have you got the sacred wallet?'

Ron pats his pocket and smiles. In Melbourne, Maggie had insisted on putting one hundred dollars into a wallet and they put two hundred. A brilliant way to prevent arguments over who pays the bill.

The dining room is empty. Their chairs scrape against the

polished wood floor. A head appears over swinging bar doors leading to the kitchen. A few minutes later, a middle-aged woman marches in, floral cobbler apron firmly tied behind her back.

'I'm Liz, and I'm your cook tonight. I can grill you some garfish, if you like?' She looks at them as if daring them to say no. 'It was swimming in the sea two hours ago.' That clinches it. They all nod. 'It comes with chips and salad,' she says as she disappears into the kitchen. Pots clatter. The whoosh of a gas jet.

'At least it's not three days old,' Maggie jokes.

Liz soon reappears with laden plates. Maggie is still arranging her napkin when, with gusto, Ron attacks his meal. He rolls his eyes in appreciation. 'This is the best fish I've ever tasted.'

Maggie keeps glancing at Ron's plate. 'If you keep eating as fast as that you'll get indigestion.'

Ron slows down a fraction, but his plate is soon wiped clean. Diane pushes some fish to one side, places her knife and fork together, and leans back.

'Finish that,' Maggie says. 'It's only a mouthful.'

'I'm totally stuffed.' Diane pats her stomach and pushes her chair from the table. Ron leans across and forks her leftover fish onto his plate. Maggie's eyes widen. Liz hurries in with three extra garfish.

'Saw your clean plates. Here's some more.'

Diane leans forward and whispers to Maggie. 'Does this put us in the 'treasured member of the family' category, or the 'uncouth mainlander' section?' The memory of the transfer from the airport and the driver's tales of a visiting football club from Melbourne greedily scoffing down food and then, stark naked, racing each other in supermarket trolleys down the main street at midnight, prominent.

Before Liz can escape back to the kitchen, Maggie asks, 'How do we get to Cape Barron?'

'If you want to know anything about the history of the island, you must visit Wybalenna cemetery.' Liz gestures towards the dining room door. 'Now you run upstairs, clean your teeth, and when you get back, I'll be free and can show you a couple of interesting places on a map.'

Definitely 'treasured members of the family', but Diane worries that Maggie will give her usual sharp reply and relegate them to the 'uncouth mainlanders'. Maggie remains silent. Diane grins, remembering Maggie's advice. Never argue with a good cook.

They arrange with Liz to hire a car.

'Where do we pick it up?' Ron pushes back his chair.

'Out front. It's a white Nissan.' Liz laughs, 'I hope you don't mind a few dents. It's Gwen McKenzie's turn on the roster.'

'Roster?'

'There's no Avis or Budget Rent-A-Car here. You'll find the keys in the ignition.'

'What a jewel of a place,' Maggie says. 'I wouldn't have missed this for the world.'

Over breakfast, the local maps are checked and a decision is made to visit Trouser Bay.

Maggie, in a thick Texan drawl says, 'Now there's gotta be a story about Trouser Bay.'

Liz explains that, after his ship wrecked, a sailor had a lucky escape when he managed to struggle ashore. His trousers washed up three days later.

'It's thirty kilometres away,' she continues. 'That's an all-day trip.'

'All day?' Ron raises an eyebrow. It only takes an hour to drive thirty K's to Melbourne.

'I forgot.' Liz gives them a pitying look. 'You're mainlanders. Are you still going?'

They nod in unison.

'Maybe we could have a barbecue?' Diane suggests. 'I'm sure we can find a picnic area and a coin-in-the-slot hot plate, like those lining the banks of the Yarra River in Melbourne.'

Liz gives them a frying pan, a box of matches and three Scotch Fillets. Laughing like school children, they set off in Gwen McKenzie's car.

Diane and Maggie sit on sun-warmed mulch under a stand of casuarinas, their legs dangling over the edge of a cliff. Below is a sweep of golden sand. The blue waters of Trouser Bay sparkle in the sunlight.

'This is God's own country.' Maggie breathes in the fresh, salty air. 'No tourists and the best food. Just magic.' She picks up a twig. 'This is amazing,' she says, turning it over in the palm of her hand. 'See the minute scale of these leaves. They are grouped in whorls of five.'

'You'd never guess you love biology.'

'Nearly as much as I love reading.' Maggie drops the twig, pulls a book from her pack and hands it to Diane. She glances at the title, *An Unquiet Mind: A Memoir of Moods and Madness.*

'It's a story of incredible loss.' Maggie hesitates, looks as if she is going to say something.

Ron flops onto the picnic rug. 'Any lunch?' He reaches for the picnic basket. Diane playfully slaps his hand.

'Come on. Give a man a break. I could eat a horse.'

Diane aims the book at him, but instead, folds back the green table napkin covering the picnic basket. She takes out four ham and salad rolls, tasty cheese, enormous homemade lamingtons, equally large raspberry slices and an apple for each of them.

Ron grins. 'This would feed an army.'

'Are you sure?' Maggie tosses him the box of matches. 'Maybe you can get the steaks going.'

Muchas gracias Senorita.

After their hearty meal, Ron stretches out on the rug, hands clasped under his head. Diane and Maggie relax in comfortable silence. The spot, a perfect place to sit and dream. Diane rubs an aching knee. Lines etch deep around

Maggie's mouth and eyes. What is her life like? What are her hopes and dreams? At least, her small body is still sturdy, her mind as sharp as ever. Diane hopes she's as good when she's eighty. But what has she achieved so far? Nothing of great note. A few qualifications. A couple of prizes for short stories, but still struggling to finish a book.

Below, white crochet foam edges the curve of golden sand, joining land to sea.

*

Maggie holds on to the panic handle as the Nissan bumps and jolts down the grassy road. They stop at a post and wire fence. A collection of headstones and neglected graves huddle beneath the only patch of tea trees on the grassy coastal plain.

The rusty gate creaks. They stroll down a windswept path lined with purple irises. Past ancient headstones. One tombstone stands proud and tall surrounded by a cluster of unmarked graves. She can barely read the inscription: Mannalargenna. Last chief of the Portland Tribe.

Perched on a stone slab, she pulls out her glasses and guide book and reads, Between 1833 and 1847, one hundred Tasmanian aborigines died on Flinders Island. The memory of an old Apache saying surfaces. There is no death, only a change of worlds. Maggie doesn't believe it.

She moves on to another gravestone. *Private Patrick Monaghan. King's Own Light Infantry. Died 1885.* The icy Antarctic wind blows in from the sea. She blows on her cupped hands and reads the epitaph on the next headstone.

Sacred to the memory of Margaret Monaghan 24 years, 5 months and her two children, James and Patrick, who were drowned 23rd of December 1840 by the upsetting of a boat conveying them from on board H M Brig Tamar to the settlement at Flinders Island.

Two days before Christmas. Twenty-nine-year-old Private Patrick Monaghan, King's Own Light Infantry, after waiting over six months for his family, stands waving on the shore. Sees them lowered over the side of the brig into a row boat. A few whitecaps, but the skies are blue. The boat cresting waves. Dipping out of sight. Flailing oars. Upturned boat. Did he plunge into the waves? Did fellow infantrymen hold him back? Dreadful if he had to watch his wife and children drown. Maggie shivers and hurries to a patch of weak sunlight.

*

Diane pushes open the dining room door. The place is deserted. Liz emerges from the kitchen to tell her that every Sunday the restaurant is closed and suggests they try the local golf club.

'It's a nice trip. Just keep the ocean on your right.' She walks them to the front door.

'I think she wants a night off,' Maggie mutters, climbing into the back seat behind Ron. 'I hope this place has decent coffee.'

The road runs through the middle of the course. Golfers, dragging buggies, smile and wave. Kangaroos prop upright and scratch their bellies, ignoring the little white balls whizzing past their ears. Ron parks the car beside the covered porch leading into the bistro.

The dining room is basic, but the menu extensive. Again, they have the place to themselves. With a John Wayne swagger, Ron approaches the bar.

'What time do you close?'

The barman looks up from wiping glasses. 'What time are you leaving?'

Maggie looks at the empty tables. You could fire a gun and not hit anyone, she says. So different from Santa Fe.

Ron ploughs through a huge mixed grill.

'You shouldn't eat so fast.' Maggie indicates his empty plate. 'It's not good for your health.' Her plate is still half full.

Ron picks up the menu. Anyone want sweets? They have a special. Ice cream with Crème de Cacao.

Maggie shakes her head.

'Sounds good.' Diane looks around for a waiter. 'Sure you don't want one, Maggie?'

'Don't worry about cost.' Ron waves the sacred wallet and grins. 'Still plenty left.'

Maggie folds her arms. Crème de Cacao? Ron nods. Maggie's mouth forms a thin line. 'I can't have alcohol.'

'Are you on tablets? Lots of people in the village say alcohol and tablets don't mix.'

'I'm a recovering alcoholic, Diane.'

Eyes wide, Diane and Ron stare at Maggie. Struggle to comprehend.

'I'm an ex-lush.'

Lush? Diane's teetotalling mother, a former Rechabite Queen of the Band of Hope, once pointed out an old bag lady sprawled against a brick wall, moaning over a broken bottle of gin. Grabbing Diane's hand, her mother stepped over the acrid contents staining the path, and preached a lengthy lecture on the evils of drink.

'You? An alcoholic?' Diane cannot visualise her Saint Maggie as a lush. 'You never mentioned it.'

Ron fidgets in his seat. 'The lemon meringue pie looks good.'

'It's not something I talk about.'

'But how—?'

Ron points to the cake display. 'What about cheesecake?'

They shake their heads. He walks over to the counter. Diane leans forward, takes Maggie's hands in hers and whispers, 'What happened?'

'I beat it. Did it cold turkey.'

Diane furrows her brow.

'I called on all the love in the universe to help me.' Maggie pauses. 'And I succeeded.'

Ron arrives with a large slice of mud cake. Maggie gives

Diane's hand a quick squeeze and says, 'But that's all in the past.' She sits back in her chair and turns to Ron. 'Did you hear about the Quaker drinking orange juice in the bar?'

Ron grins. Diane smiles automatically, her thoughts elsewhere.

With an outrageous Texan drawl, Maggie recites, 'A drunk wanders into a bar and sits next to a man drinking orange juice. Why do you drink that stuff? the drunk asks. The man replies, Because I'm a Quaker. Then talk some Quaker talk, says the drunk. The Quaker raises his glass and says, Fuck thee.'

Ron slaps the table, throws back his head and laughs. Diane feebly smiles. What else has Maggie failed to tell her?

*

Diane dashes from room to room. Is the porch light on? Cutlery out? *Yothu Yindi Tribal Law* CD playing? At least the marinated chicken wings, Hungarian meatballs and Welsh rarebit are in the preset oven. A fruitcake sits in pride of place on the table. As long as there is plenty of food, the night will be a success. She stands back. That will do. What isn't displayed now can be dealt with later. She glances out the window. Fifteen years ago, the detractors moaned that this would be a mosquito-ridden swamp. They were wrong. A large moon illuminates an indigo sky. Lights from the houses opposite strobe calm water. Strident calls of plovers, protecting nests, eggs, or young, interrupt the soft night sounds. This is why she loves living on these manmade canals.

The doorbell rings. Diane's friends and neighbours ebb and flow, smiling, joking and making welcome her special guest. Maggie sits in a chair at the end of the table.

'Migod. All this fuss,' she says to Diane. 'I've been celebrating for over two weeks. What's so special about turning eighty? Next they'll want me to wear a party hat.'

One of Diane's hairdressing friends has already had more than her fair share of wine. Sashaying in her three-inch-high heels, juggling a tray of petits fours, she quaffs from a wine glass constantly refilled from a four-litre cask. Calls it her Chateau Cardboard. She glares at Diane's straight hair.

'Call me if you want a perm.'

Maggie watches her with anxious eyes. 'Does she know about AA?' she asks Diane. 'Maybe you could have a quiet word with her later.'

Loud laughter and the buzz of conversation drive Diane and Maggie out on the deck. A family of ducks make a vee to the opposite shore and the slap of water against the sides of moored boats drifts across the canal. Earlier in the day, between the shade sail poles, Ron had strung fairy lights. They give the deck a festive al Fresco look. Just right for the occasion. Two birthdays to celebrate. Two Leos. Two lions.

'Wait here. I have something for you.' Diane disappears inside the house then emerges with a mauve package tied with a large, pink bow.

'It's too nice to open,' Maggie says. Barb wraps her presents in brown paper and ties them with string. Maggie slowly unties the bow, removes one sticky taped spot after the other, taking care not to tear the paper.

'Rip it, Maggie.'

The search for the perfect present had taken Diane weeks. It had to be light enough for Maggie to take home with her, but not jewellery. Maggie wears only gold and silver. More than Diane can afford. She considered several nice tops, but Maggie is not one to dress up, preferring to wear shirts and slacks, except the odd free flowing mu mu, on special occasions. Like tonight.

Finally, ribbon wound into a neat circle, paper smoothed and flattened, Maggie holds up a long, hand-painted, silk scarf.

'The ochre colours are the earth, the aboriginal patterns will remind you of Australia, and when you wear it'—Diane gives a little laugh—'think of me.'

Maggie slips the soft silk around her neck and flicks an end back her shoulder.

'Do I look like an author? My writing group will be so impressed.' Diane sighs with relief.

Maggie leans forward. 'Give me your paw,' she commands. Turning Diane's hand palm upwards, she cups it in her own. Taking from her pocket a silver and gold entwined necklace, she curls it into Diane's palm. 'Happy Birthday.'

Diane gazes at the gleaming coil. Noticing Maggie's bare neck, she shakes her head. 'I can't—.'

'I want you to have it.'

'But—'

Maggie gently folds Diane's fingers and holds her fist closed.

'It's yours. And no arguments.'

Diane hesitates. Every instinct shouts to give it back, but one look at Maggie's stern face tells her not to try. The decision has been made. Accept the gift with grace.

With both ends of the necklace pinched between thumbs and forefingers, Diane clasps it at the back of her neck. Holding her head high, she pats the gift with her left hand. Her eyes shining, she gives Maggie a hug.

'I'll wear it always.'

'Are you two going to sit out there all night,' Ron calls. 'Maggie has a plane to catch tomorrow.'

*

Diane's Journal: Australia.

You gave Maggie a copy of your writing group's latest anthology signed by all the members. Something light for her to read on the plane. Your short story on page nineteen, a celebration of your twenty-two years of pen friendship. Maggie admired the seascape cover, with 'Casting a Line' scripted in a fishing line cast across the page.

*How does a writer choose a title? Christina, founder of
your writing group, when walking with her two girls
along the Kubunji Beach pier watched an angler's line
snake into the water. Imagined it forming into words. Or
it could be a line in the text that leaps out at you. Maybe
for this work in progress 'What Time is it There'? It
reminds you of Maggie.*

*You pick up a long, white envelope with a red-and-
blue striped border. A dark blue PAR AVION AIR MAIL in
the left hand corner. How many years have you
corresponded? Over thirty? Where has the time gone?
You still write long, newsy letters, but these days, apart
from your letters to Maggie, you rely on emails. It's hard
to remember a time when letters were written by hand or
typed on a typewriter.*

*

After removing the rug from her knees, Maggie slowly climbs
the stairs to her study. With a sigh, she sinks into her chair
and searches for her yellow pad and favourite slim-line pen.

1/27/2000

*Dear Diane, I hardly know where to start. Barb has been
taking care of me with really 'tough love'. Of course there
are times when I resent it, even though I know she is
right. She sometimes gets mad at me because I don't
follow her orders properly. She is an extraordinarily good
caregiver. She looks up drugs I've been given and their
possible side effects. As a result, with my consent, we cut
back on many of them, and what a great change. Before,
my memory was terribly impaired, and I felt dopey too
much of the time. I was not helped at that nursing home.
The beds were uncomfortable. The food damn near
inedible and the care varied a great deal.*

Barb brings her a cup of coffee. She stops, stares at Maggie's neck.

'Why are you wearing that chain, Moth-er? Where is the one you usually wear?'

'Which one?'

'You didn't leave it at that nursing home, did you?'

'I have trouble remembering what day it is. Why should I worry about a necklace?'

'I hope you haven't lost it.'

I can't believe what a snob I am, Diane. Not a social one at all. About books, yes—with no basis in fact, just my twisted mind. As you know, I continually escape in mystery books, but get quite snooty about romances. Mills and Boon? No! Readers Digest? No!

Because of that I missed a most wonderful book that it seems everyone else has read and loved: '84 Charing Cross Road' by Helen Hanff. My friend and neighbour, Jane Watkins, lent them (there's a sequel—'The Duchess of Bloomsbury Court', or is it Street?) to me the other day. Tiny little things and powerful. I sat down to look at them and don't usually like letters (except ours, of course), but I couldn't put that first book down. Now, I feel like a fool. I bought '84' and have ordered the 'Dutchess'. Have you read them? If not, please let me send them to you. The edition I bought said that Helen died in '97 and I grieved. Also, a movie was made in 1986 with Ann Bancroft and Anthony Hopkins. Was I on this planet?

In the midst of my reading and 'living' with Helen in New York and in London, I kept thinking about you. Your anthology story about our friendship touched me deeply. Maybe one day you could write more? It would make a good book. Looking back, our friendship seems almost unreal, but how I love living and getting to be part of your family.

*

Diane's Journal: Australia.

*Reliving your first meeting and ensuing pen-friendship,
and Maggie's prompting, planted the thought to write a
longer version of your story. It would be an opportunity to
publish her poetry, limericks and double dactyls. A mark
of respect for someone who was the catalyst for your
writing journey. The thought 'There is no greater tribute
than to lovingly record a life' jumps into your mind.*

*Maybe it could be like 84 Charing Cross Road? You like
the simplicity of the letter format and understanding how
powerful it can be. It could be a small intimate book so
different from the epic proportions of your mother's story
That covered two world wars and a depression.*

*This would be an uplifting little tale of two women, who,
in spite of differences in age, culture and countries, formed
a lasting friendship. A common story. True, but one that in
troubled times reinforced the good in human nature.*

*And underlying all these lofty aims was the thought
that it would give Maggie a lift when she needed it most.*

*

Diane wanders back from the letterbox with a stack of mail.
Nothing from Maggie today. She spies a stamped, self-
addressed envelope. She rips it open and hastily withdraws a
single page.

*Greensleaves Publishing Pty Ltd
31 Collins St
Melbourne*

*Dear Diane Simpson:
Thank you for sending us your manuscript, but...*

Diane sighs. Another rejection to add to the mounting pile upstairs. She'll soon have enough to wallpaper her study. Seventeen in all. All for different reasons. The manuscript was engaging, exciting, interesting, well written, but was not what we are looking for, the wrong genre, not marketable, too similar to one we have recently published. Or, the manuscript needed to be expanded, shortened, and—best excuse of all—we only accept manuscripts from an agent. The trouble being, to get an agent you need to be published. And to be published, you need an agent.

At least this time, the publisher hasn't returned another pristine, first three chapters that never left the packet. A coffee mug ring or a mustard smear on the title page would at least indicate someone actually read her submission. But this rejection slip was a doozy.

Thank you for sending Ossie Mumma.

Ossie Mumma? The working title of Diane's book is *Valerie G.* Diane laughs. This is a new one. Rejected for the wrong story. The writer of Ossie Mumma will receive her letter saying, 'Thank you for sending Valerie G, but unfortunately...' If only Diane and this other writer could get together and share notes. What a laugh that would be.

The letter goes with the others on top of the manuscript in the bottom drawer.

7/6/2000

Dear Maggie, I'm getting used to publisher's rejections.
So far, I've sent Mum's story to Giramondo, Hardy Grant,
Penguin and Picador to name a few. Don't get excited.
I've done a basic outline for our story, but it's hard to
find time to write. I'm sitting, here with the gas heater
sounding like a helicopter, the garage door keeps going
up and down, and the washing machine vibrating its way
out the laundry door.

*The old saying is that troubles always come in threes
so this should be it, for this week at least. I'm currently
studying playwriting at Holmesglen TAFE. Our teacher
says to write about something you know. Of course for
me, it has to be the hairdressing salon.*

The clients watch Diane's every move. They chatter amongst themselves, well aware of their place in the hairdressing queue. She works as fast as she can, but the pain in her left knee creeps up into the thigh, her leg a log of wood. She glances at her watch and grimaces. Another two hours before she can have more painkillers. She grits her teeth. No time to stop, not even for a cup of coffee. Grabbing a mug, she fills it with hot water from the tap and sips it between scissor snips.

The pressure is constant: help her elderly clients over to the basin, wash and condition the hair, place rollers, position ear-guards, cover the lot with a net and pop under the dryer. Today, she will put the timer on for thirty minutes instead of the usual twenty. The extra ten minutes will give her time to clear the backlog.

She glances at the waiting faces. Eve flips the pages of a magazine. Maureen holds up her knitting. 'Look how much I've done since I've been here.' Margaret passes round a box of chocolates. She'll give chocolates a miss today. Diane's stomach turns at the thought of the gooey centre clinging to her teeth. She must have done ten clients already this morning and still the queue is out the door. Who'd want to be a sole trader?

The pain nags Diane, worries her, frays her nerves. She is constantly evaluating distances. How far to the basin? How many steps to that chair? She should do something about it, but the x-rays taken five years ago were fine. It must be vascular. She just needs to lose weight and exercise. An image of Maggie, eighty and walking a kilometre every day, makes her sigh with envy.

The village notice board posted line dancing classes with

Ruth at Two p.m. Saturday. That should get the circulation going. It will be fun to wear tight blue jeans, a western shirt, large Texan hat and move in time to twangy bootscootin' music. She laughs at the mental picture. Maggie would be horrified to see her in such a get up. It's like imagining Maggie going bush dancing with corks dangling from her hat.

Ruth shouts and claps her hands. Vine to the right. Clap, clap, clap. Billy Ray Cyrus belts out *Achy Breaky Heart* from a CD player in the corner.

Vine to the left. Tap, tap, tap. Diane, hands on hips, swings her bottom and stomps her boots, but when she gets home, she'll crawl up the stairs hoping against hope to make it to the bed, perhaps to sleep.

Each evening, a pillow under both knees helps... for five minutes. Between her legs. Ahhh, better. For five minutes. Maybe at her back? Then back to the knees. The physio says to exercise through it. No pain, no gain. When her legs are fit and strong, the problem will go away.

Niggling at the back of her mind is, could it be her hips? Of course not, the most severe pain is in her knees. And the achy stiffness in her lower back? Sciatica, of course. Her back always the weakest link.

A memory of leaning over the bath to wash her small daughter and being stuck in that position for several days still causes pain. And when she pulled out shrubs? It went again. That time she gave a credible impersonation of an orang-utan, knuckles dragging on the floor, as she tried to keep the household going.

Eve suggests swimming. Diane pulls on old bathers abandoned for years. Modesty skirt in front, flippers on her feet, boogie board under her arm, every morning she launches herself into the sea. She ignores a teenager's laughter. Just wait till she gets older.

Thelma suggests bike riding. Diane's legs become slimmer, body leaner and she feels better than she has in years. But when she walks, her right leg insists on dipping and clients keep asking about her knee.

*

How I wish you could be here, Maggie. We opened last night at the State Theatre. It was wonderful to see my girls romp across the stage. The audience laughed, yes, really laughed. I've included a program from the Fertile Ground New Plays Festival.

Hair Today, Gone Tomorrow

A modern bittersweet comedy

There are ten women to every man living in the Palm View Retirement Village. Lisa, the village hairdresser, does the same clients every Friday. After many busy years, her elderly clients are coming to terms with no longer being needed. They also fear illness and loneliness, but the greatest fear is Alzheimer's and being sent to a nursing home. They cope by being cheerful, cynical or downright difficult.

The combined ages of the four actors exceeds two hundred and sixty years theatrical experience. Playwright, Diane Simpson...

Lights dim and the rustle of sweet wrappers and programs gradually cease. Diane slips into the back row of the theatre, her fingers crossed. She'd cross her eyes if she thought it would do any good. Ron and Kerry have front row seats. What will they think? The curtains open to the tune of *When I'm Sixty Four*. Diane looks at the crowded stalls and hugs the thought that these people have paid. Yes, paid good money to see her play.

Reflecting on the roller-coaster ride this play has taken her, she is aware that to have made it to production was due to never giving up. And luck: blind, wonderful, fantastic luck. Diane rubs her scalp. This stress would give anyone alopecia. Limping is bad enough without her hair falling out in clumps.

171

A small price to pay. Her palms tingle. She had never felt so alive in her life. She wants to pee. Desperately.

What if the play doesn't work? What if the characters, so alive in her head, die on the stage? Too late to run now. Lisa, in three-inch-high-heels, mini skirt and jangling bracelets, totters across the stage carrying a cup of tea with teabag string dangling. She waves her tail-comb in the air. Hi Jean, she says. The audience laughs at the play on words. Lisa nails the part, telling joke after joke, and the audience laughs. Not a titter, but a good belly laugh.

Diane is on the edge of her seat. The more the audience laughs, the more her girls come alive. Merl taps her foot as she sings *You Are My Sunshine*, Jean tosses her hair and snaps at Merl, Lisa twitters and dithers around the stage, fluttering and fussing, and Elizabeth silences them all with one withering glance. The finale. The 'special' light shines on Lisa and Jean with their arms around each other, then slowly fades to black. The audience stands and claps and Diane's girls are called back time and time again. Lisa beams at the wolf whistles and waggles her bottom when she leaves the stage.

The after party is a blur of congratulations, champagne and back slapping. Ron and Kerry stand to one side, until Diane finally makes her escape.

'It was fantastic, Mum,' Kerry says, kissing them goodbye.

When they reach the sanctuary of their home, Diane breathes a sigh. 'What did you honestly think of it?'

'Not bad,' he says.

She punches his arm. Her bed has never felt so good. She has never felt so good.

'Happy?' Ron asks: but there is no reply, Diane is dreaming of her girls.

'Jean,' she murmurs. 'Stop it' Put her down.' Diane giggles. 'Lisa. Lisa. Sort them out.'

In spite of her brief success, constant pain has Diane refusing social invitations, hoping there is always a seat on the train, and swallowing too many over-the-counter painkillers. She can't close her bathroom cabinet because of herbal remedies.

One day in the hall mirror she is shocked at the haggard face, bent body.

Dr. Hughes slides four x-rays into a backlit frame. The winged image of Diane's pelvis, resting on the bulbous tops of her leg bones, flank two, knobbly knee bone films. He stabs a forefinger at the x-ray. 'Your pain is caused by severe osteoarthritis in your right hip.'

Diane shakes her head.

Dr. Hughes is sympathetic. 'The cartilage has gone. It's bone on bone.'

'It's my knee that hurts.'

'When someone has a heart attack, often the pain extends down the left arm and into the hand.' Dr. Hughes scrawls on his prescription pad. He tears off the page and hands it to her. 'Face it,' he says, looking her squarely in the eyes. 'Your hip is stuffed.'

Finally, the words sink in.

Osteo.

Osteo equals old.

Her grandfather sourly muttering with pain as he stomped around the house leaning on his cane.

Her mother in a wheelchair, teeth clenched, declaring, 'They're not going to cut me. Remember Else?'

Aunty Else, who had the operation only for the hip to dislocate. 'You've never heard a scream like it, dear.'

Dr. Hughes is insistent. 'You need a total hip replacement. Ring me when you are ready.'

Diane limps out of the surgery.

Hip replacement. She imagines cut muscle, cut bone and a metal rod. She'll wait a bit longer, but the debilitating pain grips her knee. Remembering her mother, Diane knows that eventually her leg will lock and the femur will crumble until there is no bone left. And always the pain. Constant, unremitting. Reaching level nine on a scale of one to ten. Diane accepts the inevitable, picks up the phone and dials.

With the operation date marked in red on her calendar, Diane visualises herself, leg up, in a wheelchair, ski cap at a jaunty angle, telling friends, I was skiing down the Woollybutt trail when I hit a patch of black ice, tried to miss this big boulder, but.... Dramatic skidoo rescue, Channel nine news, hospital and a hip operation. It will make a good story for Maggie. Or she can limp up to the admissions desk and say, 'I'm booked in for a new front suspension, and while you're about it, I'll have my fifty thousand kilometre service.' Whatever the story she tells, Diane is determined to be a happy hippie, dancing, studying and living again with a smile on her face.

*

7/30/2000

> *Dear Diane, No real need for this letter as not much has happened here. Early morning exercises take half an hour, and I'm back walking two miles a day. My doctor says if I was fitter, I'd be dangerous. Barb and I co-exist amiably, but it is crowded with so much of her life cluttering every room. Santa Fe is becoming busier every day, and we are thinking of building on my five acres at Gateway. I'm sure I'll be fine on my own down there. I...*

The pen clatters to the floor. Maggie rubs stiff fingers. Bending to pick it up, she half expects to see Hank's chair in the corner of the room. Forgetting it has long gone to charity. She shivers and pulls on a sweater. There is a darkness in that corner. A spot where the sun doesn't reach. She shivers again. Maybe the front door isn't closed properly. It could be wide open, like the other day when she came back from the library. Barb swears she closed it when she left.

Kicking a snake draft-stopper back against the gap beneath the door, Maggie still feels a flow of cold air. A new crack in the adobe wall close to the door jamb makes her blow on her hands for a little warmth. This place is falling apart. Barb complains that the roof still leaks, wardrobe doors refuse to slide, and that's just a couple of the repairs she's listed on the kitchen whiteboard.

Maggie glances at the half-finished letter, hesitates then enters her study. Maybe some time spent reading old friends will settle her down. Barb will soon be home with potatoes and coffee. She won't be able to read then. They'll spend the afternoon thumbing through books featuring designs for cabins, beach homes and straw bale houses.

John Master's name in gold stands out from all the others in the bookcase. You know you've arrived as an author when your name is more prominent than the title. Perfect choice, but how to get to his books? Barb's stuff is everywhere. Everything she has collected over her lifetime is stored in this house. Boxes fill every room, some stacked ceiling high in Hank's garage. Eight years since he died, and she still won't let Maggie throw out a nail.

She's stuck between two boxes marked Bathroom/towels and Clothes/cushions. The front door hinges squeak and moan.

'You should give half this junk to charity,' Maggie shouts.

'I got the Kenya coffee, Moth-er.' Barb dumps parcels on the kitchen counter and fills the coffee percolator.

'When will you use any of this stuff?' Maggie extract herself from the overcrowded room.

'They were all out of Dakota Chief potatoes.' Barb measures coffee into the pot and wipes a spot of water off the counter.

Maggie escapes outside and juggles her writing pad on her knee. She wishes she could talk to Diane but she never knows when to phone. Damn the time difference. And Diane is always busy. Too busy. Maybe if she wasn't always studying she would have more time to talk and write to an old friend.

Should she tell her she is burning the candle at both ends? And for what? It's great to have an education but what's it going to do for her in the real world? God knows it's hard for any woman to get any sort of recognition in male dominated societies. But what would telling her achieve? Better to keep things bright and breezy. She won't say anything. Not in this letter anyway.

> *I should follow Hank's example, Diane, and keep copies of the letters I've written to you because half the time I can't remember what I've told you, so you'll just have to ignore repetition.*
>
> *If you haven't read 'My Ishmael' —the third in the saga —do try and get it. It's really the best. Then, a friend of Barb's gave me her copy of 'Tuesdays with Morrie' by Mitch Albom. It's a small book, but super-powerful, and leaves you with a wonderful feeling. It's about an old sociology professor who is dying of ALS (Lou Gehrig's disease, which killed my brother). The author was Morrie's student and had attended Tuesday class. When he got news of the illness, he flew to visit him every Tuesday until Morrie eventually died. Trust me. It is not depressing. You'll love it.*
>
> *For doing my volunteer work at the library, I can choose a book to have my name inscribed inside. I suggested they get at least three copies, for I'm sure it will take off as more people hear about it.*

The shopping bags jiggle and bounce in the back of the four wheel drive as Maggie tries to miss deep potholes in Terrillos Road. Barb wanted to drive, but this is Maggie's car and she insists on driving. If Barb drives, they'll be gone for ages. She won't go over forty miles an hour. Maggie wants to get the Goddamn groceries and head for home.

They pass clusters of tacky little boxes that pass for houses fronting bitumen roads. Many with a square of green lawn out front. Maggie shakes her head muttering. Migod. What will happen to the water table in a couple of years? Cars beep and speed past. Young men, one hand draped across the steering wheel of their souped-up cruisers, wait at traffic lights. *Doof, doof, doof.*

When they enter an area of old adobe homes with Madonna blue gates and sparse desert gardens, she relaxes. Remnants of the old Santa Fe. But it was depressing living in Santa Fe back then. More-so now that smog has become part of everyday life. The only thing she will miss is the library. But Ginny already knows her in the branch in Gateway, and the air will be fresh and clean. Unpolluted by progress. Maggie thinks with affection of the sleepy hollow at the base of the Chiricahua Mountains and how that wonderful old Apache name rolls off her tongue.

The housing design books are neatly stacked. Spread over the table is a floor plan for a spacious doublewide home.

'I don't like the rectangular shape,' Maggie says.

'Then let's move things around,' Barb suggests. 'The kitchen could be a little larger, and if we move the garage to here—'she points to the plan'—it will be perfect.' A bedroom and en suite at this end for you. A sitting room in the middle and a bedroom and en suite for me.

Maggie needs a porch front and back. She imagines reading outside on balmy evenings. And more room in the laundry.

Barb marks the proposed alterations onto the plan.

'Let's give it to Doug's son. He's a builder. We'll see what he says.'

Barb rolls up the plans and places them in a cylinder ready to post.

After weeks of waiting, Maggie finally collects the professional blueprints of their house from the Santa Fe Post Office. They are perfect. Everything is where she wants it to be.

Are you sure you want to live there,' Barb says. 'It gets so hot in summer.'

'It cools down at night.'

'Where will you get provisions?'

'I don't need much, and Geriton is only seventy miles away.' She doesn't mention Maggie's age.

Diane, I'm busy packing more boxes to take to Gateway.

'Just sign here. Where there's a cross.' The attorney points to the bottom of several official documents. Maggie signs.

'And here.'

He witnesses her signatures. The title papers to the Santa Fe house are pushed over to Barb and the procedure is repeated. Barb gives the attorney a hundred dollars, and he hands it, and a receipt, to Maggie.

'Cheapest sale of a home I've ever witnessed.' He stares at me over the rim of his glasses. 'You're sure you know what you're doing?'

Maggie sits exhausted, surrounded by half-filled boxes. What to pack next? And where to put it.

'Do you want these?' Barb asks.

'What?'

'I wish you'd get hearing aids, Moth-er.' She points to shelves stacked with Maggie's mother's needlework. Rosebud garlanded tablecloths, crocheted doilies.

'When will you use them?'

Maggie shrugs her shoulders. She's worn out trying to decide what she wants. Not much. No more clutter. Her greatest problem is her books. Every one a treasured friend. She must cull, but how will she decide between them? A mother cannot choose between her children. And it's too expensive to ship books to Diane.

Eventually, a small box is packed and ready to donate to the Santa Fe Library. Let them do with them as they will. Turning to her journals, she throws up her hands.

'Leave them here,' Barb says. 'I'll look after them.'

Maggie sighs with relief. She can visit them when she

comes to Santa Fe. But before she follows Barb downstairs, she grabs her Kenya journal and adds it to the books to go.

They arrive at the house in Gateway. The shady porch protects the front door from the hot Arizona sun. Before Maggie turns the key in the lock, she closes her eyes and listens to a desert wind rustling grasses and the week-week call of a Common Poorwill. Peaceful gentle sounds, undisturbed by man. This is her Africa. She is home.

Barb bustles around, unpacking, stocking the refrigerator, filling the pantry and making up beds.

'Migod, where do you get your energy?' Maggie flops into an armchair. An oasis in the middle of chaos. 'I'm pooped.'

'You've been great, Moth-er. I didn't think we'd be in by now.' Barb wipes sweat from her forehead with the back of her hand. A smile illuminates her face. It's been a long time since Maggie has seen her so happy.

'Look.' She points out the kitchen window. 'Musk hogs drinking from our dish.'

Maggie relishes Barb's delight. Lifting the footrest of her favourite chair, she leans back, folds her arms and closes her eyes.

*

Diane's Journal: Australia.

*Hazy images of beeping machines drift past your slitted
eyes. An inflated balloon hand with jutting fingers white
against a blanket. The hand of your childhood
nightmares fills your mind. It smothers everything,
fingers expanding, about to explode. You open your
mouth, but the scream of terror never bursts from your
swollen throat. Is it a dream? Blue leads snake across the
bed. You try to push them away. The balloon hand
refuses to move. Deep shit.*

179

An intensive care nurse at the foot of the bed drops her file into a holder. Two fingers grasp her wrist. The nurse studies her watch.

'You'll live,' she says with a smile and pats her hand. I'll tell doctor you're awake.

*

Diane's legs are strapped on either side of a wedged pillow. She feels like a new born mewling, I want. I'm thirsty. I'm wet. Change me. I'm hurt. Make it go away. Her raw quivering body the only reality. The nurse pulls back the covers, bowl of hot soapy water on the bed.

'Ups a daisy.' She rolls the fragile quivering body onto the side, sponges and dries Diane's back.

Sighs of relief, the soapy flannel caressing her bruised spine. Slowly the room comes into focus. Voices. Other beds. Other patients. She is back in the world again.

In North Ward, Diane wants to vomit. A repugnant smell comes from a needle bin on the bedside table. Her stomach heaves. What is it about the smell that revolted her? Is it connected to her traumatic time in the ICU? When Kerry was four, she heard a tune playing on the radio. Upsetting a tumbler of milk, she slapped her hands over her ears and screamed, 'Turn it off. Turn it off.' It was the relaxation tape playing while Diane gave birth to Kerry after a long, protracted labour.

Diane throws a towel, smothering the needle bin.

The anesthetist stands at the foot of Diane's bed. 'You've been to hell and back.'

Diane raises an eyebrow.

'You swelled, turned red, blood pressure dropped to forty and your heart fibrillated.'

Diane's fingers tighten on the blanket.

'But you stabilized. We'll check you for a stroke and any heart problems before you leave.' Walking towards the door, she turns, 'If you hadn't been in this hospital. You wouldn't have had a chance.'

Diane smiles her thanks.

The last rays of a setting sun shine on her bed. Who or what saved her? A talented anaesthetist? Dedicated doctors and nurses? A well-equipped hospital? All the love in the universe? Maybe all four.

Diane lies on top of the bed, her feet encased in a pair of bright yellow, furry blobs resembling chicken feet, complete with stuffed red claws. With her white elastic compression stockings, she feels like Foghorn Leghorn from childrens' cartoons. She's ready to kill Kerry for pulling them onto her feet, and then leaving. Diane can't reach down to take them off. But the sight makes her laugh.

The door opens and her specialist walks in. He takes one look at the outsized chicken feet. Tries not to laugh. Tries to talk sternly to Diane.

'You're not going to try to walk in those, are you?' She vigorously shakes her head.

Diane is home convalescing when Kerry arrives with a new laptop.

'Thought this might come in handy. It's better than your old one. It has windows 7.' She places it on the kitchen table. The array of icons at the top of the screen impresses Diane.

Click, click, and she is on Google. Click, click, and folders are opened or filed for future use.

During Diane's childhood, she attended many magic shows where magicians extracted gold coins from people's ears, doves appeared from under silk scarves and rabbits emerged from hats. This computer has the same spellbinding fascination. She wants to know more.

Kerry shows her how. 'You just click this, then this, and then this happens. Go on Mum, have a try.'

From the start, Diane has trouble. She clicks. It flashes a warning. Clicks again and an hourglass refuses to budge. She waits, but it will not move. It sits there, humming tunelessly, just like Ron sits in the car, engine running, waiting for her to slam the front door and jump in.

The screen freezes. She switches it off. Waits five minutes. Presses the on button and cracks her knuckles until the blue sky screensaver appears and fluffy white clouds scuttle across the screen.

Diane constantly telephones Kerry asking, 'Why won't it print?' Or, 'The screen's a funny colour.' Or, 'Why does it keep saying the program will terminate?' Kerry patiently tells her to press this, click that, and order is restored.

Slowly, Diane solves the problems and eventually wonders how, in the early days of her study, she managed. In the beginning she just had an exercise book and pen. Later, her first computer became a glorified typewriter. This computer now keeps her accounts and pays her bills. Organises holidays and collects and delivers letters. Plays soothing CDs and stores her memories. Diane has learnt a new language and has a new name. *disimpson@yahoo dot com dot au*. She sends perfect emails and the red underlining of mistakes and green for grammar in the text reminds her of Maggie. Her work edited and neat on the page, she spends hours everyday tapping away at university assignments. Maggie's story on hold.

*

Diane's Journal: Australia.

You glance back over this last section and can't help laughing. Computers are supposed to make life easier. They allow the writer to cut, paste and move script

*from one section to another, but on this computer
keyboard the 'e' key keeps sticking and 'edited '
becomes 'ditd' and 'neat 'nat'. It makes for crazy
reading. Your work ditd and nat on the page. You may
even resort to writing longhand if this persists. You
still send Maggie handwritten letters rather than neat
computer printouts. Maggie feels they are soulless and
scrawled scripts are 'real' letters that capture the
emotional essence of the writer. You notice when
Maggie writes a comment about the American national
debt it is always in short, angry strokes. Stories about
Elizabeth are in soft flowing script, while entries in her
hiking journals march across the page.*

*

11/14/2000

*As soon as the house is finished, Diane, why don't you
come and stay in Gateway? I'm sure I've accrued
enough frequent flyer points to get at least one of you
here. Tempted? We can work on our story, and I can
take you to all my favorite places. The canyon is
beautiful at any time of the year. In August, we could
celebrate our birthdays together. I, too, have thought
often of our long friendship and marvel at it. Would
that our turf were as close.*

*

2001: Gateway, Arizona, USA

*Dear Maggie, When I see your writing on the envelope, I
drop everything to catch up with your news.
We are experiencing a most unusual summer. We haven't
been able to open the door leading to the deck because
the wind has been incredible. It sweeps in violent gusts
over the roofs of the houses across from us, hits the water*

183

*and riffs forward like a dark sea serpent until it breaks in
choppy waves onto our sandy beach. Today, the tide is
the lowest I've seen for a long time and our dingy is
nearly suspended above the water. The ropes to the jetty
are as tight as banjo strings. At this time of day, the big
brown dog in the house across the water usually plays
with his plastic ice cream container, but today he just
stuck out his head then scuttled back inside. However,
the man across the way, with three boys under five years
of age, is braving the elements to sit and have a beer and
some peace. But that's enough window gazing.
Gateway sounds like a great place. Is it really as idyllic as
you describe? It's amazing that so many of your friends
from 1945 still live there. I can't wait to see...*

Diane drags a backpack out of the bottom of the wardrobe.
At the last minute Ron has decided to come. The list of
comments, *Too tired*, *What about my heart tablets*, and *Nothing
for me to do* suddenly replaced by *You can't manage on your own.
I'm coming with you.* Had he thought she would back down? Not
make the trip without him? How much time will she have
with Maggie on her own? She yearns to talk face to face, hear
Maggie's voice, watch her expressions. To learn first-hand
about her new friends, Pete and Junella, and the tiny hamlet
of Gateway. But this time it will be different. Maggie and she
will discuss books they've read. Evaluate the writing.

Diane lifts the backpack onto the bed. On top of a package
containing the now obligatory, homemade fruitcake, she
slides the creative writing component of her latest course.
She also adds a hastily cobbled together thirty pages of
Maggie's book. The flight of fifteen hours and fifty-two
minutes will give her an opportunity to revise. The poor
standard of her writing bothers her, but what an opportunity
for Maggie to wield her red pen.

They will sit at the kitchen table, heads bent over a stack
of bulldog clipped pages, and thrash out issues of omission

and addition. But will Maggie agree to any deletions? In her last letter, she insisted every person involved be included in the story. It means a cast of thousands. Diane has tried to write and explain, has even telephoned, saying it is impossible. For the sake of the story, many people must be left out.

'But they were there,' was Maggie's unyielding reply.

*

Diane raises her right arm, takes a quick whiff and winces. She smells like Wombat road kill. She's experienced plenty of those on their outback travels. What a trip. Fifteen hours from Melbourne to Los Angeles. Two hours in another plane to Tucson. Four hours in Barb's four wheel drive to Maggie's home in Gateway. That is bad enough, but when Barb picks them up at 10:00 a.m., she wants to show them everything along the way. Add to that a detour to shop at Trader Joe's.

Bouncing in the back seat of the four wheel drive, Diane's eyes cross with fatigue. She can't focus. Several hefty digs to Ron's ribs are necessary whenever his head falls back and his mouth becomes a bug catcher. At least, he doesn't snore. An unexpected thunderstorm saves them. Barb heads straight for Gateway without any further detours.

Six-thirty p.m. One hundred degrees. Long shadows promise relief from soul-searing heat. Diane slumps on the high-backed, bottom-polished church pew on the front porch of Maggie's new adobe home: a strange piece of furniture for a self-proclaimed atheist. Ron is prostrate on the double bed in the second bedroom. His bare feet dangle.

The adobe home is just as Diane imagined. Situated on five acres surrounded by mesquite bushes and desert dust. Jack rabbits, pigeons and even fickle musk hogs drink from several water dishes tucked amongst native grasses. In her letters, Maggie gave a detailed description of solid beams called vigas, ceilings lined with natural wood panels, brick floors, and a

185

steep galvanised roof. She refused to have a traditional flat adobe one like the constantly leaking roof in Santa Fe. Thick walls of sun-dried clay bricks and straw help keep out the extreme heat of summer and the bitter cold of winter snow. The home is comfortable and inviting.

A sizzling early morning sun sucks at an already dry land. The day promises to be a scorcher. A ceiling fan above Diane and Ron's bed slowly circulates hot air.

'Do I smell coffee?' Ron levers himself up on one arm.

Diane drags on shorts and a top then pulls on runners. Only afterwards does she remember Maggie's warning to look for scorpions hiding in the toes. In the kitchen, her friend boils eggs. Barb slices apple cake.

'You're up early.' Diane's smile is cheerful, but guarded.

'Not for us.' Barb points to a clock with her knife. 'We left at 6:00 a.m. for our walk with Pete.'

'You must be keen.' Diane likes the idea of an early morning walk, but 6:00 a.m.?

'If you can get up early enough tomorrow, you should—'

'Hi everyone.' Ron sniffs the air. 'Do I smell toast?'

'Is the toast ready, Moth-er?' Barb taps her mother's arm.

Maggie looks up from the stove.

'What?'

'The toast.' Barb points to the toaster.

'I can't do two things at once.' Maggie hastily drops in two slices and stares at them as if willing them to be done.

She picks up the chicken-shaped timer, checks the front and holds it to her ear. 'I'm timing the eggs.'

'Why don't you use the timer on the oven?' Barb impatiently flicks back an escaped strand of hair. 'It's more reliable.'

'I like this one.' Maggie shakes the chicken then places it back on the counter.

Barb looks at Diane. 'The stove timer's more accurate, isn't it, Diane.'

Clattering forks in the cutlery drawer, Diane pretends she

doesn't hear.

Maggie places a plate containing several supersized iced donuts and four wedges of orange cake in the centre of the table.

During breakfast Diane has one donut, but Ron has three. Diane looks at his ever expanding waistline. He will become more than His Roundness if he stays here too long.

The Nissan Pathfinder is backed up to the garage door. Barb is anxious to begin the eight-hour drive back to Santa Fe.

After she has gone, Diane helps Maggie by folding the tea towels and napkins.

'Trying to look good?' Ron asks her. 'You were never that tidy at home.' Is she trying to impress Maggie? Trying to fit in with Maggie's lifestyle? Not wanting to rock the boat? Why stay two weeks instead of one?

'You can't come all this way for a week,' Maggie argued in her letters. 'I want to take you to my writing group, and there is the Desert Museum down the road, not to mention the mountains. A week isn't long enough.'

Diane already regrets giving in. Will this visit prove the old adage that fish and visitors stink in three days?

After lunch, Maggie settles into her favourite lounge chair. Beside her several bookmarked biographies, spectacles, a box of tissues and small tumbler of water.

'Barb is a wonderful help,' she says, kicking up the bottom of the recliner. 'But I'm exhausted when she goes.'

Diane washes the dishes and Ron dries, making sure they don't spill water on the floor.

'Rinse them well,' Maggie calls. 'When I was at your place, I thought I'd get chemical poisoning from detergent residue.'

How has her family managed to survive so long? She, and even her mother, always filled the sink with hot water and added heaps of dishwashing detergent. The foamier the better. She used to scrub the dishes with a scouring pad, place them in a drainer, then wipe them with a tea towel. Rinsing after washing is only a recently acquired habit. Diane suspects it may have been promoted to sell double sinks or to scare people into buying dishwashers.

Maggie looks at her watch. 'Siesta time.' She gestures towards their room. 'Off you go.'

Ron's jaw drops in surprise. 'Now?'

Maggie checks her watch again. 'It's one-thirty. Everyone has a siesta after lunch.'

He obediently heads for the bedroom door, muttering, 'When in Rome...'

'Do you always have a lay down in the middle of the day?' Diane asks.

'Hens lay, people lie,' Maggie corrects. 'If you doubt that's right, check with Theodore Bernstein.' She nods towards the bookcase.

Diane's face warms and she takes a deep breath.

'I'll take your word for it.' She hurries to join Ron.

Closing the door of the bedroom, she lowers her voice before she explodes.

'This is like a constant grammar lesson.' Diane sits on the side of the bed. She drags off a hiking shoe and lets it drop to the floor.

'Sent to our bedroom with no discussion. And no thought that we might want to do something else.' The bed squeaks. A second hiking shoe hits the floor. 'Maggie assumes we will do as we are told.' She plumps her pillow into shape then lies next to Ron. 'Worst of all?' She turns to him. 'She's right.'

Ron's belly is shaking.

'It's not funny, Ron.' Diane punches his arm. His belly wobbles harder, and he snorts with laughter.

'It's the middle of the day,' he whispers.

Diane can't help snickering.

Ron holds his shaking sides. 'I feel like a naughty kid sent to my room.'

'Shhhh.' Diane covers his mouth with her hand.

Pillows in front of their faces to deaden the sound, they

laugh until tears stream down their cheeks.

'I'm so glad you came,' Diane finally manages to gasp. 'A fortnight of afternoon naps will drive me crazy.'

'I'm a good buffer, aren't I.'

They count wood knots in the ceiling. One hundred and fifty-three.

Diane opens the back door.

'Don't go outside.' Maggie warns that packs of musk hogs lie in wait to attack and scorpions hide, tails raised ready to sting.

'Only mad dogs and Englishmen go out in the noonday sun.' Locking the door, she tells tales of friends who live in the mountains putting metal plates across outside stairs to stop marauding bears.

'People are the problem. Stupid people. They travel to national parks to see wild animals and leave their picnic scraps behind. The bears soon learn that picnic baskets are found in the back seats of cars.' She puts up two hands as if warding off evil. 'They've been known to eat the leather upholstery.'

Maggie's eyes blaze with a passion bordering on anger.

Diane places the draft of what she now calls The Book in front of Maggie. 'Any chance of working on this?'

Maggie glances at it. 'We'll look at it later.' She turns her back and walks away.

Diane places it back on the buffet and sighs. Diane the student. Maggie the educator. What happened to the dream of talking as equals? Each empowered in their own field?

'I'm going for a quick walk,' Diane calls.

'But it will be dark soon.'

'I'm not going far.'

'Ron. Go with her.'

'It's just a stroll up to the end of the road. I'll only be ten minutes.'

When Maggie has finished with them, Diane and Ron look ready for an African safari. Long-sleeved shirts, hiking sticks, whistles in case they get lost. Maggie has already insisted they wear their hiking boots. Diane has a survival pack on her back containing a flask of water and tourniquet in case of snakebite.

'All we need is a cut lunch,' Ron mutters. Maggie hands him a torch.

'It's still sunny.'

'It gets dark quickly in the desert.' She gives Diane an extra stick to ward off rattlesnakes.

'Be careful of the musk hogs. They often feed under the large juniper tree at evening.'

Rugged up and armed, they set out for their ten minutes of freedom. Ron stomps down the dusty drive, muttering, 'I'm not going to last two weeks.'

Diane sighs as she takes off her boots. 'Am I doing anything wrong?'

Ron shrugs. Suggests that maybe house guests are too much for Maggie at her age.

*

Diane's Journal: Australia.

There had been no hint of friction in Maggie's letters. In retrospect your letters to each other were only ever filled with stories of everyday life, funny incidents, amusing anecdotes, never anything personal. No grief or despair. It took you hours to write to Maggie. Labouring over sentence structure, correct spelling, and ensuring the content safe to be read aloud to the Cochise County Writing Group.

They love your letters, Maggie said in one of hers. You cringed at the thought of your letters as performance pieces. Knowing there was an audience made you change the way you wrote. You got quite carried away and added and subtracted. Made sure each story had a beginning, a middle and an end. Began using metaphors and wrote about constellations of daisies, and described baby plovers as cotton wool balls on toothpicks scampering along the beach.

*Before posting you re-read every word, changed
anything too personal, aware that your words were being
shared with others. Bright and breezy is your definition
of what you wrote, but a later letter from Maggie
revealed it was pride in the writing that made her share
selected sections with her friends. You would never have
thought to read Maggie's letters out loud. Not even to
Ron. So you swapped recipes, travel stories, shared the
odd hope and dream, applauded successes and only
rarely revealed anything emotional or controversial.*

*

Later, in the lounge, Maggie paces the floor. 'I'm glad I left
Santa Fe,' she says. 'Can't stand the place.' Diane raises a
questioning eyebrow.

'Too many Goddamn Americans.' Maggie pushes her hands
deep into the pockets of her jacket.

'They keep building tacky houses and creating ghettos of
concentrated charm. Can you understand people who move
to the desert and plant a lawn? Why don't they leave their
Goddamn city culture behind?' She stares at Diane, daring her
to disagree.

Maggie is angry at the world. Angry at her loss of status,
that Barb has tied up all her money and controls everything
she does. The don't do that, don't buy that, is transferred to
Diane. Maggie constantly tells her what to do, where to sit, try
this, put that there, close that, lock this.

Diane walks away. It is a small distance from the back door
to the low rock wall by the side of the house. Yet it is a world
apart. Doves coo, finches scratch and flutter and she can sit
and gaze at blue-hazed mountains.

*

Diane waits patiently while Maggie backs the Rav Four out of
the garage.

191

'Get in, Diane, I'm taking you to the Desert Museum.' Despite a cushion, Maggie can barely see above the steering wheel.

As they drive down to Cave Creek Road, Diane clutches the seat, hoping Maggie will not pick up her nervousness. A tiny gold elephant on a chain swings backwards and forwards, hypnotising Diane. The sun flares through the windscreen, and she relaxes in spite of herself.

'Where is my Goddamn sunshade?' Maggie drives one handed and bends down to look in the side pocket. The car drifts to the wrong side of the road. Diane's stomach lurches. Hoping her intake of breath isn't too loud, she resists the urge to grab the steering wheel.

'Careful, Maggie.'

Maggie doesn't answer. Finding the shade, she drops it onto her lap, pulling the car back on course. Diane sighs with relief, until Maggie, using both hands, pulls down the sun visor. The car drifts again.

'Last year, Ron hit our letterbox when he was looking for his sunglasses.'

Maggie pulls up in front of the museum. Looking around the deserted car park, she says, 'Can't see any mailboxes here.'

The museum is a large PVC weatherboard-clad building on the edge of the road to Rodeo. It shimmers in the afternoon heat, the only building for miles in the treeless desert.

'Mike's a wonderful young man. I helped him organise an exhibition of our groundbreaking research.' Maggie pushes open the large, wooden door and points to a glass display cabinet featuring reptiles.

She introduces Diane as *my friend from Australia* and proceeds to talk to Mike about famous people and exotic places. When Maggie over-emphasises her role in Hank's desert expeditions, Diane shifts from one foot to the other. Looks at the ground.

'Come into the back, Maggie,' Mike says. 'I have a rare *Micruroides euryxanthus* you'll be interested in.'

He leads the way until they stand in front of glass case containing a brightly coloured coiled snake. Maggie leans forward, gushing like a mother seeing her newborn for the first time.

'He's exquisite.' She peers through the glass. Motions for Diane to come closer.

'See the unique red and yellow coral bands.' She smiles and chants. *Red bands next to yellow, harmful fellow.* 'Have you taken pictures, Diane? You'll want to share this with Ron.'

Back in the museum shop, Maggie still glows with pleasure. Turning away from her animated conversation, on the pretext of admiring a collection of turquoise Indian jewellery, Diane works her way over to a stack of souvenir clothing. Placing both hands inside the bottom of a XXX ochre t-shirt she stretches it. Perfect for Ron's ample frame, but she can't imagine him displaying a snake, crawling out the eye socket of the skull of a longhorn steer, at the coffee shop in Kubunji Beach. Maybe a cap with *Arizona Desert* emblazoned above the peak? Definitely a turquoise necklace for Kerry. Diane glimpses herself in the mirror on the sunglasses stand. Are the multiple silver chains with tiny charms looped around her neck and matching silver bracelets a bit over the top? The younger university students assure her they are trendy.

Maggie prattles on about desert critters, reptilian breeding habits, snakes, and Hank's pioneering herpetology research. Work done thirty years ago. Maggie a widow of many years, yet still playing the part of the famous man's wife. Still wanting to be important.

Mike stands first on one foot and then the other, his hands busy tidying the counter. He turns a yawn into a cough, covering his mouth with his hand.

Diane keeps her distance, as Maggie, in a loud voice, recites scientific names an average person needs a dictionary to understand. What happened to the woman who inspired her for so many years?

*

Diane's journal: Australia

> *You wonder if Maggie has always been an elitist, using language to bolster her self esteem? How could you not have seen this? You stare at the diminutive figure and feel numb. The striving to emulate Maggie has gone. The Book isn't meant to be Maggie's biography but somehow you have slowly developed it into an unrealistic hymn of praise. Maggie wants it to be true. But true to what?*

*

Maggie carefully places her coffee mug onto a coaster and picks up the draft of the biography. Settling into her chair, she scrutinizes the scrawls, circles and connecting arrows of Diane's outline. Trying to take it in, she gazes out the window. This is her life, recorded, preserved. She smiles. At last. Something tangible to prove that she was the one who did all the work. She was the driving force behind all Hank's achievements. Her story will prove to Barb the personal sacrifices were worth it.

She twists her neck from side to side to release pressure building at the base of her skull. But what has she achieved? Most of her life was spent supporting Hank. There is always her poetry and limericks, but are they good enough to be forever preserved in the pages of a book? Fear knots in the pit of her stomach.

A jack rabbit hops into the clearing, distracting her. It cleans its whiskers and wiggles its ears, which delights her, makes her feel at one with the land and its creatures. The beauty of the place must be included in her biography.

Maggie flicks through page after page of prose. her photographs will put some life into it, but how to decide from the albums lining the shelves in the study at Santa Fe? All represent a special time and place in her life. She looks again at the sketched outline, but cannot see where Diane has indicated which pages the photographs will go. And what about her friends? How will Diane fit it all in? Maggie presses her fingers hard into the back of her neck and winces. What about Anna?

*

Propped on the side of the bed, Diane ties tight the laces of her hiking boots. Maggie would not approve of sloppy laces on the walk to the library. Diane can't risk another black mark, yet another part of her wants to let the laces flop. And to hell with it.

'You go,' Ron says. 'Don't worry about me.'

Diane waits for the gulp guaranteed to make her feel guilty. His crestfallen look says abandoned. Unloved. Without a television to veg in front of, Ron is lost. Maggie's television is being repaired.

Diane points to the bookcase. There's a huge selection to choose from. 'Read a book?'

She should have known better.

*

Diane's Journal: Australia.

You emerge from your study with A4 paper in your hand.

'You're not going to read it to me are you?' says Ron recoiling from the very suggestion. This was the man who revered television and never read a book. You had long learnt to keep your studies separate from everyday life. You knew he wasn't interested in your courses or what you had been doing but lately you had noticed that he had been very aloof and even more distant. Was it the trouble with the couple in the unit behind them? Was he caught up in their lives? Was she complaining to him about her partner and was he listening?

*

Giving him a quick hug, Diane strides into the kitchen. Maggie, in Gore-Tex safari outfit, complete with boots and peaked cap, leans on two hiking sticks. She surveys Diane's footwear and nods approval. What is it with Maggie and good boots?

Handing over a spare backpack, Maggie hunches her own into a more comfortable position on her bent spine. Diane wants to shoulder it for her. The determined stride tells her not to try.

Humidity hits them like a sloppy tongue, and already Maggie mops her neck with a kerchief. Diane stops, sniffs the air, revels in the smell of dry grasses carried on a hair-ruffling breeze. Listens to the soft sounds of desert creatures— a rustling of lizards, chirping birds, and the faint cry of an eagle, soaring high over mountain tors. So different from barking dogs and slamming car doors back home.

Crunching on gravel, they hike down the dirt driveway to the main road. Maggie sets a cracking pace, breathing in and of her mouth in gusty breaths in time to her steps. Diane's long legs a definite advantage. They smell the garbage collection point before they see it.

'A dollar a trash bag,' Maggie gloats. 'How cheap is that?'

Two small wood buildings, flanked by Ocotillo cactus, huddle close to ancient ash trees. American flags flutter patriotically from their roofs, the whitewashed library and Gateway Post Office ooze decaying pride. Originally a school, but the young people have long gone. Gateway reminds Diane of the retirement village, only here the houses are spread out, hidden within the vegetation and away from prying eyes. Maggie checks her post office box before mounting wooden steps leading into the cool recesses of the library.

Ginny, the librarian, hurries over and takes Maggie's backpack. As wide as she is long, her eyes sparkle when she grabs Diane's hand. Shaking it heartily, Indian beads dance on the t-shirt with the message: Behind every great man is a woman rolling her eyes.

Diane is once again an Australian friend. Maggie hurries over to her favourite Classics shelf to search for Catcher in the Rye. Diane, browsing for books discovers the library's public computer. She asks Ginny for the internet password and begins typing.

'There you are.' Maggie drops the book on the desk beside the keyboard. 'I've been looking everywhere for you.'

'Emails,' Diane says, beaming. 'I haven't been near a computer for a week, and they're stacked a mile high.'

Maggie glances at the screen, before hurrying off to ask Ginny about a book by Alice Brown.

Diane looks in dismay at the list of unattended mail: coursework to download, deadlines for her Lakeside and Postgrad Writers Groups, friends wanting to catch up and innumerable communal internet jokes. She vows to remove her email address from all joke lists, but doesn't want to hurt her friends. It is their way of keeping in touch. Better to delete them unread, although sometimes she is tempted to play a potentially funny video clip.

Maggie stands behind her. Several books in her arms.

'Ready?'

'In a minute.'

'We need to get back.'

'Won't be long,' Diane says, tapping furiously on the keyboard.

*

Maggie feels a stab in her heart. The similarity to Anna is uncanny. The blonde head bent over the keyboard, the intense face totally focused on the task in hand, oblivious to everything around her. Maggie would stand by the window of their New York apartment, searching for Anna's brassy, orange halo bobbing in a sea of brown, as she strides up the hill. Maggie would grab a book, drop into her armchair, pretend to be reading, but every sense tuned to the sound of the key in the lock.

'How was your day?' Maggie would say, holding her breath, knowing she could be greeted with either a smile and bright chatter, or a grunt and shaking plaster when her bedroom door slammed and the bolt shot home.

Night after night Maggie woke and saw the light shining under the door, Anna's constant raids on the refrigerator their only contact. Finally, she would emerge with red-rimmed eyes and blink as if seeing Maggie for the first time. She never allowed her to read her long stories or completed novels, but sometimes Maggie would sneak a peek. It helped her understand the wild swirls of paint erupting on the art class canvas. Ferocious fire and black despair in abstract confusion.

She always knew when things were not right with Anna. The locked bedroom door and the same tape over and over again. The sun has drowned in a deathly sea. Lyrics of misery and hopelessness. Lost in her own world for days, only to emerge to hurt and destroy.

Maggie's mind races back over the years. Lesbian? It explains the crew cut hair and denim overalls. Lack of male friends.

She would never tell them. What would Hank say? He wanted her genes to perpetuate his dynasty. Brilliant grandchildren to succeed and excel. How he revelled in the accolades, the incredibly high marks, the flashes of academic brilliance and consistently ignored Anna's weird behaviour.

Maggie tries to understand her eldest child. Reads every book she can about mental disorders. *You Never Promised Me a Rose Garden* the closest she comes to understanding Anna. Schizophrenic? Maybe. Manic depressive? Certainly. Every time she suggested a specialist, Anna would say, 'There's nothing wrong with me. Go see him yourself.' Barb knew to keep out of her way. Wounded too many times.

Maybe if she'd handled it better. Maybe...No. Maggie

shakes her head to clear it of memories. Feels the anger rising. She did the best she could at the time. Made her choices. Now, she has to live with them.

Maggie dumps the books into her backpack, waves goodbye to Ginny and marches outside.

*

'Hurry up, taxi's here.' Ron drags his suitcase to the front door.

In the bedroom, Diane folds the last t-shirt and places it into the suitcase on the bed. Why is it so hard to pack everything back into a case at the end of a trip? She hadn't bought much, but the case is overflowing. Maggie hurries into the room with several shirts and a pair of pants, tags dangling, draped over her arm. She hands them to Diane.

'They should fit.'

Diane recognises expensive Gore-Tex clothing. The same brand as Maggie wears on her trips to Africa. Always silently admired by Diane, but far beyond her budget.

'That's lovely of you, Maggie. But I can't take them.' She indicates her brimming case.

'Surely, you can fit them in. They pack down to nothing.' She places the clothes on top of the pile.

'I appreciate the thought, but...' Diane puts the clothes back onto the bed. Maggie grabs the pants.

'The legs zip off,' she says and demonstrates. Holding up shorts, she twists them to and fro. Suitcase wheels click clack past the bedroom door. A car door slams. Diane grabs the shorts and throws them into the case. Maggie stuffs the two severed pants legs into a small gap between some undies and sandals.

'And the shirts have vents under the arms.' Maggie shoves them into Diane's hands. 'Wonderful for hiking.'

'They are amazing, but—'

'No buts. Put them in.'

Diane hesitates. The taxi horn honks. She shoves the clothes inside, leans heavily on the lid and, with difficulty, zips the case secure. She'll worry about it being overweight when she gets to the airport.

Ron's head appears in the doorway. 'Get a move on,' he says before striding back down the hall.

Diane envelopes Maggie in a hug. Feels the brittle bones. 'I can't thank you enough—'

'Wait.' Maggie's hand grips her arm. Diane glances at the door expecting to see Ron's anxious face. She doesn't want him to have another heart attack.

'What is it?' She grabs the case.

Maggie's nails dig deep into her skin. 'There's something I have to tell you.'

Diane stops. Maggie's face tells her something is wrong.

'Anna is...' She hesitates.

'What about Anna?'

'She... isn't in Alaska.'

Diane straightens, rests the case back on the bed and waits to hear what comes next.

Maggie stares at her, trying to find the right words. Finally, she blurts out, 'She's dead.'

Diane shivers and, instinctively, her hand goes to the hollow in her chest just above her heart, and she drops onto the bed. 'When?'

'The fourteenth of April.' Maggie bows her head.

'Oh, Maggie. How terrible. How on earth have you managed to cope with this?'

Diane leans forward to embrace her friend, but Maggie holds up her hand.

'You don't understand. The fourteenth of April—1974.'

Outside, footsteps on gravel. Muffled voices. Ron's voice in casual conversation with the taxi driver.

'Before we met? The marriage? The new business?' Maggie doesn't answer.

'Why didn't you tell me?'

'I meant to.'

Diane shakes her head, 'You let me believe…'

Maggie looks pleadingly at Diane. 'In my letters to you, I still had Anna.'

Diane faces her. 'But all these years.'

'I'm so sorry.'

Diane's voice catches.'But I believed you. Believed what you wrote to me.' Tears sting her eyes as she snaps. 'Was anything you wrote true?

'It didn't seem a lie at the time,' Maggie pleads. 'I just wished it was true.'

'What else did you lie about?'

'You didn't always tell the truth,' Maggie snaps back.

Diane heaves the case off the bed. 'Stretched it maybe, but I never lied.'

'I'm sorry, Diane. It just happened. And once I'd started—'

'I feel such a fool. I trusted you.'

The taxi horn honks twice. Ron hurries in, his face flushed. Mopping beads of perspiration off his forehead with a handkerchief, he grabs the case out of Diane's hand and starts towards the door.

'Come on, you two,' he says impatiently. 'Taxi's waiting.'

At Kubunji Beach, Diane glances up from rinsing dishes in the double sink and stares at the picture-filled corkboard. How many times has she done this in the past, always with a sense of escape, a sense of adventure? Mentally joining Maggie riding an elephant through tall African grass, hiking Coyote Trail, dancing at an Indian Pueblo, munching crusty corn bread. But it is more than that. There are other photos. Maggie and her reading side by side, standing in front of a chilli-framed doorway, arms around each other's waist. Amigos. How had she been so easily deceived? Why hadn't she asked for photos of Anna?

She slowly removes the photos from the board and drops them into the rubbish bin. Ron scowls his disapproval.

'The old girl's in her eighties.'

'So?'

'Imagine carrying that grief for all those years. I think you're over-reacting.'

'For twenty-five years I believed her lies.'

Ron crosses his arms. 'Is that so bad?'

'I told everyone about Anna living in Alaska. About her husband, their life, the falling out with Maggie.' Diane draws indignation around her.

'In the book, I have Maggie with two daughters. I've workshopped sections at the writers' group—'

Ron gathers Diane in his arms. She pulls away.

'She was the one insisting on facts. For it to be true. Now, she's made me a liar too.'

*

Diane's Journal: Australia.

> *With so much time on his hands Ron has fallen under the spell of the woman next door. Dawn is now on her own and looking for company. You wonder if the study and academic journey is worth it. Do you want to live alone? Over the past decade, a number of your friends have been widowed or divorced. Did you want a life where you would end up alone? No! No! No! But you must finish your degree. You have come too far to give up now. It is so much a part of who you are. But you cannot live with a man who sees you as a hindrance. Who has no love for you in his heart. He can't have it all. He must choose between you both.*

*

3/19/2001

> *I'm sorry I didn't tell you, Diane, but Anna's death was too raw. I couldn't say I only had one daughter when I'd had two. Letting you believe she was still alive helped*

202

*keep her alive for me. Let me imagine what her life might
have been like if she had lived. Put yourself in my place.
What if it had been Kerry? What would you have done?
Please write.*

Maggie reaches for the envelope. Will Diane open her
letter, or toss it in the trash can? She hasn't answered the last
two, or returned her calls. She checks the contents of her post
office box hoping to see Diane's handwriting below colorful,
Australian stamps. Ginny keeps asking after her.

She misses Diane's letters, full of fun and domestic
details. Of sunshine when outside there is ice on the ground.
Of soft-footed kangaroos when Maggie hears a dying jack
rabbit scream.

*

Diane sighs as she flicks through the mail. Nothing different.
Just the usual advertising leaflets for carpet cleaning, and real
estate agents offering to sell their house. Glancing out the
window at clouds reflected in blue water and three pelicans
waddling along the beach, she screws up the leaflet. Throws it
in the bin. She sighs at a letter from Red Energy, obviously a
bill, and one from Civic Compliance. Either Ron or her caught
by a speed camera. Probably her. Life is hectic lately. She
always seems to be preparing lessons for her creative writing
students, racing to Sandston University, or the shops, or
Ron's doctor's appointments. He keeps telling her to slow
down. Telling her she is a lead foot.

At the bottom of the pile is a familiar striped Par Avion
aerogram with American stamps. It tugs at her heart. She's no
longer angry, or upset. It's just that some unspoken bond of
trust has been broken, and she doesn't have the same joy or
interest in reading about Gateway any more. Maggie's last
three letters all the same. How the lie kept the dream alive.
Should she offer the olive branch? After all there are many
deep dark secrets she has not revealed to Maggie.

Diane glances at the cork noticeboard. Alongside a newspaper clipping featuring Elizabeth Jolley in her grey cardigan, there is one photo of Maggie. The strong face is pensive, arms folded on her lap, lines etched deep into her face.

What would she have done if, heaven forbid, Kerry had died? Diane shudders. To lose a child is unimaginable grief. But to be part of a lie for twenty-five years? She feels a fool. How easily deceived. Never questioning, believing everything Maggie told her was fact.

Even with The Book. She argued with Maggie, fought tooth and nail to be able to use her imagination. Call it fiction. Maggie insisting that every minute factual detail be recorded. What a laugh, when all the time, she was living a lie.

*

Diane's journal: Australia

> *From now on, you will allow your imagination to fill the gaps. It will no longer be Maggie's story, or Diane's. For so long you have dithered between fact and fiction, not knowing the boundaries, trying to balance between a hymn of praise to Maggie and a genuine warts-and-all account of your long friendship. Hopefully now, it will reach beyond auto/biography and become a story about women's lived experiences. Moving into fiction will give you a creative freedom you have never had before.*

*

Diane knows she should forgive, that Maggie is old. Knows she should pick up the phone and pretend it never happened. After all, she guessed both of them shared a common problem. Both had been abused by selfish men. Should she contact Maggie? Share with her the buried childhood abuse? It could bring them closer together. Shared experiences usually did. But why leave herself open to be deceived again? What would she, could she say? Maybe one day...Why not send a bright breezy postcard from a conference? Anyway texting and emails has made letters a thing of the past. Diane opens her laptop, signs in and checks her emails.

To: Diane Simpson <dsimpson@yahoo.com.au>
Subject: Premier's Awards

Dear Diane Simpson,

I am delighted to inform you that your manuscript,
Valerie G, has been shortlisted in the Victoria Premier's
Literary Award for an Unpublished Manuscript. The...

She reads the email several times, before dissolving into tears of joy. Her mother's story finally accepted.

Diane glances at the cork board. Elizabeth Jolley, first-time author at fifty-five. What would she think of Diane? I'm older and don't own a grey cardigan, Diane whispers. Elizabeth smiles down in a whimsical way.

'You've got mail,' Ron calls, throwing a stack of letters on the table.

Diane reads the Victorian Premier's invitation and shivers with delight. Ron sips coffee, black and strong.

'Any tea cake left?'

She shakes her head.

'Come with me?' She shows him the invitation. He raises his eyebrows and rattles the sweet biscuit tin.

'It's the Premier's Literary Awards presentation night.'

His eyebrows lift higher. 'Are you serious,' he says.

She nods.

Shaking his head, he opens the newspaper. 'Not my scene.'

Diane sighs, but doesn't give up and appeals to his addiction to movies.

'It's the academy awards of the literary world.' He doesn't look up. 'And dinner is included.'

He laughs. 'Forget it. You're not getting me into a monkey suit.'

*

*You raid your wardrobe and drag out the peacock blue,
pure silk jacket you had made for a wedding. It still looks
great, even over your t-shirt and jeans. It will be perfect
over black slacks and top. The matching scarf and bag
the finishing touches. Finding a padded hanger, you
hang the jacket on the bedroom doorknob, stand back
and look at it. It's still fashionable, and will certainly
save a fortune. But this is your big moment. You will be
mixing with interesting, influential people. Without a
partner beside you, you will need to feel confident. At
least look like an author, whatever that means. You run
downstairs, grab your purse, drive to Southland
Shopping Centre and buy a stunning black-and-green
flowing jacket. To hell with the cost. You will sashay into
that room and enjoy every minute.*

*

The train rattles into Flinders Street Station. Diane joins the throng of Saturday night revelers. Gaggles of shrill girls in skimpy dresses totter on outrageously high heels down crowded streets. They remind her of plovers strutting the beach, calling their mates.

Trams clatter past, but tonight, Diane hails a taxi.

'The Sofitel.' With a grin she settles back in the seat.

The taxi sweeps into the forecourt of bud-lit potted palms, glitz and glamour. A doorman swings open the door and, in true Hollywood style, Diane alights one foot at a time. Feeling like Scarlett O'Hara, she sweeps up the staircase and into the atrium. If only Rhett Butler was beside her. If only Ron had changed his mind.

She is early, but deliberately so. She wants to savour this special occasion. To see and even meet the Crème De La Crème of her literary world. Helen Garner, Brian Castro, Andrea Goldsmith, Tim Winton, to name a few. To have her name on the same program is a dream come true.

Dinner is served, cutlery clinks, expensive wines flow and the awards begin. First the keynote speaker, then The Vance Palmer Prize, Alfred Deakin Prize until finally,

The nominations for an unpublished manuscript are, Caroline Robin, *Nature's Gap*. Maria Maionchi, *Maria's Choice*. Diane Simpson, *Valerie G.*

Diane crosses her fingers. The envelope is opened. She holds her breath.

And the winner is...

Diane didn't win but remains optimistic. She is happy to have made it this far. To be shortlisted validates her as a writer and might tempt a publisher to take a punt on *Valerie G.* She makes a vow: The day a publisher accepts her manuscript, she will give up hairdressing. She just wants a book to hold.

*

Five a.m. Maggie hits the alarm button on the silver clock before her ears are blasted. Why does she set it? Eighty-six years of rising at five a habit. The sun forces heat through the crack between sill and open pane. It is hot, but not too hot. Not yet. By late afternoon, stucco-adobe walls and Madonna blue gates weather and crack. An owl, winging home, screeches to its mate, wind rustles sun-baked grass, and there is the familiar chuk, chuk, chuk whaaas of a covey of quails. Throwing back the sheet, she sits on the side of the bed and blows a kiss to Ndume, her silverback gorilla, his image forever captured and framed. His wise eyes penetrate her soul. Two antiques, bound together by fate after a chance meeting in Rwanda. Is he dead now? Murdered by poachers?

She spreads a thick Indian rug on the terracotta floor. Half an hour of exercise always puts her into a positive frame of mind. What other eighty-six year old can do twenty back rolls, twenty sit-ups and twenty full-body push-ups...at least ten on their fingers? She may be short and fubsy, but even Diane thinks she's a fit old girl.

The coffee percolator burps. Outside the kitchen window, pesky musk hogs grunt and snuffle under a mesquite bush, searching for tender roots before the Arizona sun dries them crisp. Hank's wristwatch tells Maggie to hurry. Pete will be waiting. She grabs her peaked cap and hiking sticks then step out into the heat and dust of another desert day. The Chiricahua Mountains glow in the distance, shadows quickly recede from the tors. The crossroad is empty, and she sits on a boulder until she sees Pete's lumbering, Texas-born frame.

'Sorry to be late,' he says, pointing to his left sneaker. 'Goddamn sore toe.'

They stroll down Cave Creek road and chat about Barb and the two dogs, Santa Fe, their grandchildren and the latest developments at the Gateway Research Station. An ancient juniper tree marks their mutual limit. She pats its rough bark before turning for home.

The phone rings. Maggie leaves Cheerios crackling in milk. Pete's voice is urgent. 'Put on your TV.'

'Why?'

'Just turn it on. We'll talk later.' The phone dies.

Maggie is transfixed. New York's twin towers spew smoke. The commentator's high-pitched voice sputters in the background. Plane hits. Thousands dead. Flames lick a black slit near the top of the north tower, papers flutter from broken windows, smoke mushrooms into the sky, helicopters circle like desperate bees watching the destruction of their hive.

This is New York. Her home for over thirty years. She grieves for the poor souls who work in those towers. Eight forty-five in the morning most are at their desk, sipping coffee or gathered by the water cooler. Talking about their children, office scandals and the photocopier that doesn't work. 'Goddamnit,' she mutters remembering her old friend Manny has his office near there.

How did two planes end up wedged into the side of those towers on the tip of Manhattan? The TV spits out statistics. How many people have died? The guessing continues. Four thousand, maybe five? Commentators grab scraps of news. Try to make sense of the unimaginable.

The south tower caves in. The second tower crumples. A thick, choking grey dust cloud billows up Liberty Street, enveloping people as they run. A deliberate, planned attack. Terrorists. The word chills her to the bone. Al-Qaeda. Osama bin Laden. Bush has a lot to answer for. She knows the history.

The image plays over and over again from every possible angle. A black-suited figure nosedives head first from the north tower. In mid-flight, he twists, sits, rolls and plummets one hundred stories, destined to repeat it a thousand times on TV. Maggie walks away, as the barp barp of fire engines, whistles, screams and loud exclamations spill into her sitting room. If only she could turn back the clock to five a.m. Back to the screech of an owl.

The pall of shock and disbelief enveloping New York spreads around the world.She punches the 'off' button. Blessed silence fills the room. Outside everything is the same. The mountain tors glow gold against a deep blue sky. What would the last Chiricahua Apache think of this catastrophe? Every day, proud Purple Plume, wrapped in his blanket stood on the highest tor, hand sheltering aged eyes gazing across his vast land. A warrior. A survivor of tribal battles and conflict with white settlers over scarce resources and the ownership of land. Personal battles, man to man. You knew your enemy.

She brushes away tears with the back of her hand. President Bush and his inane policies. There's so much machismo going on in the world. When she tips out soggy Cheerios, her hand shakes.

Outside, the sun shines. Nature's cycle continues. Birds

sing, rattlesnakes curl in the shade and the ditch is dry. She wipes her eyes. Nothing will be the same again. Maggie glances at the clock. Nine-thirty.a.m. Sixteen hours ahead, Diane is asleep, unaware that the known world has changed forever. Lucky her. The ramifications of this tragedy will soon hit Australia's shores.

*

Ten-thirty p.m. Diane folds the last of the ironing and glances at the TV. John Wayne lumbers across the screen, both barrels blazing. True Grit. Ron is stretched out on the couch, remote control in hand, watching a cow-hand beg for mercy.

'Coming to bed? '

'In a minute. This is the big shoot out.' Ron pats the seat beside him. Diane has seen this movie countless times. Can almost quote it word for word. What is the fascination with the American Wild West? Countless 'classic movies' have emerged from the era of gunslingers, bandits and Indian wars and taciturn, dangerous men.

Diane flops onto the couch and rests aching legs on the ottoman. Tom Chaney tips back his Stetson, hand hovering over his gun. John Wayne's lip curls. He rocks on the balls of his feet. Diane slowly mutters, 'You better believe it, pilgrim.'

Ron laughs and rubs the nape of her neck. 'Tired?'

She nods. The video credits scroll down the screen. Ron flicks to channel nine. There might be some late night news.

Diane's heart lurches as she watches the twin towers fall. Someone has attacked America. Thousands of innocent people have died. All she can think about is Maggie. How devastated she will be She used to write about New York and the people she knew there. It was her home for twenty-five years. Diane tries to ring but she can't get through. She'll try again tomorrow.

Diane pours coffee from the percolator into an extra large mug: the one with the Christmas tree design.

210

Wrapping a woolly dressing gown close, she steps out into the cold, early morning air. Rainclouds smother roofs. No hope of a glorious sunrise painting the sky pink today. She has a close connection with America and its people that began long before she met Maggie. Stories her dad told of World War Two driving trucks loaded with medical supplies and food to American army bases all over Victoria.

Her mum, sleeves rolled to her elbows, baked dozens of scones to fill hungry bellies. The next-door neighbour's three teenage daughters appreciated gifts of nylon stockings as 'scarce as hen's teeth'. Mary, the gorgeous one with big blue eyes, received more than her fair share ostentatiously ran a licked finger up a back seam to check it was straight.

Photos in the family album of gum-chewing, brash young men with cheeky grins and knife-pleated caps. Australian and American sailors travelling from Melbourne to Crib Point, relaxing at her parent's rambling old house beside the Stony Point train line. A perfect halfway point to sleep it off overnight, even if it was beside the fishpond, after a night on the town.

A photo of Navajo Steve playing cricket in the backyard. Where is he now? Later, Maggie's letters revealed a hidden world of literature, and Purple Plume's Chiricahau Mountains towering over a hamlet called Gateway.

A finger of sunlight pokes beneath lifting clouds. Plovers call. It has been a long night. Many times today, she will see the twin towers fall. A gentle breeze rustles palm leaves and boats bob beside jetties. The early morning light catches the gold and silver necklace around her neck. Instinctively, Diane strokes the strands.

*

> *The tragedy of the terrorist attack and to see the twin*
> *towers fall puts all of life into perspective. You can*
> *understand everything that is happening in your life: the*
> *study and why getting your doctorate is so important,*
> *why those academic put downs hit home, why you have*
> *to prove something to yourself and why you don't want it*
> *to cost your marriage. But even that is beyond you now.*
> *There has been a diagnosis next door of terminal cancer.*
> *And there is Maggie... always there is Maggie.*

*

All Maggie sees on television are images of tortured metal, and emotional eyewitness accounts clog the airways. She can't turn on the television without hearing the *Star Spangled Banner* or *God Bless America* sung, played or strummed. She cringes at a photo of a fire fighter placing an American flag on a pile of rubble in a deliberate replication of the famous flag-raising on Mount Suribachi on Iwo Jima. Is the nation gearing up for war? Her pen skims across the page, the writing ragged. She doesn't care.

2/20/2002

> *Diane, the more this goes on, the more I worry and the*
> *more anti-organised religion I become. I am patriotic, but*
> *I don't want to see 'God Bless America' emblazoned on*
> *billboards at every corner or stamped on my drugstore*
> *receipts. There is an excess of flag waving. It reminds me*
> *of Samuel Johnson's observation, 'Patriotism is the last*
> *refuge of scoundrels'.*
>
> *I also fear we will not be able to make critical remarks*
> *about the government or the president without becoming*
> *suspect. Bush is an idiot with foreign policies to match.*
> *Will I be incarcerated for chanting this limerick? Mr.*

Maggie reads through the letter, putting a comma here, full stop there, then scrunches it into a ball and throws it in the trash can. One phone call from Diane is not enough to mend all bridges. She begins again, this time she leaves her political opinions out and concentrates on the safer ground of books she has read and writers she admires.

*

Pigeons flutter to coo and peck at Diane's feet. She shakes the last muffin crumbs out of the paper bag and looks at her watch. Five minutes before the bus arrives. Five minutes to bask in spring sunshine before making her way to Sandston University. She coughs, blows her nose, but nothing will clear her nasal passages of petrol fumes from the continuous ebb and flow of cars around her bus stop island in front of the supermarket car park.

The twelve forty-five Warrigal Road bus hits the kerb when it pulls into Mordialloc. Diane groans. Cowboy is at the wheel. No hope of writing during the trip today. It is not just his distinctive cowboy hat, or the way he twirls his mobile phone and 'holsters' it in his side pocket, but the way he tailgates and bullies the cars in front, and pulls back on the steering wheel when forced to stop. Passengers barely have a foot on solid ground before he lurches off, bumps over the kerb to force his way into the stream of traffic. Regulars know to hang on tight when he is at the wheel.

Diane grabs her satchel and jumps clear of the door. She must not be late for supervision with Jason Walder. She calls him Mr. Do-able. His students huddle around, and he convinces them that anything is possible. He is considered the highly motivational 'football' coach of the creative writing world and he has agreed to read her manuscript.

The traffic lights turn green. Across the busy intersection, the main entrance to Sandston University is roped with blue-and-white-checked crime scene tape. Hoses snake across wet concrete looking for prey. Fire personnel drench white-hooded, space-suited rescue workers, standing legs apart, arms outstretched. Police cars block the side road, blue lights flash. Diane pulls up the collar of her jacket and hurries to join the students sheltering from the cold wind in the heated comfort of McDonalds. Threading her way to the counter, she orders a Mc-latte.

What on earth's happened? she asks the trainee, who flicks a stray strand of lank hair out of her eyes.

Anthrax, she replies. Do you want fries with that?

Juggling her polystyrene-cupped latte, Diane pushes through the crowd, trying to find a seat. A youth stands. She smiles her thanks and sinks onto the stool. There are some advantages to being a mature aged student. You are often mistaken for a lecturer. It is inconceivable to some students that anyone with wrinkles would study, just for the love of it. The door opens and a blast of cold air chills the room. A collective whisper runs through the crowd.

False alarm, the student next to her says. Talcum powder in the envelope. His smile stretches from ear to ear. The creative writing building is closed for today. Diane is disappointed to miss her appointment with Mr. Do-able, but as Maggie would say, there is always an unseen benefit. Cowboy is not driving the bus on the hour-long trip home.

*

The paper crown on Maggies head tips over one eye. Junella quickly straightens it.

'Smile.' Junella points the camera. Flash, flash. 'Hold it.' Maggie plants the smile back on her face. Flash, flash. Blanche lights the candles on a large sponge cake. Maggie is afraid the icing will melt. The Cochise writers gather around her and lustily sing. All this fuss over being ninety. What's the big deal about living that long?

8/9/2007

> *It's very strange, Diane. I'm not morbid, but I think often of death. And oddly, it's because I feel good. When I was angry and depressed in Santa Fe, I found myself wishing to die and get out of life. But here, where I am happy and want to live, which I frequently consider a selfish wish, I do think of death.*
>
> *At this very moment, I think I know why. Because I am healthy, I find myself making, in my mind, ridiculous plans. I hear of trips going to some great place in five years and want to sign up. Then, reality sets in. I may not be alive then. Quite true. That's why I think of death, and it doesn't scare me at all. Like everyone (who does think of it) I hope for a quick and easy one. An assisted one, if necessary.*
>
> *I am amazed at the number of people who don't want to talk about it, or make plans. I know I'm not as strong or agile as I used to be and, yes, there are always accidents. I'm aware of the need to pay attention to driving or moving about the house, but my mind does wander and, fortunately, considering the world's population, no one can live forever. Now that's a happy thought.*

One day a colorful postcard of Sydney Harbour Bridge arrives in her mailbox. Brief, chatty words in Diane's familiar handwriting, bridging the gap between them.

Ginny sits beside Maggie in front of the library's computer. She peers at the screen. A small black mark flashes. Ginny nods, and Maggie begins to type,

Dear Diane, Maybe I should call you dsimpson@yahoo? Kind Ginny has set up this email account for me at the library, but I still don't know what I am doing.

*

Diane breathes a sigh of relief. It is so much easier to communicate with Maggie this way. She has to admire the effort. Quite an achievement for a ninety year old. Maggie can't grasp how to create a new email, but at least she can click the reply button and send an answer.

From: Diane Simpson

Sent: 10th October 2008

To: Maggie Jackson <libGateway@yahoo.com>
Subject: Amazing

Dear Maggie,
    You are amazing. I couldn't believe the email was from you. I'm so pleased Ginny is there to help. Emails are a great way to keep in touch.

Diane finishes the email and clicks send. Rubbing aching shoulders, she sighs. Enough emails for today.

*

Diane's Journal: Australia.

You feel guilty when Maggie asks for a newsy, handwritten letter, but there just isn't time. You forward the odd internet jokes and pages of literary fun that argue that English speakers are verbally insane. Strange plays on words, such as, we recite at a play, and play at a recital. Ship by truck, and send cargo by ship. You flick

216

them off to Maggie, who shares them with her writing group friends. Life is busy and you seldom lick a stamp these days, but you constantly email. How easy it is to send quick snippets of news, and stay in touch.

You understand Ron's dilemma. He has been trying to have it both ways these days but that doesn't work. Not for you anyway. You don't write, or talk to anyone, apart from Kerry. She listens, tries to help but this is something you must sort out for yourself,

*

'Coming to bed?' Ron calls. 'It's past eleven.'

Diane feels guilty when she hears the bedside lamp click off, but turns to the final task. Just one more email to open before she can call it a day.

To: Diane Simpson <dsimpson@yahoo.com.au>
Subject: Valerie G

Dear Diane Simpson,
I am delighted to inform you that your manuscript, Valerie G, has won the Winton Press International Fiction Quest.

Winton Press
12 Duberry Lane
Victoria, Australia

*

Diane can't stop smiling. The Melbourne Writers' Festival is in full swing and the marquee at the old Sugar House buzzes with excitement. Winton Press have placed posters featuring the launch of *Valerie G* in prominent places. Diane weighs the book in her hands, admires the cover. She hugs her mother's story tight. Revels in the feeling of having stepped over some obscure literary line. Her brother has already pointed out that she is not a J.K. Rowling. Already he wants to know how many books she will sell, what is the profit margin and suggested not giving up her day job. So what if this is not another Harry Potter success story? The glow of satisfaction and joy is indescribable.

Sitting beside her university supervisor, who will introduce her as The Author, Diane's knees shake. Every chair is taken, but they are people she knows: family, friends, the Lakeside Writers' Group, postgraduate group and many others. With so many supportive familiar faces, all fear of public speaking falls away. These people are here because they care. She blesses them all and wishes Maggie sat in the front row. This journey began with her. She was the one who made Diane think, search for answers, look up words. The catalyst of this incredible journey.

Diane stands in front of the microphone and opens *Valerie G.*

*

8/22/2008

*Dear Diane, I'm sending you a real letter because
yesterday, I nearly drove Ginny out of her mind. I tried
three times to email you and lost it each time. How I wish
I could be with you, but I'm with you in spirit and as
proud of you as if you were my daughter. Just don't get
caught up in all the hype.*

*Today was our writers' group meeting. They all asked
after you and send you their heartiest congratulations.
Halfway through the morning, Blanche asked us to write
for fifteen minutes without lifting our pen. I wrote
something stupid, for it's hard for me to write on
command. I should have written about hugging a tree in
Botswana and apologising to it because one of my kind
had carved initials in its lovely skin. Still makes me
furious to think about it. One gal, a new member, wrote
an excellent piece. She is going to mail me a copy since*

*she lives quite far out of town and doesn't come to the
post office everyday as I do.*

*I'm still walking daily (6.a.m.) with Pete, but I limit
the distance to just over a mile. Partly because of the
beastly heat and also some arthritis. Today, Pete and I
had to look out for traffic. Pete said if it gets any worse,
he will have to move. I said 'Where'?*

*Have you read any of Barbara Kinsolver's books? I
hadn't, for some reason, but I took 'The Poisonwood Bible'
out of the library and was so impressed by it that I've
bought a paperback copy to send to you. Then I started
on her earlier works. Gad, she is so talented.*

*

At the Qantas boarding gate every seat is full. Cranky toddlers run endlessly up and down luggage-laden aisles, suck their thumbs or scream and struggle in their mother's arms.

*Attention all passengers on Qantas 477 travelling from
Melbourne, via Sydney to Los Angeles. Due to mechanical
problems, your flight has been delayed.*

A collective groan rises from the waiting crowd.

Diane glances at her watch. Three hours to fill. She strides over to the newspaper stand, glances at the titles of several books, ignoring the copies of Valerie G. Finally settling on *We Need to Talk about Kevin*, she makes her way to the counter, handing the shop assistant the exact change.

'Have a nice day.' The sales girl takes another look at Diane. 'Aren't you the author of...' She points to the stack of featured novels. Diane nods.

'I loved it,' she says, placing Michael Shriver's book into a plastic bag. Diane smiles her thanks, flips her long scarf over her shoulder and heads for the Qantas First Lounge.

The New York bookstore is filled to overflowing. People sit cross-legged on the floor. All clutch copies of *Valerie G.* Diane grabs both sides of the podium, prepared speech ready. So many hopeful faces. How many have novels stuffed in bottom drawers? They look at her with anticipation. She can see the thought: If she can do it, so can I.

Diane taps the microphone, adjusts the position and smiles. She imagines she is in the Eltham Regional Library talking to a group of friends.

*

Diane's Journal: Australia

> *You forget the formal speech, and talk about the passion of writing. Of jotting notes in an exercise book and the advantage of reading, and learning from other writers. How to smile and keep typing after the seventeenth rejection. The benefit of writing classes, writing groups and university courses. You share how researching and writing the novel became a journey of self discovery. Emphasise the invaluable support of others. You talk about Maggie.*
>
> *Your watch shows you still have seven minutes left. They wait for you to continue. Deciding to recount an anecdote, you launch into the story of the time you were in the middle of the editing process, tripped over a mat and broke your right wrist. You unconsciously rub the spot.*

*

In plaster up to her elbow, Diane paces the floor. The last chapter of the novel still unedited, the launch of *Valerie G* a month away, and she can't type. Kerry arrives, flowers in one hand and a box in the other.

'Try this.' Kerry holds up the box titled *Dragon Naturally Speaking*. 'It's a speech-activated computer program.'

Two hours later, Diane sits in front of her computer, headphones clamped to her ears, the attached microphone curved in front of her mouth. A good imitation of a telephone switchboard operator. Or a performing rock star.

'Just tell the computer what you want to type, Mum.'

'This is great,' Diane says. Delight turns to amazement when 'This is great' magically types across the screen. She laughs.

'HA,haaa haaaa, haaaaaaaaaaaaaaaa' appears.

She learns to voice punctuate by chanting. Full stop. Comma, Capital T. Scratch that. Bracket that, etc.

Diane relaxes in the chair, confident the novel will be ready in time.

But it was not all smooth sailing. There are problems. Once she told the program to type, *Dulcie struggled to escape her restrictive culture.* Dragon printed *Dulcie struggled to escape her restrictive cold chair.* And the time she dictated a letter to Maggie, telling her how much she enjoyed being a guest speaker, concluding with, I had a *terrific time in Yarrawonga.* Dragon printed that she'd had a *horrific time in Rwanda.* After that, Kerry did most of the typing.

Encouraged by the swell of laughter, Diane waves a copy of her book above her head.

'As you can see, *Valerie G* made the deadline.'

In her room in the Hilton Hotel, Diane kicks off her shoes and sighs. It has been an exhausting week of author signing from Miami to Washington, New York and Boston. She checks her diary. Finally, the rat race is over. Time to head off for some R&R. Time to visit Maggie.

*

2009: Gateway Arizona

Diane dodges slow-moving commuters and races past passengers using the moving boardwalk in the Albuquerque airport terminal. The wonky wheels on her pull along case click and clack. She glances at her watch. One p.m. Drawing a deep breath, she lets it go with a gusty sigh. A strong headwind from New York has resulted in an hour's delay. Barb will be waiting in the basement car park of the Grand Hotel.

'It's cooler for the dogs,' she said on the phone. 'Give me a ring as soon as you arrive.'

Frantically pressing keys, Diane tries to use her mobile phone, but the international roaming hasn't worked since she arrived. When she finds a public phone, her haste makes the required coins nearly miss the slot. They clatter into the change receptacle underneath. She takes a deep breath. Surely Barb understands that airlines are often delayed.

Using quarters, rather than dimes and nickels, Diane tries a second, third and fourth time. She wants to kick the phone, pound it with her fist and shout, 'work, damn you, work,' but to no avail. If she had taken the bus to Gateway, she wouldn't be in this predicament. All she wants is five days on her own with Maggie. For the first time in their lives, they can ignore family commitments, chat, laugh and share memories. They'll sit on the old church pew on the front porch, watching the sun set behind the mountains and laughing at squabbling pigeons scratching in the dust. But Barb had argued that the trip to Gateway was too far, too difficult, and she had to see her mother anyway.

'You see,' Barb had said on the phone,' if I take you, I can bring food down and do the cooking for you both. My mother essentially eats micro meals, which are very salty. In exchange for that, maybe I could go hiking for a few hours, while you keep an eye on the dogs.'

And now, because of the blasted delay, Diane has to worry about the two dogs stuck in a hot car.

Her case clacks through the exit doors and a blast of heat adds to her rising panic. Are the dogs dehydrating? Oh well, she is in America and hot dogs are part of the scene. Diane smiles at the flippant thought, glad she is regaining her sense of humour. It has been an exhausting day. A woman standing next to her talks on her mobile phone. When she finishes, Diane asks if she can use it to make a call.

'Where are you from?' the woman asks.

'Australia.' To forestall a lengthy conversation, Diane

explains that Barb has already waited over an hour. When the woman hands over her phone, Diane nervously flicks back her hair and beams her thanks. What Maggie said is true. People in New Mexico are a friendly bunch.

The battered Nissan Pathfinder pulls into the arrivals bay. Barb's mouth is set in a firm line. The hug is brief. She grabs Diane's case and lifts up the back of the 4x4. It is crammed to the roof. Portable coolers at the bottom, bulging garbage bags overlaid with bedding. A fox terrier, asleep in a cage, opens one eye. Barb holds up a finger in warning. When she shoves Diane's case on top of the wire before slamming the door, he doesn't bark. Barb's top-dog status confirmed.

Diane pushes a bottle of water and several bags to one side with her foot, then hoists herself into the passenger's seat.

'This reminds me of the time I met your mum in outback Australia.' She tries to move the seat back. 'We had to pack everything but the kitchen sink. Are you staying a month?'

'I always have to restock Moth-er's fridge.' Barb stares at the twisted gold and silver strands of Diane's necklace. Her face hardens. 'And she hasn't enough bedding for you.'

Diane squirms in her seat. For the second time in ten minutes, she feels she has inconvenienced Barb.

'How is Maggie?'

'Moth-er is well, but very forgetful. I have to ring her daily, or she wouldn't cope.'

Diane expects changes in Maggie's appearance and health, but her last email was clear and concise. Her current theme the environmental destruction of the planet, and she has George Bush firmly in her sights.

'I hope I'm as good when I'm over ninety,' she replies.

The seat is so far forward, Diane's chest is two inches from the dashboard. A bulky garbage bag behind her headrest threatens to tumble forward. Hopefully, Barb will not brake too hard. Something slimy drops onto Diane's shoulder. There is a panting sound and a musty animal smell behind her left ear. She turns her head and looks directly into curious brown eyes. A kelpie cross, tongue lolling, sits on a cushion on top of a pile of bedding level with Diane's head. A long dribble of drool stretches to Diane's shoulder. She moves closer to the passenger door.

After what seems an eternity, Barb speaks. 'Good trip?' Without waiting for an answer, she grinds the gears, grips the wheel and they speed off over the overpass, through town then onto the Interstate Highway. Barb's face is taut, her knuckles white. She is leaner. Not one ounce of excess fat. Her face is more angular, as if the skin has been stretched tighter over the bones. Diane regrets the bars of chocolate responsible for her 'love handles', although Ron doesn't complain about the extra kilos. He wouldn't dare. Barb's luxurious hair, gripped in an elastic band at the nape of her neck, hangs to her waist, swaying when she leans forward and looks from left to right. Well brushed and shiny, it must still be her pride and joy, even with the streaks of grey. Who does Barb take after? Definitely not Maggie in stature or features. Barb has Hank's height, but that's where the resemblance ends.

'We'll stop at McDonalds.' Barb grinds the gears. 'Give the dogs a break.'

Diane dreams of a Big Mac with extra pickle. Leaving too early for the sumptuous breakfast at the Hilton she's only eaten an in-flight takeaway bowl of instant noodles.

'I have vouchers for free thick shakes.' Barb dives her hand into the side pocket of the car to produce two dockets. 'That should see us through.'

A deep-throated growl followed by a sharp bark, makes Diane jump. Matilda, pricked ears turning like radar, has spotted grazing cattle. The dog barks at any moving animal, but cows are top of the list and require a more vocal warning.

'Matilda is so clever.' Barb beams her approval. 'She won the Talented Dog section at the Santa Fe Dog Show. I made her a pink tutu, and she stands on her hind legs and spins.'

Diane smiles her interest, but her back is killing her. She is grateful that Barb's mood is lighter even if the conversation is only about the dogs.

At MacDonalds, Barb hands the small dog's lead to Diane who can hardly stand. Her right leg is numb, which is more than she can say for her back. If only she could get some painkillers out of her suitcase, but one look at Barb is all she needs to change her mind. The small dog, called Imp, pulls and tugs, aiming for a straggly tree. The landscape is a dustbowl and the heat intense. Sweat beads on Diane's forehead, but she would face the fires of hell to stand and stretch. The dogs back in the car, Barb hurries into MacDonald's.

Diane's nose quivers at the smell of an all beef patties on sesame seed buns. Although she hadn't insisted on having a Big Mac, she will definitely have a whinge about the seat.

Maybe they can rearrange the luggage. Maybe she can move the seat back before Barb returns. Diane slides her right hand along the base of the seat until she finds the adjustment button. She tries to move the back of the seat into a less upright position. It refuses to budge. There is too much pressure from the luggage behind.

Barb shoves a thick-shake through the window, They wouldn't honour the vouchers, she says. Diane offers to pay, offers to buy coffee, or a burger, but Barb refuses. Diane winces as Barb says,' Make yourself comfortable. It's eight hours to Gateway.'

The headlights cast shadows amongst the mesquite bushes on either side of the mile-long gravel drive. Animal eyes gleam then fade. The small adobe house with its high-pitched roof comes into view. Maggie waits under the porch light. She hurries to the driver's door.

'Why didn't you call me?' Maggie's brow is creased with worry. Barb mutters something and lets the dogs out.

Like a giant bear, Diane wraps her arms around the short

fragile frame. Maggie is smaller, more stooped, the osteoporosis hump obvious under the African shirt. Her short, curly hair is grey, the face more lined, but her smile is genuine.

The dogs bark their delight at being free. Refusing to participate in the joyous reunion, Barb unloads the car.

Maggie grabs Diane's arm and hurries towards the door. 'It's good to see you. Remember when—'

'Moth-er,' Barb calls.

The kitchen is a chaos of boxes, bedding and food, all unloaded with military precision.

'Put this here. That there. That goes in the refrigerator, Moth-er. Not that one, the one in the garage. Don't put that bag on the coffee table.'

Diane stops what she is doing like a guilty schoolgirl and winces.

'It will scratch. Dad made that table and it's worth a lot of money,' Barb said.

*

Diane's Journal: Australia.

> *The topic of money came up frequently on your drive*
> *from the airport. Barb mentions that she can't afford to*
> *go to a hairdresser, or buy more than two coffees a week.*
> *Then there were the complaints about how Maggie made*
> *poor investment decisions without consulting Barb and is*
> *not looking after their Gateway home. You just nodded,*
> *offering a brief word now and again, when given the*
> *chance, especially when Barb said that she had to shout*
> *because her mother was deaf. You commiserated*
> *because Ron has two hearing aids and you told Barb*
> *hearing loss was just a part of growing older. You wanted*
> *to say more, but decided against it.*

*

When all has been sorted, stacked and put away, Diane closes the bedroom door and sighs. How will they all get on together for the next five days? Diane must be up and dressed by 5:30 am in readiness for the 6 am walk up Cave Creek Road. Will she be able to sleep? Diane laughs at the thought of Ron counting knots in the ceiling. Misses his laughter, wishes he was here. This is not going to be the relaxed reunion she imagined.

Heaving her case onto the big double bed, she finds a couple of spare hangers in the wardrobe. The size fourteen t-shirts and bulky jackets, too big for Maggie, must belong to Barb. Diane pushes the clothes back along the rail and hangs up her shirts. The rest of her stuff goes into an empty chest of drawers under the window. Had Barb cleared out her things to make space for her, or is this kept for guests?

The room is as neat as a new pin, and Diane wants to keep it that way. She would have willingly taken the couch in the lounge, but Barb insisted on giving her the room. Diane is glad she did. Having a room to retreat to will be her salvation. But the thought of Barb on the uncomfortable couch takes the joy away.

'I'll be all right.' Barb throws a pillow onto the couch. 'Don't worry about me.'

On the big double bed, watching the ceiling fan circulate hot air, Diane absentmindedly smooths the sheet beside her. She misses Ron's familiar shape. It is early morning in Australia. He is sitting on the side of the bed, planning the day. Was it fifteen years since the shock of Ron's retrenchment?

That Tuesday, he started work as usual at 7:00 a.m. When everyone had arrived, management called a meeting. The workshop was closing and the sixty odd workers were to collect everything from their lockers and go home. They would not be back to the workshop again.

Their first reaction was disbelief, followed by the purchase of several cartons of beer. Diane would never forget picking up the phone and hearing Ron's slurred words, 'Come and getsh me.'

Of seeing Johnny Bolton, tears streaming down his cheeks, arms flung around Ron's neck crying, 'I'sh luvs yu, Ron.' Sobs wetting the shoulder of Ron's grimy dust jacket.

Has she ever told Maggie how profoundly retrenchment, and Ron's subsequent heart attack, affected them? Or about their decision for him to retire? How much do they hide from each other in their letters? When did Hank retire? It must have been before they met, but Maggie never talked about that.

*

Diane's journal: Australia

> *You look back on the years spent working, skimping,*
> *saving and then blowing the lot on travel. But had that*
> *been wise? Did you act out Aesop's fable of The Ant and*
> *the Grasshopper? Laughing and dancing throughout the*
> *summer without a thought of the financial winter*
> *ahead? Is Barb right to look after every penny?*
> *You couldn't afford Ron's fare for this book tour.*
> *A lucky escape for him. You smile at the thought of*
> *dragging him around the book circuit. Not his scene.*
> *If only he was here to talk to. To laugh and count one*
> *hundred and fifty-three knots in the ceiling. This time*
> *you are the odd one out, a shag on a rock, spreading*
> *your wings.*

*

Dit,dit,dit. Dit dit dit. Diane rolls over, grabs the travel clock and snaps off the alarm. Five-thirty a.m. She pulls on slacks and t-shirt then sticks her head outside the bedroom door. The lounge is in darkness. On the couch is a hump of bedclothes with Matilda at Barb's feet. Imp pushes a wet nuzzle through the dog cage wire and sniffs in anticipation. There is no light under Maggie's door. It is not like them to be late for anything, but it had been a long day yesterday. They must be exhausted. Should she wake them? She goes back to her bedroom and leaves the door open.

Propped up by pillows, Diane double checks the clock. Five-thirty-seven a.m. With a sharp intake of breath, she realises the clock is set to a different time zone, and she is an hour early.

She absentmindedly runs her thumb and forefinger along the interlaced necklace, feeling smooth metal. Will it be a better day today? Maybe Barb will get up and smile at her mother, relaxed and refreshed from a few hours sleep, the stress of the trip forgotten. Mothers and daughters. They can't live with each other and can't live without each other. Families and relationship can be so different. At ten, Diane already knew her mother's beliefs and view on life and had accepted them as her own.

Buy a car and forget carpets. A car took you out into the country. It meant camping holidays, adventures, laughter and, because the cars were always old and needing repair, plenty of drama. Like her mother always said, today's tragedies are tomorrow's funny stories. The motto they lived by was seize the day. Use the good crystal. Don't cry if it breaks. Pick flowers.

What memories does Barb have of Maggie? Did Barb give her flowers? When Diane was eleven, in minute letters within a scrolled floral border, she printed her mum's favourite poem and placed it in a tiny frame. Her mum kept it on her bedside table until the day she died.

I'd rather have one little rose from the garden of a friend,
than all the choicest flowers when this weary life must end.

Diane dreams of her childhood. Picking wild flowers in the vacant block next door and placing them carefully into the pocket created by grabbing the bottom of her skirt and holding it up against her waist. Yellow dandelions, white onion weed and native grasses. 'Mummy,' she calls, racing through the squeaking flywire door. 'These are for you.'

Her mother smiles and takes the offering, arranging them in the special vase from the crystal cabinet. Ruffling her hair, her mother sniffs the flowers and inhales deeply. 'They smell of spring,' she says, wiping a blob of pollen off the end of her nose.

'Are you ready, Diane?' Barb's voice is impatient.

Diane jumps off the bed and hurries into the lounge. Should she salute? Leaning on a hiking pole, Maggie looks like an intrepid hunter setting out for an African safari. But she has no waist. Her ribs appear to rest on her hips.

Barb buzzes around, snapping leads on the dogs and shouting, 'I've told you before, Moth-er. Use two sticks.' She looks at Diane's court shoes. 'You can't wear those. Where are your hiking boots?'

'I didn't have room,' Diane protests, thinking of the glamorous outfits and strappy sandals needed on the tour.

Barb takes a spare pair of boots out of the wardrobe, insisting Diane put them on. It is a small victory when Diane, with a pained expression, is adamant they are too small.

Maggie insists on driving to the turn off.

'Don't park there.' Barb waves her mother forward. 'Move up further.'

'But I always park here.'

'Up further, Moth-er.' She points emphatically to a spot further up the road.

'But—'

'Someone will come around the corner and hit you.'

Maggie slams her foot on the brake. 'Goddamnit gal. You've got a bug up your butt today.'

Barb leads the way, the two dogs, like miniature harnessed huskies, trot up the winding road. Walking beside Maggie, Diane's feet march to an unheard beat.

I'd rather have one pleasant word in kindness said to me, than flattery when my heart is still and this life has ceased to be.

She wants to yank the bouncing pony tail. To shake Barb. Tell her that her mother will not be around much longer.

Diane's journal: Australia

You know only too well what it is like to lose a mother. The feelings of helplessness, the constant questioning. Did you do enough? Could you have done more? It is dark outside your study window. The words of the long forgotten poem keep time with your memories and computer keyboard typing,

> *I'd rather have a loving smile from*
> *friends I know are true*
>
> *Than tears shed round my casket*
> *when I bid this world adieu*
>
> *Bring me all the flowers today,*
> *whether pink or white or red.*
>
> *I'd rather have one blossom now,*
> *than a truckload...*

Maybe you could have tried to have a heart-to-heart talk with Barb. Would it have helped? But you realize that no one understands the loss until it happens to them. Once you are home you'll send funny emails and write literary jokes. Barb will be the one who cares for Maggie in her old age, but you worry, will all of her decisions will be in Maggie's best interest?

*

Diane hums a few bars from *Fiddler on the Roof. Sunrise sunset, sunrise sunset, swiftly flow the days.* Two out of five gone already. She sips from a mug, grateful for the jar of instant coffee from New York she threw into her bag at the last minute. Long fingers of shadow creep towards the porch. A cool breeze stirs the mesquite leaves and the plastic bowl of water for the native birds and animals is half empty. A pot clatters to the floor. Angry words force their way through thick adobe walls. They are at it again.

She squirms in her rickety folding chair and gazes with longing at the distant mountains. The last rays of sun skim across purple shadows in deep ravines. An owl answers its mate. Nature is peaceful, like a softly clucking hen fluffing its feathers and settling down for the night. Why can't Barb be the same? She bickers, argues, fights and snaps. If only the serenity of the mountains could encompass the house.

'Two packets of cookies open, Moth-er? Why do you do that?"

Diane tries to concentrate on the book Maggie gave her. *Breakfast with Buddha*. Roland Merullo questions the busyness, the stress of modern life. What does it matter if Maggie opens two packets, or has a little sugar, a little wine. Relax. Have some fun.

'You should finish one before you buy another. Don't you keep a list?' Barb clatters a spoon around a pan.

'What?'

'It's wasteful, Moth-er. Cookies cost...'

Picking up the folding chair, Diane moves farther along the porch away from the kitchen window and strident carping voice. Ever since she arrived, Barb has been cranky.

Yesterday at breakfast, Diane left half an oily croissant and was surprised this morning to see the Glad-wrapped, microwave-heated remains on her bread and butter plate. At her request, Barb tossed a packet of bread onto the table. Diane deftly removed two slices.

'And they're full of sugar. Five grams per cookie. Do you want diabetes Moth-er? No. Well read the list of ingredients.'

Diane wants to stride in, grab a packet of biscuits, throw a couple of coins on the table and eat the lot. Her stomach rumbles. A wrap with hummus has left a gap that only a packet of biscuits will fill. But there are side benefits. A pinch of her love-handles convinces her they are smaller.

Maggie drags a folding chair out the back door. Diane opens it and places it beside her own. Maggie's sweeping gesture encompasses the mountains and valley.

'Magnificent, isn't it. Now you know why I live here.' She slumps and angrily wipes away the tear trickling down one cheek. 'Damn blocked tear duct. They can't do anything for it.'

'Are you okay?'

Maggie pats Diane's hand and nods. Suddenly she smiles and from inside her shirt produces a packet of Trader Joe biscuits. Noticing Diane's surprise, she says with a wink, 'What the eye doesn't see, the heart doesn't grieve.'

Chomping a biscuit, they giggle like school girls.

'What happened to the old church pew?' Diane brushes crumbs off her t-shirt. Ants scurry towards the unexpected bounty.

Maggie sighs. 'It's in the garage.'Diane raises and eyebrow. 'Barb says someone might steal it.'

Diane can't control her mirth. 'That pew is as heavy as lead. It would take two men to lift it.'

They press fingertips on their lips, shoulders shaking.

Wiping their spectacles with tissues, in companionable silence, they watch Jack rabbits, large translucent ears twitching at the slightest sound, drink from the dish beside the dry ditch. A slight breeze carries with it the heady scent of yucca plants and the saguaro cacti stand tall and proud against the skyline.

'She means well. I don't know what I'd do without her. Goddamnit, she had a tough time as a kid. Hank was always hard on her.'

Maggie points to the book on Diane's lap. 'I was always a reader. Always had my nose stuck in a book. A couple of years ago, after an argument with Barb, she showed me a photo taken when she was a baby. I was sitting on a couch with her in my arms, giving her a bottle with one hand and holding a book in the other.'

'Nothing wrong with that.'

'My head is turned away.' Maggie stares at the ground.' I'm reading, Diane. I'm not looking at her, cuddling her. I'm reading while I'm feeding my baby. Sometimes I dream that Anna is calling me and I don't hear. My nose stuck in a book.'

'I put Kerry in her pram and propped the bottle up on a pillow. It doesn't mean we're bad mothers.'

Maggie pats Diane's hand. 'I'm glad you came.' Dark clouds appear above high tors. A flash of sheet lightening brightens the sky.

'I love summer storms.' Maggie leans back in her chair, watching nature's display.

The song of crickets hangs in the air. Forked lightening streaks to the ground.

'One thousand and one. One thousand and two, One thousand...' Diane counts. At one thousand and six, thunder rumbles.

'The heart of that storm is six miles away,' Diane calculates. Odd drops of rain splatter thirsty ground. Maggie pushes her chair back further under the porch. 'You've done so well. It's a great book.'

'What about our book?'

Maggie tugs at her ear. 'Do what you like. Maybe add some fiction. I'm not an interesting person.' She runs her fingers through her hair. 'Hank wanted me to be.' She laughs. 'But not for my sake. Only so it would reflect well on him. He said I could have any interest I wanted outside the home, as long as it didn't interfere with researching and typing his latest paper. Nothing fitted apart from hiking.' Maggie rubs the palm of her hand with her thumb.

'He abused me you know. Abused me in the bedroom.' Diane wonders if this is the moment when they share their deepest thoughts, share their common plight as girls and women. She opens her mouth but quickly closes it when Maggie continues. 'It makes me angry, but it's my own fault for being a doormat and putting up with it so long.' She scuffs the patio bricks with the toe of her boot. 'I wanted to leave, but I was afraid. Who would take care of the kids?'

Diane leans forward in her chair, staring across the valley. Maggie indicates with her head towards the kitchen. 'Barb had enough nerve to walk away from her marriage when her kids were grown. By then, I'd adapted to my life.'

'We all do the best we can at the time.' Diane starts to gather her things, but Maggie resumes talking.

'We never worked well as a family. When Barb was eighteen, she begged for my permission to join the army.'

Diane waits for more, but Maggie is lost in memory.

'What did you say?'

'I said no, of course,' Maggie snaps.

Diane's intake of breath is audible.

'I couldn't let her go. Not that it did me much good. Ungrateful gal eloped with Ted three months later and—'

'Where's Matilda's bowl, Moth-er,' Barb calls.

Maggie slowly rises to her feet. 'Don't forget to put your chair back in the garage.' She indicates her head towards the kitchen. 'We wouldn't want it stolen.'

Diane sits in silence as rain hides the mountains and the night creatures emerge.

*

Barb arranges slices of carrot cake on an earthenware plate. 'What are you taking to the luncheon today, Moth-er?' she calls.

Maggie produces a packet of frozen miniature wraps. She slides the Alfoil tray out of the packet and puts it in the oven.

Barb grabs the empty packet and reads the label. 'You can't take this tasteless trailer trash food.'

'But I like them,' Maggie says, looking at the bite-sized wraps through the glass front of the oven.

'What's in them?'

'Meat.'

'What sort of meat?' Barb turns over the packet and carefully reads the list of ingredients.

'You take your cake,' Maggie snaps.' I'm taking my wraps.'

Barb grabs a tissue and eradicates a spider crawling up the wall.

They pile into the car. Barb drives, Maggie is beside her and Diane is behind them, nursing the tea-towel covered tray of miniature wraps. Ten minutes later, they arrive at Nancy Chow's home for the monthly meeting of the Cochise County Arts Network.

Over twenty people gather in the large room packed with tables and chairs. Maggie introduces Diane as her Australian pen friend who has just published a book. Diane blushes at the obvious pride in Maggie's voice. Barb appears with a stern face and, taking her mother's elbow, steers Maggie away. This outing reminds Diane of the Australian comedian Rolf Harris's three-legged character Jake the Peg, de da duddle dee da dum. She is the extra leg.

Women greet Maggie and peck her cheek. Men shake hands and offer their seats. A new member of the group gives Maggie a hardback copy of *The Arabian Nights*.

'Found it in a yard sale. Thought you might like it.'

Maggie fingers the silk endpapers, checks inside the flyleaf.' I'm overwhelmed. Clever you. This edition is by none other than Richard Burton.'

'I've scored big this time,' the new member whispers as he passes Diane.

She debates whether to stay with Maggie or let mother and daughter be together. Deciding on the latter, she wanders over to the kitchen. Surely they will have a couple of bottles of wine. Red or white, it doesn't matter, but Sauvignon Blanc if there's a choice. Wine will calm her , relax her so she is able to cope with anything. Stemmed glass in one hand, the other resting on her hip, she will confidently move amongst the crowd, chatting on any topic they like to introduce. But too much and she will slur her words before the world spins and her eyelids droop with fatigue. All she can find is orange juice and lemonade. Maybe a blessing.

The kitchen bench is covered in food-laden plates of all shapes and sizes. At potluck luncheons it is grab a plate, stand in line and help yourself. She tries a bit of everything. Sour belly pork, sweet potato pie, hot chilli and, of course, some of Maggie's 'trailer trash'. She makes sure she finishes with a slice of Barb's carrot cake. She does not want to be accused of favouritism.

Diane finds herself sitting next to Junella, who survived two awful marriages before a failed attempt at being a nun. Now, she writes murder mysteries.

*

Diane's journal: Australia

> *It never ceases to amaze you how easily some people tell a condensed Reader's Digest version of their lives to a complete stranger. It happens often, in buses, trams and trains as you travel back and forth to Melbourne. Why you? Is it your age? You have turned sixty. A milestone in anyone's language. Or does it show somehow on your face that people and their stories fascinate you? Often you weave some aspect of these shared lives—a mannerism, dress, or event—into the narrative of your next story or even into your current book.*

*

Junella's life story intrigues Diane, and she leans forward to hear every word. She observes the flowing orange jacket, Medusa-like black hair and unexpectedly small stud earrings. Why so small when large hoops would have completed the wanton gypsy look?

Ding, ding, ding. Nancy Chow taps a teaspoon on the rim of

a glass. 'Quiet everyone. The entertainment is about to begin.'

'Have you got any poetry to read?' Junella asks Diane.

She shakes her head. Junella assures her presenting is not compulsory.

At the end of the room are a piano, podium and microphone. Maggie breaks away from her group of friends and sits beside Diane.

'Aren't they a great bunch,' she says. 'We—'

'There you are, Moth-er.' Barb drags up a chair.

Diane glances around. Barb and she are the only people under seventy years of age. It's like stepping back in time to the family get-togethers of her youth. Her mum insists on dressing her in the pink frock with the frills so she can recite a poem in her plumiest voice for the assembled extended family.

Missing by A. A Milne, she says in a high-pitched, ten-year-old voice.

Has anyone seen my mouse? I opened his box for half a minute. Just to make sure he was really in it.

Will she be expected to perform here?

The first person today is Jeannette Blondell. Nancy hands over the microphone to a buxom woman with *I Don't Think So* written on her Tee-shirt. Jeannette grabs the podium with both hands, leans forward and, in a loud voice, recites twenty-five verses of a dubiously funny poem. She waits for the applause to die before asking if maybe everyone would like her to read another.

When a male member offers to recite a poem, she reluctantly releases her grip. He has written it for his wife's seventy-fifth birthday. She sits directly in front of him and, with misty eyes, treasures every word.

The only thing missing is a string quartet in the background playing *Sweet Mystery of Life*.

An ancient couple sit together on the stool in front of the old upright piano and play and sing their own composition. It is a light-hearted, upbeat tune which has Diane tapping her foot. They bow in unison.

Nancy Chow opens a blue leather-bound book, adjusts her glasses and reads about running barefoot through grass, searching for arrowheads amongst Indian ruins, morning sun on mesas and the challenges of growing old. The poem concludes *Away from mechanical racket, bird sings.*

There is a moment of silence, recognition of artistic beauty and eloquence, before the applause.

'Who else has something to contribute?' Nancy asks. Her eyes search the room and settle on Diane. 'What about Maggie's Australian friend? Author of *Valerie G*?'

Diane flicks back her hair, prances across the room and grips the podium. The majority of people are smiling. To hell with Barb's crossed arms and thin line of a mouth. Diane takes a deep breath and says, 'I would not be here today if it hadn't been for a chance meeting in 1975 with an amazing and inspiring woman.' She indicates Maggie.

Diane is relaxed, confident that she knows Maggies poem by heart. She looks around the room at Maggie's friends, hesitates, and finally says,

'This is by my friend and mentor, Maggie Jackson.'

> *Cyanide Jar*
> *How many hours have I spent*
> *Thoughts beating in my mind*
> *Pinning down a sentiment*
> *When suddenly I find*
> *That words so nearly sentient*
> *Can die when too confined.*

Diane waits for the applause to die down before continuing, 'And this was obviously written by Maggie. Quizzical Quartet.' She pauses, then slips into theatrical mode, ready to deliver every line.

This craze for youth is quite uncouth.
That age is bad is very sad.
Forget your looks.
Just read some books.

'That's our Maggie,' someone calls. Laughter ripples around the room.

No tummy nip.
Go on a trip.
You want to live?
What can you give?

Diane leans forward to engage her audience.

No angry shove.
Invest in love.

She smiles at Maggie. 'Thank you for thirty-five years of love and friendship.'

Amidst applause, Diane makes her way back to her seat. Maggie's cheeks are pink. She leans close to Diane.

'Our friendship is precious,' she whispers, eyes shining.

'Maggie!' someone shouts. 'Have you something for us today?'

Maggie grins and hurries to the podium. Nancy lowers the microphone. Maggie looks over her spectacles at her audience, 'You all know what I think about politicians.' Hoots of laughter. A wicked smile highlights her face.

'A senate leader named Dole,' Maggie begins.

Several men in the audience whistle their delight. Apparently senator Dole is not popular in Gateway.

'Is thinking about a new role. He used to be witty,' Maggie pauses for effect. 'But now he's just shitty. And totally losing his soul.'

The clapping extends for several minutes and Maggie makes her way back to her seat.

'That should stir them up.' She adjusts the cushion before

settling. 'I'll never forgive Dole for sending our troops to Bosnia.'

Junella leans towards Diane and whispers, 'Our Maggie can be seen as opinionated, but we always rely on her to enliven things.'

A feeling of camaraderie overwhelms Diane. When the room is divided into three and a song sheet with the words to the musical round *Row, Row, Row Your Boat* is handed out, she is not surprised.

At first, her voice is a whisper, but she is soon caught up in the enthusiasm of her group and sings with just as much gusto as Junella. Diane has forgotten how much fun singing a round could be. Her group finishes with 'Merrily, Merrily, Merrily, gay this life must be.'

Barb taps her watch. 'We have to get going soon.'

Maggie hurries off to chat with friends. On her own, she is animated, her face flushed with pleasure. She laughs, argues, is opinionated and is the Maggie Diane remembers.

She leaves Maggie chatting with her friends and wanders into the back garden. Strolling down an ochre brick path winding through flowering cacti, she admires huge bumble bees pollinating purple Echinacea. Eager sprinklers pump scrawny desert plants to artificial splendour. All around her, couples and groups of friends sit on seats carved out of native wood, animatedly discussing literature, art and everyday life. In spite of the singing and fellowship, she has never felt more alone. She leans on the gate leading to a chicken pen and listens to the clack and bubble of bickering hens.

Back at Maggie's house nothing has changed. The constant nagging, barking dogs, and extra house guests tire Maggie. Her normal routine disrupted, her home and life chaotic. her laughter full of small humiliations. On her own in this tiny Gateway community she has self worth. This group of tolerant, happy retirees appreciate and love her. Diane decides to leave a day early.

*

Maggie leans forward to peer at the large road map spread over the kitchen table. Barb stabs a forefinger at a red spot.

'It's two and a half hours to Sierra Vista,' she says to Diane. 'I'll be gone all day. You can look after Moth-er.'

Maggie walks away before she says something she will regret. Does Barb think she's a child? She starts clattering dishes. She's quite capable. She lives here on her own on five acres, cook clean and shops for herself and walks every day. And helps out at the library. But she doesn't want to drive to Sierra Vista just to service and re-register the car. Barb wants to add her name to the title. Is she worried that she won't get it when Maggie dies?

Maggie flops into the battered recliner chair she brought from Santa Fe. One of the few pieces of furniture from the old place. She left most of her stuff behind, but the new bed with a double mattress is heaven for her old bones. And how many Indian rugs and artworks does she need? She leans over and rubs the stone belly of Kokopelli, the dancing humpbacked flute player with huge phallus and feather antenna. The old Zuni woman in the Santa Fe Plaza told Maggie it brings good luck.

Her hand automatically reaches for the book beside her on the coffee table, but she hastily pulls back. Barb hates to see her reading. Says she loves her books more than her. Is she is right? Books never answer back, or berate Maggie for scraping a chair or opening two packets of cookies. Barb blames her and Hank for all her troubles.

Maggie lies back, folds her arms across her chest and closes her eyes, but her right knee aches and pains. Rubbing helps a little. She glances at two heads bent over a map. She didn't tell either of them about that Goddamn fall until well after the event.

The road to Cave Creek stretches ahead. So early in the

morning, yet hot sun scorches Maggie's back.

'Sorry, I can't make it this morning,' Pete said on the phone. 'The grandkids are here.'

She misses his lanky frame and gruff good humour. Preoccupied with the titles of books she wants Ginny to get for her, she trips and goes down hard. She manages to roll onto her butt and hug her right knee. Blood oozes. 'Goddamnit,' she mutters, 'I've ruined my brand new hiking pants.' Pain sets in.

Junella's van chugs up the road and swerves to the shoulder. Sticking her head out of the window, she shouts, 'What are you doing there, Maggie?'

'I hurt my goddamn knee,' she shouts back.

Junella helps Maggie into the van, takes her home, washes and bandages her grazed knee, a bruise already forming.

Weeks of treatment follow. Ice packs, then heat and heavy duty painkillers. Maggie's doctor in Geriton is away. Her replacement puts a pressure bandage on upside down and Maggie's foot balloons. It takes two weeks before Junella gets her to a doctor in sinful Sierra Vista.

After hobbling around the house on a walker, she is full of self-pity. In her letters to Diane, she writes about her latest book and the weather and forgets, for a brief while, the pain of her injured knee, osteoporosis, the wheeze of emphysema and loss of hearing. Barb soon finds out about the results of the fall when she does Maggie's accounts and pays the bills.

Barb's hand waves from the driver's window. Maggie's little RAV Four disappears down the gravel driveway, tiny gold elephant cheerily swinging from the rear-view mirror. If only her daughter could be as freewheeling. Maggie loves to see Barb, but it's time she left. Maggie is tripping over dog cages, blankets are stacked on the couch, nothing is where it should be. She feels too old to cope but worries that she is turning into a selfish old hag.

Maggie throws the keys to Barb's Nissan to Diane. She has

no intention of driving a gear-changing tank when she's used to her fully automatic RAV. Diane walks towards the passenger side of the car.

'Where are you going?' Maggie points to the keys. 'That's the passenger's door.'

'I forget that you drive on the wrong side of the road,' she says.

'No. We drive on the right side.' Diane gets her feeble joke, at least it gives them a laugh.

'I wondered why there was no steering wheel,' she says. She walks to the other side.

Grabbing the panic handle, Maggie hoists herself into the passenger's seat. Diane crunches the gears, and they lurch down the left side of the road.

'Keep right,' Maggie shouts.

'Relax. I've been driving for forty years and have an unblemished record.'

'Forty? More like sixty for me. I used to turn the crank handle of an old Ford before it would start. Nowadays, you turn a key.' Maggie puts her forefinger on her lips. 'And don't forget, not a word to Barb about where we are going. If she asks, say we've been to the post office.'

Diane crunches the gears and nods.

The Nissan's wheels bounce over a dry pebble ford, then grind up the gravel drive leading to the Southern Research Station. Before they reach the main building, leafy ancient elms— a welcome sight in the extreme heat— replace the cottonwood trees lining the track.

The office is deserted. Maggie hands Diane several information pamphlets on palaeontology, geology, archaeology and astrology. The familiar words roll off her tongue. She feels at ease. Here is respect and recognition. Here, she's still known as the famous Hank Jackson's wife.

Diane looks through racks containing information about flora, fauna, hikes and tours. On the counter, Maggie finds a brochure entitled Western Research Station, American Museum of Natural History, Gateway, Arizona. Subheadings include history, location, facilities, volunteer program, grants and accommodation. She grabs Diane's arm and steers her outside. She wants to show her the cabins where she used to live.

A group of young people splashes, shouts and plunges into the Station's swimming pool. Their shrieks of delight make Maggie wish she could join them, but she is not the young woman she was in 1947. There's no way she'd show these young ones her ancient body.

'Don't you wish you were a postgraduate researcher, Diane?'

'I'd love someone to fund me to jump into that pool. Why didn't we bring our bathers?' She chuckles.

They reach the old cabin tucked against the canyon wall. With a sigh, Maggie lowers herself onto a wooden seat in the shade of an old alder tree. Diane joins her. Childish spirits ride the winds, laughing and whispering names.

'Let's go to the summit,' Maggie suggests, pointing to craggy tors. 'The view is breathtaking.'

They park under a canopy of dogwoods near the start of a trail. Canyon walls rise steep and high as they follow the winding forest track to the summit. Even with her wilderness boots and the two obligatory hiking sticks, Maggie is soon bent over and wheezing. Diane slows down to match her pace. 'Damn cigarettes.' Diane slows down to match her pace. Maggie pretends to admire the view, but she's angry at the memory of constantly patting her pockets to reassure herself she had her cigarettes before she could leave the house. Of the death rattle of a cough that disappeared after three weeks, but she still got emphysema.

'Maggie, we've been walking a long time. Do you want a break?'

It's been several years since Maggie has been there. She looks around. Trees grow, bushes die, but rocks always stay the same. She points to two pinnacles side by side, recognising them and the magnificent view over the valley far below.

They flop onto a groundsheet thrown beneath a tree and Maggie rubs aching bones. Tall cedars, strong arms reaching to a canopy of blue, frame the mountain range rolling into the distance.

'It is breathtaking.' Diane's camera clicks.

They sit close together, the fitful wind fans their faces while the sun takes flash lit pictures of the baked earth. Grass shrivels. Diane follows Maggie's silent lead. There is plenty of time to talk. A plane drones overhead.

'Remember when we first met, Maggie? How many years ago now? Over thirty? What a blessing that was.' Diane wraps an arm around her friend's shoulders and gives her a squeeze.

Maggie glances up at the speck of silver. 'I wonder if the pilot can see us.' She avoids looking at Diane. 'All he sees is pristine forest.' Bile rises in Maggie's throat. 'At least here, man has not chiselled the mountain, built tacky houses, drained the water or put up fences.' She stops herself before she goes too far. Diane waits for her to continue.

'Here, the world is as it should be. A peaceful place. '

A small lizard scuttles under a fallen log.

'The gals were happy at the Research Station. Barb was only six, so she doesn't remember much. Anna was nine.'

'Time passes too quickly.' Diane gazes into the distance. 'Look at us. You're in your nineties and me? I'm over sixty. I often think about Kerry when she was small...I'm so proud of her, Maggie, and the woman she has become.'

Stupid tears sting Maggie's eyes, and she blurts out, 'This is where I scattered Anna's ashes.'

Diane's mouth opens, but soon closes. She looks around as if seeking a marker. Maggie is surprised at the intensity of the hurt after all this time, and yet she feels an overwhelming urge to talk about Anna. She wants Diane to know her. To understand.

The comforting weight of Diane's arm still rests on Maggie's shoulders. A stray ant struggles past carrying an outsized load.

'You never get over it.' The words are no sooner out of Maggie's mouth than anger wells up again from somewhere dark inside, like a rattlesnake uncoiling to strike. She wants to lash out, to shout and scream Anna's name. She picks up a stone and throws it as hard as she can down to the valley floor far below. It clunks against the nearest tree. Anna. Her name pounds in Maggie's head. She feels it, tastes its bitterness on her tongue. Diane holds her, trying to comprehend the agonising grief of losing a child.

A jack rabbit screams and Maggie shudders.

'I'm not going to pretend that I can begin to feel your depth of pain, Maggie,' Diane whispers. 'But I will always remember my grief and despair when my mother died.'

Trees move gently in the wind rising from the valley. Cranes fly overhead, half angel, half bird.

'Tell me about Anna.'

Maggie's mind slips back thirty-six years to the apartment in New York.

'She was... ' She can't find the right words, but soon they tumble out as if they will never stop. She talks about Anna's genius, her incredible ability to succeed. Unlimited energy, artistic flair and the drugs, drinking, sex, violence and depression. Her complete lack of a moral compass. How Maggie never knew who Anna would hurt next. Usually it was Barb. Always Barb. The fear. Constant fear that Anna would wreck a car, steal Barb's boyfriend or smash a priceless statue.

'I'd stand at her door,' Maggie confides. 'Only to be told, Go away. You're not wanted here.'

Diane winces and squeezes Maggie's hand.

'Two in the afternoon. Cops knocking on the door... I... They found her in Central Park. Overdose. A suicide note in her pocket.'

Diane's arm tightens around Maggie's shoulders,

'I always knew there was something drastically wrong with her. Hank put it down to rebellion. He couldn't accept she was mentally sick. You know what Hank was like.'

Diane nods.

'Anna was the apple of his eye.' Maggie wipes her face with her handkerchief. 'She was in a coma for two weeks. Liver gone. Then lungs.'

Maggie's eyes are dark, her mind back in that stark white room, listening to the beeps of the ventilator. Anna looked so young, so untouched. No accident scars, no blood, no bandages. Maggie stroked her cheek half expecting her eyes to fly open. Afraid of what she might see in them. But she was dead. Brain dead.

'After four days we turned off the life support.'

Tears trickle down Diane's face. She roughly brushes them away. An eagle cries. Sweat and tears drip off the end of Maggie's nose. Vanish into thirsty soil.

'She's at peace now, Maggie. Can you be too?'

'Maybe you believe in an afterlife, Diane. I don't.' Maggie crosses her arms tight across her body. 'The pain never goes away.'

'What do you believe, Maggie?'

'I don't know.' Maggie cries, raising her eyes to the clear blue sky. She gathers her thoughts before answering. 'I often sit and think of Anna and my parents. People I knew and counted on. I don't talk to them, but I'm communicating. My father always said, If you remember me, I'll come back. That's something anyone can have. You don't have to believe in anything. It's just there.'

'When my mum died, I was touched by how many people were there for me.'

'Hank always said that people are no Goddamn good. I don't agree but they do make me angry. Especially if they ask, When did you lose your daughter? What a stupid thing to say.

I didn't lose her like some purse or object I left behind. She didn't pass on. She died.'

Diane hugs Maggie tighter. Thirty-five years of grief pours onto Diane's shoulder.

'I let both my daughters down.'

'Mothers always take the blame,' Diane softly says. 'There were two parents, not just you. And Anna was forty, not four.

*

Diane's Journal: Australia.

> *You escape to your room, clutching the well-worn book Maggie has given you to read. On the cover of I Never Promised You a Rose Garden is the shadowy photo of a young woman, head bent, half her face covered by wispy hair, her thin arms crossed protectively across her chest. Her expression is one of intense sadness as she hides from life in the seductive world of madness. You devour chunks of words and add your tears to stains already there. You learn about schizophrenia, chemical imbalances of the brain, mania and depression and the anguish of a mother and child. At the same time, problems at home have sorted themselves out. The woman in the unit has died and it is empty and up for sale. Things are not the same with Ron but you trundle along. You never wanted your academic journey to affect your family life, or to end up alone. You had been there, done that. But did your study cause this problem? Would it have happened anyway? These days there is always study and writing but you now know what is important to you and your self esteem. Finishing this PhD.*

*

Outside Diane's door, Matilda and Imp yap, Barb carps and controls and Maggie twists and turns, forgets and stumbles. She seems to be shrinking into her skin. Two women, two dogs are too much for her. It is time to leave. Barb does not query her reasons.

'I thought you were leaving Friday?' Maggie says, but accepts the excuse that it would be better for Diane to leave Thursday and get a good night's sleep in Albuquerque before the long trip home.

*

12/12/2009

> *Dear Diane, I'm such a procrastinator. It takes me ages to start a letter. Here goes. I wish we'd had more time together. Maybe then it would not have been so tiring for this old hag. Too much going on all at once, and I'm no longer used to it. But I am now, more or less, recovered and back to normal. So I hope you know how happy I was to see you. I just wish Ron could have been here as well. Even if it meant an added person.*
>
> *I had to go to Geriton yesterday, and it was an ordeal. Kept waiting, at the doctor's for an hour, another hour at the place to get new glasses, and I spent too much for the latter. I was really done in when I got home. Amazing this morning that I was able to go out at six walking with Pete.*
>
> *Love, Maggie.*
>
> *Ps. Your 'prime' proofreader caught you on the first page of your letter. It is 'fewer' not 'less' people. Check your 'Careful Writer'. This is done lovingly as I trust you know.*

*

Diane's journal: Australia

> *Three a.m. Maggie fills your thoughts; the laptop open at the first draft of What Time is it There? As you now call The Book. Writing the story of your friendship means you*

can stand back. See yourself and Maggie as you were so long ago. Reflecting on the past allows you to be more objective, to question and hopefully see both pen-friends, warts and all.

A crescent moon is suspended in indigo. You cross to a folder of Maggie's letters, amazed that you have kept so many. The last two years are in loopy script scrawled on bright yellow paper. Opening the folder at random, you look beyond Maggie's words. Hidden beneath descriptions of blooming yuccas and the ditch running dry, you see again the probing, questioning, prompting that always spurred you on.

Maggie saw in you a potential you never knew you had. The ability to learn. To question and explore and an insatiable need to make more of yourself. The desire to discover new worlds. You laugh. Little did Maggie know what she was starting when she first recommended you buy a dictionary. You glance at your bulging bookcase and row of certificates on your study wall. Guiltily, you re-read Maggie's email, your fingers automatically tapping the computer keyboard.

*

11/2/2010

Dear Maggie, I can't believe I'm actually typing a 'real' letter. It is so long since I have sent anything via 'snail mail'. How life changes. Everything seems to be emails these days, and people keep in touch via 'Facebook' and 'Twitter' and Internet sites. I thought computers would lighten the workload and give me more time for myself. Instead, they are so time-consuming that there is often no opportunity to sit in the sun and watch the seagulls line dance.

I think one of the main reasons why I felt so relaxed and at peace at your place, after the frantic pace of the book tour, was not having to worry about replying to

*emails. Those glorious Chiricahua Mountains dragged
my gaze up to the sky to cloud-watch and daydream.
Nancy Chow had it right when she wrote, Away from
mechanical racket, bird sings.*

Diane hesitates. What to write next? What can she say
about the visit?

*Has Barb got over her hissy fit? Does she comprehend
that it doesn't matter if you have a chocolate biscuit? For
crying out loud, you are over ninety. I hope when I'm
your age, I can have all the chocolate biscuits I want.*

Diane deletes the previous sentence and starts again.

*It was so special catching up with you. Barb did a great
job driving me all the way to Gateway, and cooking for
us. It was hectic for you having not only myself and Barb,
but also the two dogs.*

Diane smiles at the memory of Barb saying,' I'm going to
wash Imp. Do you want to watch?' and being offended when
Diane had preferred to sit in the shade and read.

*Maggie, I know how I felt when Kerry came to stay the
week before I left. She slept in my study, which made it
difficult to organise any paperwork to take with me. You
know what a night owl I am. I got on the plane hoping I
had managed to gather enough documentation together
to see me through the tour. I loved having her and
wouldn't have missed it for the world, but I was also out
of my routine and the house was a shambles. I'm sure
this is how you must have felt with all of us there. But I
have enough heart-warming memory pictures of my stay
with you to keep me warm all winter.*

Pulling her woolly dressing gown around her, Diane turns
the heater up another notch.

*

Diane's Journal: Australia.

Soon you will quietly slip back to bed. You often get up at 3:00 a.m. to study and write. The next day you will be sleep deprived but secure in the knowledge that your passion for writing doesn't upset the daily routine. Ron is not interested in writing. His passions are food, a warm bed and you leave him alone to do what he wants to do. Whenever you are tempted to share your world you remember the time when you saw his relief when a sheet of paper you wanted him to read was the telephone bill.

*

I arrived home to the coldest winter temperatures Victoria has had for years. Rain, hail, sleet and snow on the hills. After the heat of Arizona, I was a little tardy in putting on my winter underwear and, without my nether regions protected, I caught a chill. But I'm fine now. All this week, I've done nothing but laze around and sleep. I guess all the travelling caught up with me. On the last leg of my journey home from Albuquerque, to Dallas, to Los Angeles and then Melbourne, our full-to-the-brim airbus encountered a headwind, and we had to divert to Sydney to take on more fuel. Ron was waiting to meet me at Tullamarine when suddenly the arrival time went from 7:55 a.m. to 10:15 a.m. Poor guy had a long wait, and it cost $45 for parking fees.

Diane wonders if he had even missed her. The house was just as she left it and the refrigerator still packed with frozen home-cooked meals.

On the plane home, I had a brilliant idea. We went straight from the airport to the Melbourne Hilton Hotel. It was bliss to share stories over a leisurely dinner. After a relaxing night we arrived home ready to face the 'mechanical racket'.

*

Diane's journal: Australia

You lean back in your chair and clasp your hands behind your head to ease the ache in your shoulders. The first light of dawn shines under a bank of clouds. Already the birds are making a commotion. Ron will stir and the day will begin. But first, you want to explore your side of the relationship with Maggie. What did you give to someone who had the associated power and status attached to her famous husband, travelled the world, wore only the best clothing, state-of-the-art hiking boots, and never wanted for a penny?

Adulation. Respect. And later?

From the filing system, you pull a folder. Copies of some of your letters sent after Kerry gave you a computer. Printed off so you could hold a page in your hand and, out of respect for Maggie, wield a red pen. Later, you learnt to track changes on the screen. Now only a folder of stored emails remain.

Words leap from flipped pages. I admire the...respect your... I wouldn't have thought of that.

*

27/7/2010

*Dear Maggie, Last Tuesday night, I went to the Palm
Beach Writers' Group. They all insisted on hearing about
you and send their love. You are obviously an honorary
member and integral part of our group. I'm sure you will
enjoy your signed copy of our latest anthology.*

*Christine Neil worked so hard to put the anthology
together, and I felt guilty to have run off and left her
with the lot. She is an amazing woman with so many
talents. Our writing groups are so alike. Wonderful,
supportive people who know how to have fun. How
lucky we are. It's so rare to find altruistic groups like
this these days.*

*I hope you like the photos. I've included an extra one
for Pete, featuring the walk up cave Creek Road. He's
such a gentle soul, who cares for you and protects you.
Must get this 'real letter' posted to you today.*

*Much love and hugs,
Diane and His Roundness xxxxx*

She checks for any red underlining and green grammar
suggestions, then deletes the tracked sections and, finally,
adds a post script.

*P.S. Would you believe we are off to Kerry's 40th birthday?
Yes. 40th. Where has that time gone? I must scan some
early photos of her for her party. Isn't that a Mum's role, to
embarrass her offspring on special occasions?*

Diane prints, signs, folds and addresses an envelope. How
long it has been since she licked a stamp?

The reply came handwritten on yellow paper.

9/8/2010

Dearest friend, It is still fairly cool, the greenery is still with us and the ditch is gargling and trickling past the pump house. The scent of flowering yuccas triggers salad-day memories. I really miss you. I console myself with a very good book written by one of your countrymen, Tim Flannery. It's 'The Eternal Frontier'. It's all about North America from its very beginning to its possible demise. He seems to feel, as I do, that we appear to be trying to hasten the latter by our greedy behavior.

If the copying machine at the library is working, I'll send you what I read to the writing group yesterday. They all sent their regards to you, and were sorry you'd left.

Are you both well? I do worry about his roundness, so please, please starve him a bit. I'd love him just as much when he's skinnier. Barb may possibly come down from Santa Fe next week and take me for my check-up in Geriton. I can't say I look forward to the trip and certainly not to a doctor's appointment. Oh well, asi-es la vida.

Love, Maggie

*

Kubunji Beach 2012

To: Maggie Jackson <libGateway@yahoo.com>
Subject: All Okay

Hi Maggie,

It's 5:00.a.m (Ron is tucked up in bed and snoring) and I'm trying to create some law and order here in my study. I've made a hot drink with a teaspoon of honey and a dash of cinnamon. I find it gives me a better boost than tea or coffee these days. I get so tired of coffee but, unlike Ron, I'm not keen on green tea.

Our weather has been up and down like a yo-yo. One day extreme heat and the next, I'm wearing a coat. Today should be about 26C, and I'm delighted to say that just when the gardens look as if they will curl up their toes and die, we get a solid downpour of rain and the plants lift their heads and smile again. I don't have to worry about a garden as such because we have no 'fragile' roses or delicate plants here. I've replaced them with wild Iris and succulents. They will survive anything nature can throw at them and generously provide the living greenery my heart craves. A small parcel is winging its way to you. I hope it arrives okay.

I think of you so often and we send our love,

Hugs from Diane and His Roundness xxx

Attached to the bottom of the email is Maggie's reply.

Dear Diane, So happy to hear from you this way as I find it increasingly difficult to write long letters (that I really prefer to get). I still enjoy my life and know that I'm lucky in so many ways. I no longer like to eat a lot and avoid as many clelbrations as I can. I think of you everyday and will try out my phone card one of these days. Love, Maggie

⁕

Diane's Journal: Australia

It is a gorgeous day today and you are cooped up at this university for at least the next couple of hours. You must write a conference paper and pull together your PhD colloquium presentation. There always seems to be so much university stuff to do and people, especially Ron, get cranky if you can't go to family occasions or spend too much time in your study. The

*other day, much to Ron's delight, you even had to
refuse a free ticket to the opera. How dedicated is
that? To keep your sanity most mornings, as the first
rays of sun creep across the water you drag your
kayak out onto the canal. Suspended between water
and sky, you dip your oar into reflected clouds. A
flock of swallows swoop and sing just about your head
while entranced, you paddle between two worlds.*

*

Diane's pull-along business case clicks and clacks down the bricked path, tugging like a recalcitrant puppy. Perched on a hill, Sandston University is a rural-style campus with rambling buildings. A cold wind twirls fallen leaves. Clutching her red poncho close around her neck, she hurries to the self-opening doors. Short hair has its disadvantages in winter. The doors part, and she hurries through, reflecting on how fortunate the new toll-way was completed just before she started her doctorate. It takes twenty minutes off the trip from home to here and still she is late.

So much to do, so little time to do it in. She owes Maggie a letter, cryptic emails a stopgap. What is needed is a two-paged newsy letter, filled with love and care, but she is already late for supervision and needs to dump her bag at her workstation.

*

Diane's journal: Australia

*At home, warm, winter sunshine streams through your
study window. Your office chair has a back support and
armrests to ensure your comfort. On castors, it rolls
easily between desk and table. Time passes and you keep
tapping, the novel slowly taking shape. You lean back,
roll your shoulders and ease your neck before quickly*

returning to your imagined world of Arizona sun and Australian sand.

Neighbours go, new neighbours come and still, you type, day in day out. From your window, you wave to the newly arrived elderly couple tending their garden. They wave back. You promise yourself that as soon as you get a spare minute, you will personally welcome them. But first, let them settle in.

Three weeks later, there is a knock at the door. you open it to find the new neighbours with a plate of cakes. When they see you, their mouths drop open.

'You can walk,' the woman says in disbelief. Apparently, seeing you sitting in the same position by the window day after day, they thought you were in a wheelchair.

*

Diane still has to pinch herself that she is at Sandston. The story slowly taking shape. When she opens her locker, seven butterfly clipped sections of the first draft of the novel, plus the exegesis, reassure her that progress is being made. Like so many other students, she is pushing to meet deadlines. Sometimes, it feels like she has one foot pinned to the ground and is spinning in circles.

Lee, in the next cubicle, cheerily waves, headphones in ears. Is she busy transcribing texts for her thesis or listening to the latest rap group? Diane checks for a smile or a frown. She sometimes dreams of being a young, international postgraduate student like Lee. Living in student accommodation overlooking a lake with only herself to look after, although the social life sounds full on.

Or even Jenny on the other side of the partition, who goes home to a mother's care. Washing done, food on the table, a room of her own. Diane is the matriarch of her family. It is her role to care for others. A role she would not change for all the spare time or space in the world. But she must write that letter. A woman in her nineties on the other side of the world is waiting.

*

3/31/2010

> *Dear Diane, Did I reply to your last email? I think I did. Maybe I hit the wrong button. I just read four books in two days, and my mind is a bit fuzzy. If you haven't read 'The Glass House' by Jeannette Walls, do try to find it. It is almost as good as Angela's Ashes and as disturbing. Made me happy I was able to quit drinking. I've just had my 48th anniversary of the event on May 22nd.*

Ginny hands Maggie a stack of books and says, 'That should keep you going for a couple of days.'

Maggie peers at the titles, some old, some new. She can't wait to get home, turn on the air conditioner and start reading.

Great t-shirt.' Maggie says pointing to the caption. Ginny throws back her shoulders. Emblazoned across her ample bosom is *Every time you destroy a book, God kills a kitten.*

To Maggie the drive home seems longer than usual. Maybe it's the heat. The sky has never looked bluer, but she pants and wheezes walking to the back door. Maybe Barb is right. Even for this short distance, she needs two sticks. Holding onto the porch post she savours the feel of warm wood. Sits for a moment on the old pew her writing group helped drag out of the garage. The gabled pump house that she's labeled *The Chapel of Perpetual Pessimism* squats beside the dry ditch overgrown with mesquite.

Unlatching the back door, she dumps her bag on Hank's handmade seat, turn on the air conditioner and fill the coffee percolator. Deciding to rest for a few minutes while it perks, she walks towards her old chair. Her head feels light, vision blurry and her left leg seems to have a mind of its own. She staggers. Sees the looming arm of the chair. Reaches out to save herself. Everything fades to black.

Maggie's hand grips the edge of a rug. The phone rings. She tries to move. Nothing works. Tries again. Pain. Soul-searing pain. Breath rasps in her throat. Something sticky is on her face, in her hair. The phone rings again. And again. She manages to move an arm. Tries to drag herself forward, but hasn't the strength. Is this it? Will someone find her dead on the floor? The coffee percolator rattles on the stove. Maggie shivers. And shivers again. Goddamn air conditioner.

*

Diane clicks the blue Skype icon on her computer. The cheapness of computer-generated international calls means she can talk for half an hour and still have over twelve dollars in the account.

Bip,bip, bip—bip **baarp** bip....Skype tries to establish the now familiar telephone link between Floral Waters and Gateway. What time is it there? Skype repeats its insistent bip,bip. Someone must be there. A ninety-three-year-old, can't stray far.

Where is Barb, or the housekeeper, Anita? Bip, bip... Maybe Maggie is in bed, snuggling under warm blankets, Nadume, in all his silverbacked glory watching over her. Someone needs to be there.

Skype keeps ringing. Maybe she is back in her old adobe home in Santa Fe? She hates it there. Santa Fe would be easier for Barb. It's hard to work out what time to ring. 8:00 a.m. Saturday in Australia—6:00 p.m. Friday in New Mexico. But what about daylight savings? Everyone forgets that.

Bip,bip, bip—bip-**baarp**. You have called 808-727-2692, Barb's recorded voice intones. Please leave a message after the beep.

Hi Barb, it's Diane. I was just wondering how Maggie is going. I'll ring—Barb's recorded voice intones. Please leave a message after the beep.

'Hi Barb, it's Diane. I was just wondering how Maggie is going. I'll ring—'

Barb's voice interrupts. 'Diane. I've been meaning to call you.' Barb hesitates. 'Moth-er died.'

'When?' she whispers.

'Last Saturday.'

'Barb...' Her voice catches. 'I'm so sorry.'

'Moth-er stopped eating. I told her the consequences. She said goodbye to Elizabeth. She didn't want to, but I insisted. I told her, your granddaughter needs closure, Moth-er.'

Diane cannot speak. Her mind repeating the words, Mother died. Diane reaches for tissues, which mush in her hand. If only she had one of Ron's large, soft handkerchiefs. If only Ron was beside her.

Barb's voice babbles on, 'Elizabeth flew from California and arrived just in time.'

Diane visualises the last goodbyes. A small, fragile body under pristine white sheets. Elizabeth crying. Maggie hated goodbyes, but would have agreed. Anything for peace. Diane catches her breath and tries to hold herself together. A voice that doesn't sound like her own says, 'I'm so sorry, Barb. Look after yourself.'

A click breaks the link.

Slumped in front of the computer screen, Diane stares at the Skype icon, her nerves jangling. Why such a shock? Of all people, she should have known at Maggie's age anything can happen.

She pictures Maggie deciding, enough is enough. But to starve to death—that takes time; a painfully slow shutting down of the body. Renal failure, blindness. Is that what really happened, or is that the story Barb wants others to believe? A flash of Maggie with a plastic bag over her face. Diane shakes her head. No. Accept the story.

Ron emerges from their bedroom, fresh from his shower.

'How's Maggie?' He sees Diane's face. His arms wrap around her and the touch of his roundness brings more tears. She snuggles into his warmth, soft velour against her cheek, and breathes in the familiar soapy, day-old sweat, woollen smell that triggers the comfort of shared years.

'She wasn't bad for a Yank,' he says.

Trust Ron to make a joke, but this time Diane can't laugh.

'Think about the good things. Remember when we first met at the Dig Tree?'

Diane's thoughts race back to the people they were then and once again blesses that chance meeting and the years of letters that followed. Letters that became the centre of her world. But the centre can move and shatter.

'I'll make you a cuppa.'

His footsteps plod downstairs and she closes the study door behind him.

9/7/2012

Dear Barb,

I still can't believe that ~~Maggie~~ your mum has died. Why didn't you tell me? You must have had plenty of warning if she decided to starve to death. ~~Although that sounds like a cock and bull story to me.~~ I think, in the end, you helped her, but I can't let my mind go there. And what business is it of mine anyway? I wasn't there. I couldn't help you. I couldn't help her.

Diane screws up the letter and throws it in the bin. Grabbing her jacket, she walks out the door, down the steps and along the sandy curve of the canal. Head bent into the wind, collar pulled well up around her neck, she doesn't hear the neighbours' dogs bark a greeting, or the wind singing through tall palms. She is back on the road to Cave Creek with Maggie and Pete, laughing, chatting, heading for the old juniper tree to give it a hug.

9/7/2012

Dear Barb,

You are in my thoughts. I still can't believe that your mum has gone. It is always a shock. I remember the feelings of loss and sadness when my mum died. All the words in the world didn't help, and the fact that our mothers enjoyed long fruitful lives doesn't make it any easier. Your mother's death has left a big hole in my life. I will always be in debt to her for her interest and concern all those years ago for a young, uneducated Australian mum.

Diane eventually seals the envelope and slips it into her coat pocket. On 21st August, an email arrives.

To: Diane Simpson <dsimpson@yahoo.com.au>
Subject: From Barb

Dear Diane,

Hope you are both doing well. Thanks for your support. By the way, have you seen the small Kokopelli statue Mother had on the coffee table beside her chair? I can't find it anywhere.

*

Diane's Journal: Australia

A box of tape recordings haunts you. Brief informal conversations you had in 2002. There are so few. When the tape recorder was on, Maggie rarely wanted to talk, and the best conversations were when you turned it off. For you, it is the sound of her deep, opinionated voice that you want to hear, but it is too soon. You must give yourself time and believe the writing will come to life, in Maggie's voice. Yet woven within the writing is your story. Maggie and you in the context of history, revealed via your recollections. You must decide how you want this story to end. With you finally getting the floppy doctorate hat. Staying with Ron as you go forward into the next stage of your life? It cannot be a hymn of praise to your friend. She has died and you have to cope with your grief. Miss her, mourn her but the story has to be revealed warts and all. No one is perfect. Everyone does the best they can with what life has given them. But how to end this story of such a special friendship? Maybe end with what you would have liked to have happened. Why not have some fun?

*

Diane gives Kokopelli's tummy a rub, runs downstairs and pulls the kayak into the water.

The End

CLIMACTERIC

Not for me the gentle tease of hesitating spring

Nor again the vague unease of gravid summer.

Exultantly, I join the trees in autumnal celebration

Blazing painted defiance of heavy, thickened trunks

The flamboyant dance subtly quickened

By the premonitory breath of winter death

 – MRB

Reading Group Questions

Thank you for reading my novel *What Time is it There?* and I hope you enjoyed it. The following questions may help you to get a deeper understanding of the themes which run throughout the novel.

1. Does the tyanny of distance add to or hinder the relationship between the two women

2. Do Maggie and Diane understand and support each other?

3. What motivated Maggie and Diane in this story?

4. Maggie doesn't share her secret with Diane and lies to her. Do you understand why she makes up a life for her dead daughter? Why didn't Maggie share her sorrow with Diane?

5. Can you understand why the main characters hide truths about their lives in their correspondence?

6. Does the Australian/USA setting reveal insights into the customs and countryside of the novel? What did you discover about those countries at this time?

7. Who was your favourite character in the book, and why?

8. Are there any characters you particularly admire or dislike, and why?

9. Do you think Diane's journey to achieve academic excellence became all consuming and alienated Maggie?

10. Did you like the story of the older Diane telling what it was like to write a novel?

11. Can you pick out a passage that you found particularily profound or interesting? Why?

If you enjoyed *What Time is it There?* please consider leaving a review at Goodreads, or the place where you purchased the book. Every online review is read by me and greatly appreciated – *Glenice Whitting*

GLENICE WHITTING is an Australian author and playwright and has published two novels. She was a hairdresser for many years before she became a mature age student. It was during an English Literature Fiction Writing course that her great midlife adventure began. Rummaging through an old cardboard shoebox in the family home she found a pile of postcards dating back to the 19th century, many of them written in Old High German.

The translated greetings from abroad introduced the hairdresser to her long hidden German heritage and started her on a life-changing journey. She fell in love with the craft of writing and decided to pursue a writing career. Her Australian/German novel, *Pickle to Pie*, was short - listed for the Victorian Premier's Literary Award for an Unpublished Manuscript. It co-won the Ilura Press International Fiction Quest and was launched during The Age Melbourne Writers' Festival.

Three years as an on-line editor and columnist at *suite101.com* introduced her to web writing and resulted in an ebook *InspiringWomen*. Glenice's play *Hair Today, Gone Tomorrow* was produced during the Fertile Ground New Play Festival. Her published works include biographies, reviews, numerous short stories and two novels. What Time is it There? is about two countries, two women and lies that lead to truth. She completed the journey from VCE to PhD when she gained her Doctorate of Philosophy (Writing) from Swinburne University in 2013.

Glenice's blog can be found at *www.glenicewhitting.com*

Acknowledgements

There have been so many people contributing, supporting and helping me on my journey. It is impossible to thank them all. Here is my sincere attempt. First and foremost, my principal supervisor, Associate Professor Dominique Hecq for her academic wisdom, poetic inspiration, and unfailing belief that this dream would come true.

I would especially like to thank Dr Wendy J Dunn, author of four books, including *Falling Pomegranate Seeds: All Manner of Things*, without whom this book would not have seen the light of day.

Special thanks must also go to Carol Anne Croker, colleague and friend, for thoughtful critique and a myriad of professional and personal reasons; the inspirational and professional Mairi Neil, Mary Jane Neil and Swinburne University.

My heartfelt and deepest thanks to Paul and Marian Whitting for personal support and professional assistance throughout my entire academic and literary journey; Cindy Vallar for the benefit of her red pen, and friends and colleagues too numerous to mention. You know who you are and I thank you.

Throughout this project I have been indebted to the love and support of all of my family; especially Alan, for being my anchor and for constant encouragement. To Paul, Marian, Jason, Karen, Tahlia and Caxton. Without their understanding and support, this book would not have been possible.

Thank you all!

Glenice